Ásmundur the magistrate travels into the remote Icelandic hinterland to hear his first case, a charge of incest and infanticide. On the journey he exchanges tales of ghosts and trolls and social injustice with his servant, Thórdur. Haunted by an ancient drowning and by his own troubled dreams, Ásmundur, the confident poet and idealist, is tested to the limit during his time among desperate people in a desolate landscape. What is the relationship between love and the law? And how might justice be dispensed in such a world?

SHAD THAMES BOOKS

Also in this series:

Brushstrokes of Blue
The Young Poets of Iceland
Selected with a Preface by Páll Valsson
(The Greyhound Press)

Epilogue of the Raindrops
(Eftirmáli regndropanna)
Einar Már Gudmundsson
Translated by Bernard Scudder
(The Greyhound Press)

Angels of the Universe
(Englar Heimsins)
Einar Már Gudmundsson
Winner of the 1995 Nordic Council Literary Award
Translated by Bernard Scudder
(forthcoming from Mare's Nest)

The Trolls' Cathedral
(Tröllakirkja)
Ólafur Gunnarsson
Translated by David McDuff
(forthcoming from Mare's Nest)

Justice Undone

Justice Undone
Thor Vilhjálmsson

Translated from the Icelandic
by Bernard Scudder

MARE'S NEST

Published in 1995
in the Shad Thames series
by Mare's Nest Publishing
49 Norland Square London W11 4PZ

Justice Undone
Thor Vilhjálmsson

Cover design and illustration by Börkur Arnarson
Typeset by Agnesi Text Hadleigh Suffolk
Printed and bound by Antony Rowe Ltd Chippenham Wiltshire

ISBN 1 899197 109

Grámosinn glóir (1986) was first published in Iceland by Mál og menning, Reykjavík.

This translation is published by agreement with Mál og menning.

Mare's Nest Publishing is pleased to acknowledge the assistance of the Fund for the Translation of Icelandic Literature.

This publication has been facilitated by the generous participation of the Icelandic Embassy, London.

This book is published with the financial assistance of the Arts Council of England.

The quotation from T. S. Eliot, 'Burnt Norton' (*The Four Quartets*, in T. S. Eliot, *Collected Poems 1909–1962*) is made by permission of the Eliot Estate and Faber and Faber Limited.

Contents

Time and the bell have buried the day,
The black cloud carries the sun away.
Will the sunflower turn to us . . .

T. S. Eliot
'Burnt Norton'
The Four Quartets

and then we continued our journey.

It was almost completely overcast. A grey sky. Growing darkness. The murmur of a river, in the distance. Ourselves travelling on the sand. And the rumbling of the sea in the distance too.

Occasional tiny vegetation in the sand. When you eventually looked for it. Had a mind to do so. And roots spread wide, like ubiquitous strands of fate.

The clouds rolled forwards, from behind the mountain, flowed across the cols. Whitened there.

The horses were bored by that landscape.

My companion never said a word. How changed he was from when we were travelling eastwards; he was full of spirit then. And held his head high.

Now he was bowed, silent.

An Act of Murder

The woman hurried after the man along the sheep track. A few sheep stopped grazing and looked towards them. The man rushed on so quickly that the pregnant woman had difficulty following him along the twisting muddy track among the tussocks. Sometimes she slipped in the puddles. Her shoes and socks were wet, and the water slopped out from them. She didn't understand where he was going, just hurried after him. Perhaps she had never known who he was, this brooding man. She could see his slouching frame, his powerful, slightly rounded shoulders; his dumpy, broad buttocks, as he slogged along on his stubby legs; his hair curling up and settling over his thin collar, a roll of flesh where the broad nape of his neck joined his shoulders; she wasn't accustomed to him telling her what he was up to.

Now they could no longer see the horses they had left behind on the edge of the lake, on the promontory which ended in a low spit.

She started to hear the babbling of the stream which was curiously insinuating and soothing in all this running. As if it proclaimed a solution of sorts. She was out of breath, and her unborn child was beginning to weigh her down. The heathland gave way to a grassy bank. She slipped on it, and almost fell; and caught hold of the man so as to keep her balance. But he didn't turn around. She hadn't seen his face since they had set off on horseback.

At the top of the bank the path continued into a hollow where the stream grew wider before plunging into a pool, encountered a boulder that diverted it as it fell. There was a patch of grass there, with water willow on the banks, crane's bill. She never saw his face; perhaps scarcely even when he grabbed her and thrust her into the pool, held her down.

And the choked scream in her eyes staring up through the gentle lapping of the water around his huge coarse hands. It oozed on until it faded out somewhere in the lake; long before it reached the horses which went on grazing on the promontory.

And the wild geese strutted around the end of the spit.

Way out on the lake there were three swans swimming, two together and one a little farther off.

When he regained possession of his faculties at last, Jón Jónsson the murderer felt that it was from this moment that he first remembered how the bulge of her belly had stood up out of the water. Later he had a feeling that he had had difficulty releasing his grip on his lover when she was dead.

Bower Scene: To the Manor Born

This melancholy wryness, it was in the music as well; it pressed its way between the palm trees with their long, shiny, slippery leaves, and stirred within him the thought of some tempting lips caught unawares by candlelight at dusk, after a soirée. The palms stood in tubs, and the flickering play of their shadows alternately turned off and reawoke the glimmering on the reddish copper where the foliage stood in a semi-circle in front of the bandstand.

This pungent joviality was not jovial, and not only bitter; there was also a melancholy undercurrent at its roots.

The man sat shawled by the shadow of a palm, beside the yellow-green lantern on top of the slender marble column with its copper cincture, pale after the winter and his illness, tall and slim with youth, his face drawn by spiritual quest.

With his long, slender fingers he twisted his beard; it was new, light as if it had grown mostly in the pale glow of the moon. The moustache – until then he had trained down the sides of his mouth; now it was longer he had begun curling it upwards, and it responded better to such grooming.

The shadow of a flower pierced the broad daylight on his hand. The man looked at the hand as if he were seeing it anew, in a new light; had never seen it before in quite that way. And suddenly he noticed that the whole world was bathed in a new light, which was corrugated by new shadows.

Everything was as if born anew. But the world was still old and established – this world with its long-acquired habits and steadfastness, its customs of quelled stirrings which had become tradition. It was the newly awakened brightness that was new to him.

Or perhaps it was only him. He was new himself, awoken again.

Scorched with fire, dissipated by the burning of fever, perhaps baptized: new.

Here. Was he here? Yes. And no. Both. Perhaps he was under some kind of helmet, transparent and intangible, which caused him to be distant from that which was closest to him. A flood of vivid flashing colours, a fermenting ecosystem of light and shadow in its indoor game, an inner world drawing its intoxicating power from the prying violence whipped up by the throng. Whirlpools of silence and sound in the turbulent music beat upon him, impossible to ignore; increasing at once his presence and absence. Something was interposed between him and what was happening here, arousing his senses at the same time; but his mind had another time, another being. As if there were two dimensions of consciousness, overlapping without encroachment. One plane drew its power from the throng, the restrictions, the walls enclosing that world, the fleeting moment; the other, by virtue of everything being the opposite there, calmly expanded his emotions and mind.

At the same moment he was present in another being, another country bearing no resemblance to this, where archetypal forces did battle. Where time was so broad that its speed vanished. With people bearing no relation to those here, people who grew and drew strength from their difficulty in reaching one another, the obstacles between people, the long routes. The silence. And the mask which toil and weather and the land with its threats and eternity froze fast, a destiny transplanted upon sensitivity and yearning which each inherited from his forebears and handled with varying dexterity in the inescapable loneliness, in the company of ghosts and monsters bred in the dark, and benign illusions. And wearing that mask, they would all inevitably fall again to the earth which reclaimed man, a trivial loan, paltry but repaid in full, in the final event. In the final event each and every one, endlessly again, each one who for a brief respite was granted to travel the land and collect its adornments for the trove of his soul. For dust thou art, and unto dust shalt thou return.

Buckled beneath the burden of repetitions, lacking opportunity, lugging their lot: the curse of their race. Tiny human beings in the vastness, the endlessness. But none the less able to grow when the first dimension of days releases its oppressive grasp; and man flees to the other dimension and embraces the land, becomes the land; and the land becomes him with its unfathomable mountains and tabooed wilderness, glaciers and hot springs, with its dark expanses and brazen peaks which glow in the breeze, with its gullies where streams bellow and tumble in their confinement, beating themselves a course through the rock; and whittle images into the bedrock which the freed man of the enslaved race perceives in flashes. And in such mercy the human mind magnifies the image of its race in the rock, reflected in rock in the world of giants and gods and dwarfs, opening up to the coarse rumbling of the river; the screaming war of stone and water. Thence, the boy departs, a poet.

And then he flies across his country on newly sprouted wings, so wide that he may hover in huge arcs with eagles up around mountain peaks. Alone in the clear tranquillity.

Circling over the cones of the mountain, honing his sight on its pillars and ledges, enriched by the wind-hewn spectres of eternal rock.

Then soaring, visionary, over valleys where rivers seen from on high glide slowly across the land; and the farms present themselves to the eagle's view.

Tufts, grassy humps whose covering of blades the winds stroke as if searching for something that could receive their signal. And in these burrows beneath the grass, your people live. As if in dens or puffins' nests. And toil at cutting blades of grass among tussocks day and night to feed these obstinate creatures which prance about the mountains and the unrecorded vastness, until the time comes to cast down the scythe and pursue them across their land, rounding them up until they flow like mountain milk around the slopes in autumn with the symphony of bleats, barks, murmuring brooks and shrill shouts, and the padding of hoofs in the moss and clattering of horseshoes against stone, or the thundering canter over fields; snorting and whinnying; perhaps the whining of wind; until drinking songs merge with the voices of children and women in the corral at the foot of the mountain, and sheep change their voices when their freedom fades in the world of men.

And man returns to his croft. Your nation, your people. Century upon century. Your lineage buried in earth, which huddles under winter snowdrifts, seeking shelter from the elements in dens of earth. With memories of mountains while darkness and the blizzard close up the hovel of man and beast, their cohabitant. But each day the byres issue their challenge to the blizzard so that life may go on, each separate time. While the ghosts roam free, and spring lives vaguely distant, so distant.

It lived in his sensibilities and defended them, preventing him from being able to accustom himself to the gaiety of company, to be fettered by adornment and clamour, the slavery of immediacy, making temptations short-lived; and consciousness awoke with a pained yearning and nostalgia for something that he only occasionally vaguely recalled, but did not know how to understand.

A haunting image remained in the flow that haunted his thoughts as he rolled his glass back and forth and searched for resonance, unyielding no matter what else appeared in its place, an ever-waking tone that served to yoke together the entire roaming performance; and in his vision the young man perceived a stone standing in mid-stream, cleaving it, continuously worn away but without relenting.

Sometimes his thoughts turned towards his mother. Who was that woman? She remained in a kind of mystical haze, far back in his childhood, emitting something he did not understand, a power that sometimes appeared to grant him grace in his sufferings. Strong and cool. A force devoid of mercy. In his mind there was an image he could not call forth at will but which appeared by surprise; most typically in times of trouble when all his paths seemed blocked. Then this strong woman appeared, her image, he did not know from where. And cleared a path for him. From where? He was so young.

He was so young when they went their separate ways. When his parents ended the war that was their cohabitation. She cold, strong, silent. His father impetuous, his rhetorical flourishes knowing

8

no bounds, vacillating from one extreme to another in an instant.

He still carried the letter his father, this unstable emotional character with his grand vacillations, had written to him about the problems and psychological battles of a judge who has to conceal any sympathy he might feel or acquire for the defendants; forced instead to show intractable resolve, donning a mask to cover his mind. The letter described in detail a case he was handling, a murder in an isolated valley. A man kills his pregnant girlfriend by drowning her. The story had often haunted him, assuming a form in which he could not tell what was his own invention, and what he had been told. But he visualized three swans swimming nobly on a lake, two together and the other a short distance away.

It was in Fredericksberg in the month of May; the entire assembly sings, locking their arms and rolling in the merry swing of cheap affinity.

He ran his fingers through his hair to tidy the waves that complemented the high brow above his perceptive eyes and splashed around the room in this stifling song, finding little worthy of himself in this joyful gathering.

He knew his stage in the vast expanses bounded by mountains, in the hall of stars, or with the play of northern lights across the dome of the skies, or in nightless summers at the far limits of the world; and again he suspected rewards from the timbered halls or palaces of muses in deliberately wrought colour and sound, where the mind is trained and cultivated century upon century, and where he knew he could expect to exert sway. And concealed his fancy in this bower where he found himself for the moment.

Then silk rubbed against his sleeve, rustling softly. He looked up and saw a pair of eyes grow dark blue on meeting his.

Yes, it definitely began with those eyes. Those eyes that darkened so intensely. What happened later began with them. Had she singled him out from the crowd? And then let her maturity take charge, one thing leading to another, as if automatically. Perhaps he had dreamed of women like her. Mature, aglow with experience, who touch a young man on their own initiative as if to tell him that he is at a pre-arranged encounter, with no one knowing or remembering how or when. I am here. Have you been waiting long? She dashed away his reserve. And tied him for a while to the stage where she reigned. It had happened without the slightest compulsion; nothing could have been more natural than for her to take a seat at his table, for them to start talking without recourse to the second-best of silence, it was *de rigueur* for him to ask the waiter to bring them a bottle of wine; and for her to begin telling him about her long dream of the night before with its mundane complexities, nothing was more pressing than to know the solution to the urban complex it described; her eyes meanwhile drinking his, his childhood, the distance that they would so soon cross; so that what occupied his mind before had vanished, lost in the dark-blue eyes with their occasional twinkle of light; like a gust of wind suddenly whipping a current of water white, starting to ripple a blade of grass, or ruffling fallen leaves on a woodland path until they end up among the trees, whispering something there. This woman's lips smiled as if asking him something there was no urgency to answer, or telling him something he would understand later on regaining his concentration; or perhaps there was nothing in particular to understand, perhaps nothing in particular said; just delighting in it while it lasted, whatever might happen later. And something would have to happen whatever it might be; a premonition flickered there, a promise making him at once rapid of thought and bold of speech, eloquent and lethargic in the silences in between.

Until a distraught man was standing over them, telling her something in such a low voice that it vanished into the clamour in the hall. The woman grew uneasy as the man spoke into her hair. She did not answer. Merely nodded towards her companion at the table. The intruder regarded him with vehemence in his eyes. But when his bossy eyes met the gaze of the rival who looked at him with guarded calm, his stare softened and he smiled foppishly; but with a hint of a smirk; put a finger to his receding hairline, and took his leave with a smarmy military farewell, which ended like a wasted punch thrown into the smoke-filled air. He turned down the corners of his mouth conspiratorially, and dimples formed on his small chin; he closed his eyes, and disappeared into the crowd.

Come with me into the glade, with its merry dance, a white sail on the bay, searching for land.

And in the forest does and stags sport with their lofty, branching antlers, and glancing rays from the foliage light them up in total tranquillity for an instant in a glade . . .

A short tunnel left the respectable street where art dealers and antiquarians had their shops with their cultivated air, and bistros on the street corners, offices, the better class of merchants. In the tunnel, a stench of beer and wine. Beyond it lay a courtyard, and a single tree growing out of the paving stones, beside railings where there were paintings of a journey through tropical countries, palm islands, on a cutter which was knee-high to the figure with his forked beard tied at his belly in a knot with a pink ribbon on one side and a blue one on the other, and butterflies flittering around with bright, colourful dappled wings. Between the tendrils of his beard was a mighty bare chest with tattoos depicting a lion cub, an anchor, two violets and three exotic women's names. He sported a turban, perhaps Sinbad the Sailor, if not Robinson Crusoe in person; and the ship had arrived after he had ceased to expect it, and he perhaps grown too huge in his solitude for it to be able to transport him away from this courtyard where he had been stranded once in the distant past.

They stopped in the courtyard, and the woman in her imitation-leopardskin coat toyed with the young man's hair. The moon was enshrouded by mist. They entered by a blue door and up a steep, narrow stairway divided by landings, and copper plates on most of the doors, sometimes knockers or bell cords, even clay flowerpots or tubs in front of them. There were windows looking out, most of them set before floor level and reaching a fraction short of the ceiling, drawn with net curtains, white. There were wooden floors shining with varnish and polish, the varnish in places clotted or dried into thick streaks. At the top landing she took out her keys to open a double-locked door with a spy hole covered by a thin plate. The door of heavy wood painted olive green, with a short, thin copper handle. It opened into a cramped parlour crammed with a variety of ornaments as if they had been brought there systematically from more spacious and complex quarters, small tables covered with cloths and upholstered chairs which more appealed to the eye than offered comfort, bent and stretched in antagonism towards the body's shape. Tall vases containing withered, odourless stalks of flowers. And a silver bird, beautifully beaten, with outstretched wings as if poised to land, or to take off into the air with its craned neck, tiny eyes in its little head and a long, squawking beak. It was reflected in the shiny surface of an oblong table with rounded edges which stood on a single, carved, three-clawed leg. Between the rooms was an arched doorway, draped with thick corduroy on brass runners, the drape held up by black rings of bone, itself dark blue, with ornately carved knobs on the ends of the pole. Within was a larger room, scantily furnished with an ancient wardrobe, two broad hatboxes and an iron bed on tall legs, made of black twisted iron with a high head and foot rest and animal heads on the four posters: an eagle, a lion, a bear and a griffin with a long, dangling forked tongue and tall lupine ears.

Facing the bed where they made love hung an oblong mirror hinged in the middle, in a frame of undulate patternwork.

He had strolled out into the city, drifted along the streets thinking of the strange adventure that had befallen him. He stood at a crossroads in his life, newly risen from his sickbed after staring death in the face. Drifting with the sea of people, an entire chapter of his life rushed through his mind: beginning when he left the taciturnity of his home country and the distance that separated people in that sparse, harsh land, and found himself in the milling city where so much was at hand to quench his parched mind, in concert halls and galleries, and libraries offering all that mankind had thought and said about its yearnings and tribulations and happiness and sorrows and dreams. And he had plunged wildly into these springs, almost over-exerting himself. And these new, time-honoured customs were scarcely familiar to the young man who had been washed ashore there, so he sought security in drinking places, in debauchery as he mastered these new postures. And in bistros, in boisterousness, he quickly learned these new postures to bring himself on to a par with any seasoned player, acquiring the skill of holding his own in the play of city life. But he could never reconcile the opposites that dwelled within him, and when the boisterousness reached its peak he was snatched by loneliness without warning. For long periods he would sit alone, propelling his tankard along the coarse-planed tabletop, steering it around an emptied schnapps glass, feeling his sight sharpen to catch the hues of light where a shadow outside passed across the glass, or a cloud crossed the sun. The light indoors changed hue with the influence of wine or beer; he dipped his fingertips into cool, southern wines, raised his hand slowly and watched the drops fall from his fingertips on to the table, and thought it somehow rewarding to do so at the time. And snatches of poetry and verses were born in his mind, which he wrote down, or sometimes automatically assumed a form that afterwards he polished into poems. And then he pored over these poems, not an easy task, painful rather. But the pain was proof to him that his life had a purpose, and was an intoxication, a satisfaction; then he could become whole, no longer divided. And he discovered that he could charm in company, could easily win admiration and the trivial acquaintances offered at celebrations, in the boisterousness of parties, in bistros and restaurants. And although he soon knew how quickly they ebb, he partook of countless temptations on offer there. And so time had passed, in pleasures and boisterousness and revelling, loneliness at the very heart of a singing and rattling herd and court.

This he saw when he fell ill and looked death in the face, which he had feared ever since childhood, which always made him feel apprehensive. When his composure returned he saw how much was trivial that he had enjoyed pursuing, toyed with. More to the point: he had often played with fire, played the ultimate stakes. Invited physical and mental disaster.

Somewhere within him was a need to perceive, understand and

know. It drove him, on the one hand, to seek knowledge and experience, and collect it; and on the other hand there was his senses' compelling and insistent urge for the transitory moment, to grip it, to stop the world, and examine and preserve an image, spin on as the earth might, and planets and sun and everything else, and the wind, and the leaves would dart astonishedly in new colours from the trees, fly, but lack wing, and would fall to earth, lose their course, and land in a heap, and an end to it, and a new spring would come later, without them. Hold an image tight from time's course. Stop time but let it pass none the less. He had wallowed in fantasies broken by amnesia, then began anew when he recovered his senses. What was time then? The war lasted for weeks. Later he was told he had been snatched from the jaws of death.

And he awoke in a completely white room among white-clad radiant figures. Time stood still. Absolutely still. And these white beings passing or hovering around him without him noticing their expressions. So am I dead? he thought with a strange feeling of calm, so composed that he could not tell whether it was sorrow. So is this what being dead is like? He seemed to hear the echo of a voice from afar, as if even in death something could be about to happen.

Yes, said the doctor to his team, to the students and the nurses and his assistant, I really think he's going to pull through.

He was sitting in an ancient basement divided up into shadowy nooks with little lamps hanging down on long leads almost to the tabletops, shedding pools of light there, lighting up beer glasses and fingers and a red rose in one corner on a long stalk held up by a woman like a torch towards a dark-eyed man with his chin on his chest. He sat there preserving this train of thought while capturing new images at the same time, testing out snatches of verse which presented themselves to him almost complete. It was as if his battle with death had changed him. Opened new space within him, unexpectedly, a kind of sanctuary with both new enchantments and dangers of different sorts, promises and disasters. He knew he could not keep it open, it was so powerful that he could not live with it permanently. But he found new security in the knowledge that he could open it again. Death's gift of life was accompanied by the wisdom of avoiding trying to live with it constantly. Then he would burn out, and true death would come. Ceasing to exist. And now he thought: When I rose from the dead I wrote a poem about a man and a ghost, the ghost of a mistress who kills the man who betrayed their love.

After several tankards of beer in the darkened chambers of the old bistro he walked out into the sun and the shadows looked blue outside, the sunshine curiously white. And the brightness sharp in his eyes.

When he returned to the woman she welcomed him; she was wearing a white dress.

You're hot, she says. Go and sit in the kitchen. Have a glass of wine. I'll fill the bath for you. And while you're taking a bath I'll cook you a meal.

He got into the bath, the hot water. The door was open. He could see her working in the kitchen in her white dress. Her skin was golden.

Come here, he said, after sitting in the water for a while watching what she was doing.

She stood in the doorway, bright, watching him naked in the water.

Come here, he repeated, gesturing to her to come towards him. She leaned over him and kissed his wet body, on the shoulder, on the mouth.

Come here, he said, breaking off the kiss. Come and have a bath with me. Get into the bath with me. She left. When she returned she was naked with her large breasts tight and rounded. Slender around the waist with wide hips. Her stomach taut. Then she stepped into the water opposite him. He lifted her thighs, soft and majestic, from below, drew them towards him and her slender legs locked behind his back, while he found her sex ready and she spread herself and opened for him. He slipped smoothly inside her. Lay still there. Started moving slowly. And they played for a while, composed, blissfully but restrained, soothingly until his ear reached her mouth while he still probed gently inside her. Come on, she said, we'll finish inside, and released him from her, and he withdrew in all his grandeur. She took the big towel, white with blue stripes, and draped it over him, and dried him with tender strokes of the towel, roamed to find out whether his cock was still stiff, knelt and kissed it with a deep kiss. Come on. And she took with her another towel which was still dry, spread it out on the white polar bearskin by the table where the silver bird stretched its wings. She lay there waiting for him, open, spreading herself apart in unpretentious eagerness, and he moved slowly on to her, supporting himself on his arms, and slipped in the head of his cock for an instant, just the head, withdrew it, put it back in, and then she arched almost violently, thrust her welling sex up, drove him firmly in as deep as he could go, and he felt her juices slide and gush in excess along his whole cock, tugging at his soul with gentle, quenching glory. And they made love. Then she said, after nimble and prolonged devotion to this play, come, come now. And tensed herself eagerly against him with maddened spasms, rolled her eyes and came in delirious pleasure. And he at virtually the same time, and fell groaning upon her on the heavy polar bearskin so its head lifted from the floor with the light-blue glass beads that were now its eyes. While the silver bird flapped its wings frenziedly into its mirror. He saw into eyes which were open then, their glint far distant, where? As her sex still oozed and splashed, flowing out of it the holy juice of the pagan world.

I don't know who my father is, said the woman. The sun was high above the house opposite. And the sounds of carriages drifted along the street, sometimes calling. She put an Egyptian cigarette in the slender holder with the golden rim. She took a long, thick match from the box in a silver frame with its fluent décor of braids and twined flowers in art-nouveau style, and you can think yourself lucky not to see Aubrey Beardsley grinning through the braids with his fingers in Oscar Wilde's locks, he thought with an allusion to his day, his waistcoat flapping and his watchguard dangling from the fob, his collar undone, stroking along her spine with his little finger and ring finger, his cigarette unlit between the other two. With his other hand

16

he absent-mindedly probed her cupped, slightly angular pelvis, and looked at a white scar on her stomach. The silver bird had still not flown from the table.

You didn't know your father? So what? Don't you suppose there are plenty like you? Who knows anyone else? Do I know you? Do you know me? Except the moment we sleep together. Make love. Enjoy each other. And become two people afterwards. What do we know?

I don't know. But I still never knew my father, she said, blowing smoke into his eyes.

And what do we know then? Even though we have slept together. What do you know about my memories? Or I about yours? Even though we're getting out of the same bed now. And maybe we think for an instant we know something now, what it is now. Something we didn't know before. That we've felt something new. But what was yesterday? And the day before? A year ago, five years ago, twenty. And if we make love again for one night, keep the spectre of the past at bay, for a while – doesn't everything that we want to avoid return? Everything that we wanted to forget. It's just like part of a story, he said.

The flash of the huge match had lit up her slender fingers with their long sharp nails shining like obsidian. Lit up inside her palm whose shadowed lifeline was intersected by another even deeper, defying all reading. The glow of the cigarette was like the single eye of an animal that had lost its other eye during the hunt; and still the woman blew out light smoke filtered through her lungs; on a whim, or affectedly, she lit another match and put it to her ear as if listening to the secret language of the flame, and lit up half her face like a carved raven's wing with dark, moist eyes, deep blue while the rest was in shadow, then snapped her hand forward to extinguish the flame.

Not like that, she said; and he saw her rounded eyelid slip down over her eye, knowing that the eyeball was hardening within, and her eyelashes like birds' tracks in the freshly fallen snow: not like your poetic fancies, my clever young man. It was the man who raped my mother. He was never caught. My father.

It came from somewhere afar, through a haze. Grew sharper sometimes, came into close-up, receded again. She had told him stories of her travels with a dance troupe to many countries. Of her childhood on the family estate, secure with her family. Until the evening came around when her maternal aunt had told her the terrible story of her origin. And changed everything. Why? And was it true? Or the mendacious fruit of a sick mind? Malice? Jealousy?

And the devil had never been far away since then. Perpetually threatening.

She had told him about a man she met on her travels in a remote country. How she had fallen in love and arranged to meet him in a small town two days later at the end of the tour. And knew he would be her first. From the moment she boarded the train for that place where their adventure would come true, and give herself to him. The train stopped. She got up, reached for her suitcase from the rack, brought it down on to the seat and held it with one hand. The passengers moving along the corridor to disembark were reflected in the glass of the window she was looking through out on to the platform, where a single inspector stood wearing his official cap with two signal flags under his arm, another train, empty and stationary, stood on the next tracks. On the other side was the station building, across from the passage where the passengers poured out with their luggage; the clamour of the people outside reached her, along with the sound of a few brass instruments. She sat down beside her suitcase, and soon the train left, carrying her away from this meeting.

She told him how she had lived with the kindly taciturn painter who not infrequently turned rough and nasty; his mild, warm eyes were chilled by a deathly cold breeze whose provenance she never knew. And he beat her, hurt her, as if he had become another man whom she did not know.

She told him of their acquaintances who had been at the Academy of Art with him and broke into this apartment one night under the influence of strange substances, and beat her near-naked friend and broke his bones, threw her on top of the unconscious man, length-ways across the bed, but without raping her, and took nothing but the silver bird with its outstretched wings, and a carving knife she had used to cut onions the night before.

The silver bird, said the young man.

Yes, the silver bird, she answered.

This silver bird here?

Yes, she said.

Really? he said.

I saw him three weeks later.

Saw whom?

I saw the bird in an antiquarian's window. On the first floor. On the square here at the end of the next street. He was trying to fly through the window. But always got reflected in the glass. Perhaps he was afraid, and stopped. He seemed pleased when I came and fetched him. Now he's dead.

The bird?

My friend. He'll never hit me again. It took him a long time to recover. And never did completely.

But the people who attacked him? And stole the silver bird.

They've been let out of prison. One of them lives in this house, downstairs. When he's not living with his friend.

And do you see them around here in the house? Do you meet them?

Of course I do. When he lives in the same house? He comes to visit me sometimes. He was the one you saw at the restaurant. Where we met. He was the one who took the bird. He hit my friend over the head with the lamp the Egyptian prince gave me. Yes, you've met him.

Prologue to the Sentence:
Emissary of the Invisible Father

Their horses ambled across the heathland which began where they left the lavafield. The lava behind them where the track curled like a wily serpent, and they had to beware of fissures and holes, and wend their way around crotchety lava trolls, which thrust up out of the stretches of grey moss in the shrieking silence of their dominion; and the two men talked loudly for a while, their horses snorting occasionally, purple hills ahead and the trail growing straighter.

Sometimes slabs of rock lay right across the track, making the horseshoes clatter when they met the stone; but most often it was the muted beat of hoofs that travelled along the threads of the land like a secret message. About the life of men, when the ceaseless motion of the deserts of trolls and dwarfs was past.

There was no sun, a light cover of cloud. His companion started muttering to himself and groping his way, found his bearings and began to intone verses when they cantered over the soft landscape. Their path lay ahead over sand-covered plains, until the land rose and became rocky. They negotiated low gravel banks and boulders. And the rock tried to impress its song upon the horseshoes. Harmonize the two without jarring on the senses. Brooks and melt streams interrupted those epics of horseshoes and rock, diversifying them with more mystical variations, and another sound was yielded when they crossed rock that water flowed over, sometimes moss on the banks or other primitive vegetation.

The countenance of the land grew harsher. Now it was deserted and gloomy. The heathland ahead with its uncertainties of weather and imminent hauntings.

Still the land rose, the vegetation grew more monotonous, though there were dips grown with heather and grass-covered hollows, scrawny and low; the wind ruffled short blades; bumps and little tussocks of moss campion, and hardy pimples of vegetation where the land fought obstinately against erosion, the abrading winds of desolation.

Afterwards they skirted the rim of a chasm where the land descended on sloping pillars towards the river which now flowed over a bed of clay but was still out of sight. The wall of rock reared up on the other side, chiselled by the river's course through the centuries as it swelled and shrank, and charged forth in the spring, roaring onwards, beating the foam-washed chasm on either side, and forced out new apparitions; newly fashioned trolls appeared in the ridges of the cliffs, and crept forth to create a faith where mysteries could be quarried from the depths of the unconscious; the soul of archetypal man.

The two men threaded their way, each along his trail, brought their horses to a walking gait, gave them free rein.

Beyond, the mountain rose above the chasm with screes on its slopes and streaks of sand; and narrow strips of grass like pursed lips spread open, green with the thin trickles of brooks. Scudding clouds endlessly transformed the colours on the upper slopes. The sky darkened, and the day grew dimmer in the great wilderness.

Two men, four horses. Gravel banks eroded by the mud with tussocks of heather and bulges of moss shot through and whitened with reindeer moss; whitening roots, naked roots above the soil; rocks with splashes of lichen.

And the reindeer moss shedding a little brief light, ashen with hues of pale violet.

Farther up, there was marshland with grassy islets. There were brooks and fens with tussocks, and hair grass. Cotton grass. Even higher, a stream flowing through the moor, above a heather-covered slope. The stream disappeared at intervals, to emerge spluttering with a low rumble and a broken babbling. On its bank stood a short, slender mushroom, white with a red blob in the middle of its cap as if splashed with blood in a folk tale. And cotton grass stood out from the light, yellow-green expanse with a damp cloth beneath it.

The drops on the fen moss trembled, glittered like delicate jewels.

Curious springs, the drops in the moss by the stream, like water shot with frost, or with veins and vaults here and there, or puddles icing or crystallizing over. Standing upright awaiting a prodding finger that would sink into the pale yellow-green moss. Trembling in the breeze. Then gaping cracks or shreds in the moss, which was crowned by crowberry; and islets of hair grass spread around.

Ochre bowls of dried-up pools; courses of streams with the flora of their beds laid bare.

Sterile screes spreading down from the shoulder of the mountain below the peak, as if poised to stalk into the ochre bottoms of the dried pools. Their ascent grew steeper, the higher they moved up the slopes. And other mountains came into sight. Fog began to swirl around their jagged tops and down their steep rocky sides. Yet parted for an instant like steam, magnifying gullies into chasms, stones into cliffs. Trolls? Waiting for something. That would be, had perhaps become. Wind whistling, the roaring of peaks, rumbling behind the mountains.

Now there were snowdrifts in the cirques they had to cross, and when they reached the shoulder a shallow valley appeared walled with massive cliffs, and unexpectedly the side facing away from the valley with its white-green lichen like verdigris, flat slabs vaguely reminiscent of marble.

The air was cloudless and pure in the chill breeze in the valley although haze and mist continued to reek around the mountain. Behind the peak in the dry riverbed which had long been on one side of them, the encircling mountains formed a cirque, snowdrifts stretching down them, as the misty cloud crawled, borne by the wind, or hovered around the peaks, gliding towards and away from their sharp extremities. Plunging over the slope, alternately revealing and covering the cliffs on the uncrossed track in a fast flow, right down to the muddy screes with their streaks of rock.

The moss on the stones in the cirque was almost black among the huge boulders. The crown of huge cliffs invited a threatening vision to be born. Vision upon vision. The mist farther off pressed the closer one tighter, gliding to and fro, hovering in the wings, as if the mountain were breathing and its slopes rippling. A single crowberry in moss-adorned rock and colourful lichen; and green dapples in the black moss like powder in the pitch of moss, with patches of brown as well, and as if emerging scorched from beneath the ice and snowdrift.

They said nothing, occasionally moving apart as if each were in his private world, with his own thoughts and perceptions and the same land, the same sky, the same weather; each swelling with what fermented in his mind; gathering playthings for his thoughts, choosing backdrops from the landscape to stage their play; outlines of images rushing past, plentiful at this moment; then spinning into an uncomposed tapestry, on the walls of rooms which were far away now, where the mind would later search for what it might own.

They had long traversed the boulders between the mountains before ascending it, the mountain which possessed its own reality. Unless it was a dream.

A dream?

Wizened blades of grass shivered between the stones, perhaps concealing a longing to be a string in a vast harp worthy of gathering whispered ciphers; which the wind had borne afar in quest of instruments to give them voice; so that it would not lose them, nor the confidence of those who yearned for colour in their silence.

To rise up against the superior force of emptiness. And root one's vision in this land which killed most living things were they not charged with magic from its own terror.

Gathered in solitude. Studied from sanctuaries, snatched from peril.

Hold me, hold me; let me go.

I left the horse to itself, allowed it to snatch bites of grass. And there I saw meeting in the rocks a kindly ogress with a child between her legs, and a dwarf-like thinker in a crag projecting from the pile of rock; an ancient noble being with a wide face and a long beard with clusters of moss at its roots and green hair down on to his shoulders.

Stretching into the sloping columns of mountain rock; the cold, defiant reply of the north, created from itself, a formal retort to those made by man on southern slopes for the pure vine beneath a sky where the sun relents only for a swiftly passing night, which is black and close and warm.

How remote now those nights and sun-drenched days, with their rapid undulations in the leagues of life in cities where I once stayed, by now as if in another life; not the one I am threading in this chapter of my life, not here with these immense distances which form between people, across these mighty mountains and moors. Wastes of silence where the scream is fettered; and the river flowed peacefully from a rock where year upon year it had beaten its course onward and down to the sea, from its roots beneath the snow, in the ring of peaks, which tolerated their silence from century to century, in the tabernacle at their source.

This rock conveyed to him, to the limits of his capabilities, wherever the eye roamed, new countenances to attend that evening assembly.

They crossed a peak on the other side of the temple where no archpriest officiated, but where visitors had to enter the land with pagan forces, and become trolls to fulfil the holy duties of yore, which was still there, when it was reached.

Now it was behind them.

The sky grew cloudy, as night approached. And something awoke softly at his ear, fragmentarily at first. The murmuring of the sea, far below. The breeze lifted itself again, trilling in his ear, singing through blades of grass and sharp edges of stones.

The travellers took a long arc, leaving a single track on the sandy bank sloping down to the mumbling of the sea. Ledges and screes below them, the odd stretch of grass; immense rocks stuck into the sand, far apart.

And now the poetic eye confronted the profile of the Redeemer himself in the manner of this Icelandic landscape, wrought in its forms, and another beside it, studying him askance, born of rock as well, a native, bearded and coarse St Peter, sworn to the renowned role of the holy book, led by a single rein into the genus of flowing words.

Slowly it grew dark. Rock crunching under hoofs. A ponderous scraping from the sea; which toys at sucking in heaps of pebbles, tossing them with crazed force back to the land, up on to the thin rim beneath the sea cliffs.

Their progress over the tongue of gravel shifted their view of the crag, moving it flush against the stone Redeemer, adding new postures to read from the play of images; and a newly awoken naked woman appeared to glide in a dance, gyrating to tempt the Redeemer from his weighty task of bearing the yoke of the world. St Peter grew reticent, abnegation still in his expression, driving wonderment away.

They left this behind them, and soon the slope removed these images, placed them beyond reach, and cut the peak above them.

Old snatches of refrains came half intoned without forming a whole in their minds, the occasional unexpected word too; and he did not know whether they came from outside or within, from some hidden order, old memories or material for a lyrical offering.

And it was in just this unlikely setting that a memory began to appear as if from ancient tales, from solitude into a clamour, like a voice whispering to him an unrelated story from a southern bower where he who sits there was once you, sitting there and scanning the road which soon would in a sense better never had been taken.

Scanning the veils winding in the air from strings of smoke. And he dug beneath piles of sand down to a land where a memory was buried: you black-browed maid whose presence forsakes me never, he repeated over in his mind in the bower with its shadow of a palm tree like an image of a scimitar chopping off a criminal's hand. A thief? he asked, exhaling smoke from a long Tuscan cigar, tightly out into the spreading veils which flowed through the air, curled slowly, dispersed, lost their endless potential for weaving, became a stupefying fog thrashed intermittently away by the motorized-fan blades which cleared the air in the centre of the room. With glowing copper wings like a propeller stirring up water at the stern of a boat.

Fettering my soul by the desert's sands, he muttered haltingly to himself, and the wind wafted it away from him, in the opposite direction from his companion.

He let it go, having no need to convince himself of his play upon this stage, with his thespian streak. There was no need for magic in the hope of dispelling a gnawing fear, a gnashing doubt, hold at bay the curse of ambush by death. Here, the land itself offered to extend the time which is your life by giving it magical depth, widening it.

When they set off he looked at his companion's face which had assumed again the mask of his life, then remembered how he stood out against the sun, there was sunshine then; smooth-faced as he rested in the dip in the land, a gentle expression, like a peaceful death mask, contented, almost euthanasian.

A swarm of birds was whisked aloft above the rocky platform.

High above, ravens cawed a pagan prophecy.

There was a panorama of the countryside below the platform, stretching beautifully in the newly awoken glow of day, towards the sea.

Beneath the slope was a plain, the land dappled.

His companion had dismounted and released his horse, unloaded the baggage from the packhorse and lay with his hands behind his neck on the soft bed of earth in the dip. Ásmundur sat down beside his companion, clutched his knees and rested his cheeks between them. Saw his companion lying beside him, in perfect accord with the land at this moment. He saw how his wrinkled face smoothed out, how the runes experience had fashioned in his face wore thin, telling of a harsh war which offered no quarter. Now, peace reigned. And the sun moved in the soft breeze from behind the low clouds when they parted.

He let Thórdur decide when to stop and rest now. Teases of words passed through his mind, searching for links without urgency. But how pleasant to hear the horses champing in the breeze which carried its messages. He lay on his back with his eyes open towards the scudding clouds.

The images, he thought; those images in the clouds which reveal themselves to the traveller on long journeys, which the solitary man can read as they gather together as if on urgent business, even a message, before they part again and something else appears. And he began thinking of paintings he had seen at galleries abroad and had captivated his imagination, painted in Italy hundreds of years ago by Mantega who had hidden among the clouds remote pictures of the beyond, coupled now with the vision of an Icelandic mountain traveller. What was his companion thinking? The thought preyed on him of how being abroad had alienated him from his origins, distanced him from his people. These bustling, dramatic formative years when he vacillated, trying to acquire an identity that might ring true, a knowledge of who he was. And there were times when he had risen from debauchery, unexpectedly baptized, he felt, in saintly solitude, had been racked with anguish, was suddenly free with flashes of inspiration, as if escaping beneath a perennial burden, and could see far and wide, when the darkness of his mind suddenly lit up, illuminating a deepness he had never imagined, although suspicion had pointed the way.

When Ásmundur saw the face of his companion, Thórdur, growing younger in front of him, he began to think of his own age. Although not considered an old man, and called young in the cities where he had stayed, he had another life over and above that of his countryman, bore another world within him which created a certainty that two men lived inside him, that he lived two lives at once. And the problem was not eased by the need to reconcile these two natures, in order not to perish. Perhaps, in consequence, a kind of exile everywhere, at odds with the law of his environment, despite momentary bargains that were struck, at once the actor on the stage and its director behind the scenes. But never acquiring complete conviction. At once a young man and an elder. He often felt a pained yearning for solitude when he mellowed in splendid wantonness, and although he still managed to enchant the assembled company he could never quite enchant himself into acceptance, tempting as it was.

Ásmundur was aware of the horses, aware of Thórdur lying there.

27

With secret thoughts, possibly even for that matter the very heritage of the nation, lying there on the short grass. You hear a language spoken, conveying mysterious messages from the spirits of the brooks which were still excavating their channels, past generations, the cryptic speech of water flowing over that land. The murmur of water. Voices of all ages in the murmur of water, making man alone and the same; flow as the centuries might out to the sea. Where there is no land beyond.

They shouldn't eat too much, said Ásmundur.

Thórdur opened his eyes and his face disappeared from its heavenly peace and back behind the mask.

Well, isn't it time to be moving along; we can't stay here all day. Lovely as it is.

Thórdur stood up and brushed off the flecks of grass with the handle of his whip, the strap wrapped around his clenched fist.

The peace of the Lord, he muttered, his face now the way such men had looked for thousands of years.

When they had bridled the horses they tarried a moment before climbing into the stirrups and swinging themselves on to the horses' backs. Ásmundur rested both hands on the horse's crupper as it champed on the good grass: Thórdur, he said, handing him the snuffbox.

Thórdur held both reins with one hand tight to the bit and the horse pressed its head against his chest, as if ready to answer a question he might ask.

What's on your mind, Thórdur?

Thórdur hastened slowly. He held the fat, short wad of snuff in the hollow between his thumb and index finger, a blue vein standing out on the back of his hand. After calmly sniffing up every grain, he said: I'll tell you what Einar said to me the other day, up here at Hóll. Strange how some people can be good company and others not. Like my father. Just like he finds it impossible to say anything at all that other people enjoy.

He mounted the horse.

The horses were reluctant to stop grazing, made a few attempts to bite again, as they plodded away.

The sea appeared, far below, infinite, woven together with the ragged backdrop of the sky. The coastline like a slack bow with its cliffs bent down as if in humble veneration.

Down the mountain the mist parted from the edge of the gully, and on the slope near by a farm lay snugly as if drawing reassurance from hardly rising up from the green pillow of the land. From the hummocky field which almost reached the edge of the patchy ridge, where a spraying waterfall plunged from ledge to ledge to end in a pool, thence a river racing over shallows, winding downwards past the outposts of the district, as if some controlling force had decided to chop it clean away from the countryside farther below, beyond the law of human society.

What dreams does a virgin shepherdess dream as she sits by the brookside? And hears the waterfall bringing her promises in its high spirits. Until a deep voice begins to growl from within the rock, heavy like all-commanding providence, shattering the dreams in boulders and tapering chasms, where everything resounds differently. And her ruffled golden hair grows hoary, her soft cheek coarse, her eyes dreamless and lethargic, as she still stands on the edge watching the pool wearing away its hole under the rigid fall of water, forward; down.

There was no sign of movement at the farm. Here I do not need to knock on the door, in the name of authority. At this outermost oasis. The limits of human obstinacy, challenging the force that governs the wilderness.

Thórdur scanned from ledge to ledge then pointed silently with his whip to where a figure could be seen heading across the slope away from them, beneath a burden that left only the legs visible, bent at the knees, and the left foot stepping a good half the length of the other, although not apparently lame, very slightly pigeon-toed.

They saw no one else, and did not tarry.

That's the sea over there, magistrate. We're getting there.

They followed the track side by side. There was drizzle.

Yes, we've got this far. But a landscape like the one we've crossed today – what effect does it have on you, Thórdur?

They rode on in silence for a long while.

Hadn't Thórdur heard him?

The woman by the waterfall. Where did she come from, into his mind? He imagined her youthfulness anew, made her sit on a rock, running her fingers through her long hair. Look down into the pool, at the water falling rigid from the ledge, though the wind sometimes whisked the stream away, and waves breaking in the dip by the edge where she sat. She did not really know how to act. Now that spring was here at last. Spring. Without darkness lying over her soul, crushing it. Yet she was not light at heart, and her fingers played lightly across her long locks, stopping still sometimes. So had nothing happened? When everything was supposed to happen that had been awaited all winter. Since when? What had changed?

The spray of the waterfall pressed back against the rock. Wiped out the images there. It was some way behind. The waterfall, and the rock where no one was sitting.

Now there was a fine rain. Thórdur pulled up the reins to stop his horse. The magistrate was a little way ahead of him.

It was the brothers from Andrídarleiti, said Thórdur. Fairly quiet people. The three of them went off together, well drunk. One of them fell of his horse on the track. And rolled down the slope, a huge fall. The others picked him up but he didn't move.

He's dead then, one of them said. And they covered him with rocks to keep the ravens off him. And went home. Their father came out and saw the brothers standing outside, hungover and tired. And saw the sable mare that the lost brother owned.

How do you think our brother Páll feels? one of them asks.

Then the old man said: Yes, your brother Páll. Was he with you then?

So they told him he was under a pile of rocks they had made. Had taken a fall and died.

The old man leapt on to the sable mare and rushed off.

And he had to go and take the sable mare, said one of the brothers.

Their father reached the pass and found a single mound of rocks. And tore them away from the man underneath. Put his ear down to him and thought he could hear breathing and some sign of life. And as he lifted his son on to the back of the horse, a hipflask fell out of his pocket where it had been buried all night, a whole flask, and the old man wet his lips with it and he came round. He had just been asleep.

He was quite unhurt, no bones broken, and could sit in front of his father on the sable mare as they rode home.

The horses stood completely still, one of them moving its ears, its head hanging down by the loose rein. Ásmundur could not think of a story to tell his companion. They remained silent a while. Was Thórdur waiting for a pinch of snuff? Hardly so soon.

They crossed the plain without calling at the farms that appeared before them. Scattered. In the rain.

The rain had a soporific effect on their thoughts. The mild features of the countryside. The long lake whose far end was rendered invisible by the long headland jutting out into it, the farmhouses on the lakeside. The magistrate welcomed being able to cross this peaceful countryside slowly. He was also grateful for having enjoyed the dramatic beauty of the mountains which lifted his thoughts so far above all that slumbered low down and was insignificant and dull. It had done him good to be forced to leave his home and books behind, the Latin poets in quest of the beautiful who rejected all that dragged one down into the tragedy and starving desperation that strangled so much at birth, crippled and distorted, making human life miserable and empty and damned. The journey had steeled his heart and his courage, fortified him to face up to the wretched and the repulsive, without letting it belittle him or clip his wings.

He welcomed this harsh, magnificent beauty, which steeled and strengthened him; and he had already absorbed mythology enough from the world of the trolls to ensure immunity from all that might impair his soaring, so strong was the urge now to console himself by writing poetry and exploit to the full his power to rescue himself, and elevate his nation to the grand role he had dreamed for it, which he suspected had been chosen for it by divine providence; that the nation might reach adulthood, live up to the destiny intended for it, and accept a flaming torch, and invigorate the man who could lead it with that torch in hand, to develop so that the whole world would listen and be illuminated by the glow; the masses in huge cities could partake of the word from the ocean shore at the farthest limits of the habitable world.

Now he felt his thoughts were clad in armour, able to dispatch his duty without losing any of his force. Without debasing himself in the slightest even when handling such a terrible case.

To a certain extent he accepted this inescapable journey. And perhaps he could learn something which would offer him a subject, at a later date, for descending from the heights of his lofty quest for beauty and returning to the garden of serpents, in a new way. Had he not previously been in the snakepit like Gunnar Gjúkason, and played his harp to save his life? And the serpent had still not managed to strike at his heart, not managed to commit him to the world beyond.

He reproached his old schoolfellow the clergyman for lacking the single-mindedness to reveal the matter earlier. Then he would have been spared having to ensure that justice was done. There had been grounds even before he took up this office. It was that recent. He no longer felt the anger that had seized him when he was sent the charge. Anger at imagining that the clergyman himself should tolerate such a criminal act perpetrated in his own house, the vicarage itself. Where should the laws of God and men be respected more than in the vicar's home?

The Reverend Stefán had ignored the unspeakable relationship between half-brother and half-sister for so long that they had been led into irrecoverable calamity, and he had evidently failed for much longer in his duties as a shepherd of souls by pretending not to see what was common knowledge, and was crying out to heaven. The whole district knew. How on earth could this happen in Iceland among what were supposed to be enlightened people, people at least who were literate? The whole district whispering about these goings-on without them reaching the correct authorities. Without anyone having the courage to intervene and prevent a further chain of criminal acts. Not just against the laws of man, blatant as that was, and intolerable. With our whole new generation of lawyers, disciples of Professor Emerich who never ceased to urge us to smother the spark before it became a burning pyre. Smother tomfoolery, make public every brutal act, every breach, before it becomes an epidemic without end. Isn't the devil trying everywhere? Is there not a continuous war being waged between good and evil, the forces that battle for the world and always have done so? What will happen if we feed the power of darkness by our apathy, indifference towards our duty to work continually for the divine nature, and justify its imposition upon the world, the society of civilized men? Uproot weeds in the plot of Christianity. He felt as though he were steeling himself for a sermon, if only he could be a homilist admonishing sinners as each demands. The word godfearing, isn't that wide of the mark? And then it transpired that this was not only an act of defiance towards God, simply by breaking the law, much grosser than that, a direct threat to the Almighty who laid down the fundamental customs of Christian society. And nature itself. Where would transgressing that end? Monstrous births. Did we not have examples from the animal kingdom? In folk tales, what was more outrageous than the offspring of fox and cat, or cat and dog? When the incompatible sported together.

The rain did not grow harder. It fell softly on to the men and horses. The stones grew darker. When it fell on to the lake, the rain seemed to be hauling ten thousand drops up out of it.

Have you seen them, Thórdur? he asked suddenly.

No.

They arrived at a river that flowed over shallow rock to reach the lake.

When they skirted up the slope on the other side, Thórdur said: Well, and paused. Then: Bjarni who brought the letter – we were talking yesterday. He really spoke quite well of them. Sort of in various ways. No complaints about their work. Really, a good pair of workers as far as that goes.

What do they look like? the magistrate asked, then thought about the picture that his companion's description conjured up. The woman: jet-black hair, small with dark eyes; a pretty mouth, with thickish lips; small hands and neat legs. She was considered attractive, but rather reticent. But quite capable of speaking up for herself when she wished and the occasion demanded. Perhaps Bjarni was quoting the vicar when he called her intelligent. With a temper too, although she usually chose to restrain it. She was around twenty, the man two years younger. Considered fairly handsome. A longish neck and somewhat round-shouldered. He had a red hue to his cheeks, freckled, his eyes ashen but capable of changing colour oddly, especially when he was in good spirits as was once the case, when his eyes seemed bluer, and shone; now it was rare for him, as he once did, to joke and lark about with the women, rollickingly at times, and was sometimes, especially at the vicarage, felt to be rather too extrovert in word and deed. He even made the old women shriek with those tricks and pranks of his, which some people called buffoonery; although they perhaps enjoyed it more than they would admit. On the rare occasions when he was in a playful mood now and his brooding lifted, the housefolk thought it unnatural and it aroused no merriment among others.

Some of this the magistrate had already heard. That they were children of the same mother but had never lived in the same place before. Both had been housed at many places in the district, the woman possibly outside it as well. But he recalled someone, he did not remember whom, saying they had spent a short while together on a farm some years ago, and he did not know why she had been sent away. He knew that she had a child several years old.

It was far from pleasant having to tackle such things. It was an imposing enough task for an ordinary official, without being a poet too, who perceives the world accordingly, and cannot entirely ignore human wretchedness and desolation.

Ásmundur also noted from Thórdur's account that the young man combed wool for his sister, while she span vigorously.

And then the magistrate remembered a story to cap Thórdur's.

34

When it had just been roused the ghost was given a name by a woman who encountered it when she was rounding up sheep on the ness. She was approached by a well-dressed man of fairly small build. She asked him who he was. Ignoring the question, he asked whether he would reach Skáli farm by bedtime. If you reach there by bedtime, I'll call you Lightning, she said. With these words, the stranger disappeared like a flash. He appeared in different guises of varying smartness. Sometimes in the form of a lad wearing a fawn jumper. Even in the shape of a dog. At other times dressed up, with a custom, when greeted politely on the street, of casually taking his head off with his hat. A smell of singeing sometimes emanated from him and this startled people who did not know its origin. He was accustomed to travelling in a grey cloud of smoke, and played various malicious and dangerous pranks on people, sometimes confining himself simply to teasing them. Some people recognized him by the fire in his eyes. He was held in fear all over the countryside.

There was a man called Ívar who lived at Vad in Skriddalur. He was considered a sensible man, titanically strong with a frame to prove it. He was wise, good at wrestling, and brave. He went to Skáli farm to make some purchases and asked to be allowed to stay there, which was granted at a price. He went out himself to lead his four horses into the pasture, but when he tried to tether them they shied away. He could not tie them up, but neither could he identify what was frightening them. He had to chase around after them and struggle for a long time before he managed to get them into their tethers; this had never happened to him before. Although exhausted, when asked if he dared sleep alone in the stable loft, he said with a laugh that he wasn't afraid.

He had a light burning while he collected his strength again, and facing him were the open stairs. After a short while a man appeared there wearing a top hat and tuxedo, elegantly dressed. He stared in silence at Ívar, and Ívar stared back, thinking: this is some gentleman who has been given a place to sleep in the next bed to me. He thought his behaviour was strange, neither proffering a greeting nor continuing up the steps.

35

Good evening to you, said Ívar.

The visitor remained completely silent.

Evening.

He stayed silent, with a mocking grin.

Arrogance, felt Ívar. They both remained silent and looked each other in the eye. Then Ívar, still in a soft voice, said: Are you visiting, or do you live here?

His counterpart stayed silent, his cold grin transfixed.

You must be a stranger here. Why don't you answer me?

Ívar, beginning to lose his temper, charged him with being arrogant. Snatched up the chamberpot and pissed into it while chatting with the unfriendly caller. The stranger started pulling faces at Ívar, who by now suspected who the gentleman might be, and dashed the chamberpot straight into his face: Take that for your pains. The stranger disappeared like lightning beneath the urinary onslaught and never approached the man again.

There was much more ado, and the outcome was all the more precarious, when Stefán the Strong tackled Lightning. Renowned for his strength and in particular for carrying a heifer from the mountain pass at Strýtufjallshryggur and far on to the heath. He called at the parsonage and accepted refreshments. The clergyman asked where he was heading.

To Skáli farm.

Tonight?

Yes.

Don't you think Lightning will block your way?

I'm not afraid of him in the least.

Have you seen him?

No. But I'd like to have a look at the abomination.

You'll get a look at the abomination if you go out along the coast tonight.

Just as I wanted then, said Stefán and left.

Stefán was dressed up in an outfit of new, strong cloth and carried a yard-long staff with a sharpened point. He was a largish man, but his stout frame made him look smaller.

The moon waded through the light mist. Not the slightest breeze. Then, as he reached the spit that stretched out flat towards the moonlit sea, he saw a grey cloud of vapour swoop down from the ridge and around the rocks above him. It rushed for Stefán and split into two around him, then merged back into one.

Stefán felt a tight grip and realized there had been something inside the cloud of vapour. This strange being thrust itself over him and shoved him closer towards the sea, blocking his sight completely. He had a strong inkling that this was Lightning, taking up the challenge. Summoning up his strength, he struck out at the vapour with his staff, but it went straight through it and broke into three. He wanted to take hold of Lightning but could not get a grip and groped right through him. He seemed to be taking hold of something so slippery that it slid back out of his grasp. It felt as if it had come out of the sea, like an oily piece of sharkmeat. Whatever it was he was grappling with released its grip and he felt himself being pushed towards the sea. And they struggled to and fro until he could not help ending up in the water, which was deep right up to the land. He managed to wade ashore and free himself. But he was still not rid of Lightning, who now stood menacingly in front of him. Stefán tried to get past by stepping to the side along the waterfront, but Lightning covered him closely, slapping and shoving at him, and did not relent until Stefán landed in the sea again, this time where it was shallow. Back and forth they went, on land and in the water, and Stefán lost both his old cap and gloves and his clothes were tattered and torn.

Then a demonic power filled the ghost and it lifted Stefán high up into the air and dashed him down into the water, knocking the breath from his body. He had to call on all his innermost resources, and it was prayer that went furthest, giving him all the greater strength the more it weakened his opponent. Filled with a manic power, he finally managed to get a grip on Lightning. He made easy work of tossing him into the air, and strode forward, holding him over his head. Yet Lightning broke loose once again and puffed himself up with taunts and jeers. Having had quite enough of such arrogance, Stefán rushed up on to a bank, and Lightning too, and they clashed again. The ghost was somewhat more substantial than before. Stefán was frenzied, chanting the Lord's Prayer and other invocations of the good at the top of his voice while they fought: and these smote the ghost so hard he was left defenceless. Stefán dashed him to the ground with such force that the blow seemed to resound in the hills and rocks around him; and then suddenly there was nothing in his hands nor in his titanic grip. His adversary disappeared with a flash and a cloud of vapour, whisked up on to the mountain like a glowing thread, and vanished completely from Stefán's sight; and the two worthies were never to meet again.

Stefán reached the nearest farm sapped of strength and in unrecognizably bad shape, all hunched up with his clothes in shreds and his old staff broken into three; and he told of the rough treatment he had been given.

Did you see the abomination? said the clergyman when they met later.

That I did, and not just see it either. If there'd been bones in that bugger's body I'd have broken every one of them. But Lightning won't dare venture into my hands again.

The Shepherd's Evening

Evening in a deserted valley. The sun was heading towards the invisibility beyond the frame of the valley, the hills in the west. The land's gratitude for the day that had passed rose as a violet mist into the distant west while the sun still had a stretch left to cross before it could hide behind the hills, its valediction spreading over this world with dainty colours. The grass turned golden, and the grey moss covering the lava began to glow.

And now the sheep on the mountainsides stood still, regretful of the heedlessness of the day when the grass was green, and earthly; and so healthy that the green juice dripped from the corners of their mouths. Now they were standing still and looking, and did not move; as if they were watching something unique, or perhaps admiring the landscape like travellers. But they went back to nibbling at the slope. Then they darted among the boulders and green patches of grass and grey screes on the slopes, bounded over the dried-up courses of brooks in spasmic leaps, where the same spring the valley had been an orchestra resounding with music and song. Above it, ochre boulders and stranded pedestals stood out against the clear blue sky.

Then a sheep bleated plaintively, moaned in its own language; and the echo opened new dimensions, multiplied the valley. Wind whispered into ears, stirred up for this evening; the shadows grew darker, like eyes about to look inwards. They lengthened, as if stretched out by the wind, although it was blowing from the opposite direction.

Two sheep were standing there, one black and the other white; and watched from afar the man moving slowly closer, alone, while each stone grew independent of its own private shadow.

And in this new, reddening light which kindled shadow upon

shadow from a holy flame, which lives all over the country, it was here that the images began to frolic on the sides of the mountain; cliffs that serve to support mythological features and events, and incidents alluding to the world of men, images that have fled human eventualities and penetrated with newly baptized proclamations the senses of the man walking there, and demanded him for their emissary.

He heard the sheep high on the mountain bleat plaintively but could not see it even if he scouted around and clambered over gullies, and the sheep which had watched him before disappeared in fright towards the pink clouds in the east.

Presently the sun faded in the west. The mountains there were violet and exhaled mist. As the outlines of nearby hills and slopes grew sharper, the land there drew closer to itself; the distance abolished all substance, and hovered above in a crescent poem.

The man knew a fox had taken the lamb from the ewe, there was nothing he could do.

Dejectedly, he walked to the lake at the bottom of the valley, and only when he had reached the bank did he see the swans on the water. He sat down on a tussock covered with moss. Saw the cob-swan approach, noble and dignified, with its neck arched and head held high, while its beak pointed downwards as if deep in thought. Then the arch in its neck smoothed out, and its throat stretched out with prolonged notes, and the song carried across the water, resounding among the hills around, as if the tranquillity of the evening had awaited just this. And it was answered from the nest where its spouse was sitting on the eggs. When the cob-swan drifted over there and crossed the final stretch at a tack against the stream it lowered its head and projected it in an almost horizontal arc in over the nest. Another head rose to greet it and leaned over, and their necks touched. Whatever might have passed between them, the one that was sitting on the nest rose slowly with wings outstretched just enough to show beneath its breast the precious eggs. It sank back slowly to tend them again, and heads and necks rose and dipped down, and span an invisible web, together; while a chill breeze arrived to stroke the water and rustle the straws on the bank.

Love

He rose up from the woman, his lips had been trembling at her neck; raised himself on to his elbows, saw her eyes soporific, contented, drunk with satisfaction; bent his elbows and eased himself slowly down towards her, sank his head on to her stomach, carefully clasped her hips and lifted her towards his cheek, moved farther down and stroked his cheek against the bristling hair, lying there on his knees with his buttocks raised; while she ran her fingers through his hair, slowly and gently.

It was so gentle and tender, then he pressed himself weeping against her: What have we done?

It was all right, she said; true. If this were wrong I would refuse to believe those values. Then I'd start to understand the fallen angel.

Words, he said, what can words do?

She gave a soft, deep laugh. There was no vehemence now: you are the fire that kindles my body, she whispered loftily; the spring that quenches my burning thirst.

The wind moved through the grass, warbled refrains to the straws, moaned in the door to the croft, howled in the rafters. And the din of the sea was louder than before, when it awoke anew.

A heavy pounding came from the beach, a sliver of moonlight cracked on the surface of the ocean; a twinge of a shiver moved through him, a chill through his nakedness; like a gust from the great stage of the world to behind the curtain where they were hidden; which the warmth of her naked skin did not manage to keep at bay . . .

At the same time most people seemed to ignore it, deliberately. Pretended not to know, but were all weighed down by it. This sad shadow rested constantly over the small community at the vicarage, dividing a handful of people. The young woman held her head high in her love, and urged her lover to ward off all worries about other people's opinions, and enjoy what there was to enjoy while the occasion lasted.

This is our moment, our day. Our night. Our moment at night. We are each other's now. And now is now, whatever happens. What comes later is another matter. Here am I, here are you. Now. Us.

She said such things to him to brace up his courage.

If God is displeased, He can just look the other way.

Remember God.

Hasn't He got enough to look after? she said. Added that He could just clear off if He grudged them that. They had nothing else. Then He would be unjust. Why should they believe in an unjust God who takes from someone who owns nothing? The only thing that person has ever had. Was it not this that made them human, lifted them out of the dust? Which blows away. Dust. Without love, what is life? What would we be? Except beasts? And would this dear God want us to be beasts? Would He have made us the way He did? Would He not have made us different? Me a mouse, you an eagle? Or a cow or a lamb, a worm, a flea? Or what?

What?

She could no longer think of him as a brother. He was her lover.

The thought that it was forbidden enraged her. It made her anger flare up. She could have screamed. Who is going to forbid me?

God?

The voice of God in my heart speaks differently. This God who forbids, who is obstructing love, the vicar can keep Him. The magistrate. The God of Life, the magistrate can't order him about, not the king, not even the Pope himself. Otherwise he would be dead, even many times over.

And I deny that. For I hear Him saying within my heart: Yes, my child. Love is always right. It is true. You love a man. More than any other. Even more than your own child, the fruit of your own body. That cannot be a crime. And the vicar, he says nothing. In fact.

He sometimes gives a peculiar look, if not sheepish, perhaps accusing, with his kindly, fluttering eyes. Maybe just inquisitive. Then he looks away immediately, somewhere else. Pretends to be observing the weather, or the colours in the mountains, flashes in the sky, or have the sheep got into the field again. Just something.

Peculiar, those eyes. It is as if they are growing pale. Although not visibly. Perhaps they will end up turning white as the snow that drifts away.

And the vicar's wife. She says nothing either. Although she is sad most of the time. So sad and seemingly shy. That short woman, plumpish, inconsequential. Sometimes she is like a spirit that dissolves. A ghost that disappears before you realize. You forget her instantly. But she is still there, always fussing with something. She is young. Only a little older than the woman who works on her farm, but still expected to intervene when she defies the Almighty. She passes no judgment. That's just the old woman. She grumbles to herself. Does not dare let me hear. She is burning inside and frightened to death of me ever since . . .

Hatred, that is the crime. That is the product of the devil . . .

He ran his hands across her face in the dark, thinking he was like a blind man. With no control over where he stood in life.

Yet he saw her before him.

Yet he saw her eyes as they were revealed to him when the moon slid from behind a cloud.

A dark cloud that became lined with silver in this flight, and her eyes so dark so dim in their blazing, their black fire.

Her hair, trimmed above the eyes, covered most of her forehead.

Her mouth half open; and in the tremendous light from the sky above a string of saliva glittered between her teeth. Like the silken thread of a lone spider spinning its enticing web.

Beginning a new contrivance.

Then the grinning moon was covered again. Its mirage.

And he ran his hands across her naked body like a crazed man in lust, and fear; and horror.

What are you so worked up about? she said, clawing at his hair, his nape, his throat, his shoulders. In spasms as if pushing him back and forth at once, tugging. Not soothingly, but provocatively: don't get so worked up, darling. Stay here for a long time, a long time.

Then he lay still and tried to calm himself so they could enjoy each other longer, their ambiguous tension. He gnashed his front teeth together, tried to be slow and composed without losing the thrill. She flowed and writhed about him. And suddenly he lost control, felt the cascade released as it poured over the ledge, and tried to enter her again, but so impulsively that all was lost, and his silvered spray broke free and foamed across her.

He slumped over her, drained. Snivelling.

It's all right, she whispered; all right. And squeezed his slender frame in her arms, making him groan. Braced. Strong. My darling. My only darling . . .

The morning seemed to bode a new world. Abandon all that had been, everything would be made new. Completely calm. As if everything were so new that all living things held their breath in expectation.

The lad lay down between the hummocks to be alone in the world. This world that was supposed to be beautiful and allow love to live. Exist. He lay on his back, wriggling to find a comfortable spot on the bumpy ground beneath him, and thought about her and himself, and stray clouds floated about the sky. Teasings. Is she sleeping? Has she woken up? What was theirs was nobody's business.

He was aware of the ewes close by, ruminating in the field. But the sheepdog sniffed him out, pounced on him, started licking his face.

He pushed the dog away from his face and pressed him to his chest. Let him lie there. He had to let the dog enjoy that forbidden pleasure. He could not betray him. He could not describe the delight he felt within. The love he fostered in transgression.

Gradually the others woke up to partake of this glory. There were signs on the occasional farm, from the delicate smoke rising straight upwards in a narrow column, pink, when the stoves were lit to make ready for those who still slept, or were beginning to stir. Thinking of this, he also heard the lapping of the sea like the epithet of fertile silence.

The dog seemed to sense what he was thinking too. It snuggled up calmly to him with a slight whimper of glee at the closeness.

He read of his promises in the images left by shreds of clouds, saw them dissolve in an instant.

When he propped himself up and reached out for a straw he chanced to glance towards the farm the moment the door was opened, and saw someone emerge and scout around in all directions. More as if sniffing than looking. For all the lad could see, it was the old woman, Járnbrá.

There was more than the sea to be heard when you listened carefully. Also the river which meandered calmly close to the farm. And the sounds began to harmonize.

Then came the distant barking of a dog, together with the peaceful bleating of sheep. It was only rarely that you felt you heard the murmuring of the river all the way to where you were lying, and the grass hardly moved . . .

The young woman watched the river.

She wrapped her arms around her legs, rested her chin on her knees, and watched. How the river flowed, swelling and rippling, meandering through the flat land, and she thought about her life.

The river flowed wide and calm until it reached a bend and rushed over shallows, crossed low ledges and steps where it narrowed. How her life had passed since she came here, and something started happening in her monotonous life, which hers had been, until now.

And suddenly it was so sorrowful, this young life, tragic – but she had acquired happiness. She ceased watching the river.

Stretched, locked her fingers together and folded her arms, lay back with them behind her head. Broke the bond of her fingers and rested the nape of her neck in her palms, raised her elbows like a rampart about her face, and watched the straws moving upside-down on the bank above her, when she stretched her neck back, long straws and single. Then she heard the barking of a dog, distant.

The breeze wafted towards her what was taking place above the hollow by the riverbank. As if from another time, on to that stage. Where the river reigned with what it brought forth and carried away.

And its enchanting murmur, the soothing current, abolished time on this day, this life of toiling man . . .

The man had been mowing the field since early morning. The day was endless, like other days at this time of year. Suddenly he stopped, leaned on to his scythe. Felt himself sinking forward, recoiled. Had he nodded for an instant? Thoughts which become dreams. Before you know it. The golden land, the promised land of golden opportunities. That strange name he had heard the vicar mention, perhaps when reciting a poem: Eldorado.

Lush grass on endless plains, cornfields as in *Njál's Saga*, and he donning the mantle of Gunnar from Hlídarendi, colourfully clad; his axe so heavy that the stalks buckled beneath it, and he there in his colourful clothes in the field, a peaceful chieftain without a spear, when they ride up to him, Otkell and Skammkell and their band of men . . .

And then he began swinging his scythe again, cutting the grass, but before he realized it his thoughts had carried him back with rhythmical strokes to golden-leafed forests in America, to the gold on the Great Prairies, where singing choirs reaped and threshed the corn; and others knelt at springs, and others at brooks sifting sand two by two, leaving gold in wet dust and lumps; and black springs of oil gushing the liquid gold of the earth, its blackness glittering like sunshine on obsidian, and the thundering of the song was magnified by his labouring motions, and the rhythm of his reaping was gladder than tended to prevail during his endless toil.

And the groups of singers stood fresh-faced and expectant on the distant shores found by Leif the Lucky, and his fellow travellers Karlsefni, and Gudrídur who walked to Rome to be absolved and do penance, and then Wineland the Good was lost again through bad luck, remained forgotten for so long, until now that a newly awoken song entices back the stragglers left on this island outpost, tempting them to seek out a living there and the good fortune which is assured to all who look for it.

Admittedly there were intrusions into these rhythmical, undulating thoughts with their regular motions, jolting them into disarray when he struck where hummocks had been levelled; then they were encroached upon by the enticing hiss from the winding serpent with its forked tongue, like a blue incantation in its metallic whistle, from the jingling leaves of golden forests, from the golden glowing cliffs of the mountain where glory revealed itself: If thou therefore wilt worship me, all shall be thine.

But what you always wake up to here. The land of our fathers and mothers. Where everyone died who could. The land. The land of ice. The frozen fences of hell. Death rock of the settlers. Raven-Flóki who gave up and left, bitter. Then it was called Gardarshólmi, after the voyager who got away again at the first opportunity. But was not named after the slave who escaped with his mistress and remained alone for the winter in his little bay. His name was grand, and appropriate.

Night-Farer.

And in the mind of the young man mowing the grass, a thought swung in of Night-Farer's winter stay in his narrow bay, beneath the towering mountains with his mistress. These fugitive, unfree people.

Slaves who first found freedom in the bondage of struggling to survive in an uninhabitable land where there was no one but themselves, and death waiting constantly in ambush, where they toiled ceaselessly with the sole aim of surviving.

The young man intensified his strokes with these thoughts, and began muttering some tripping rhyme to the movements of his toiling body, singing to the scythe, singing to the grass, by the winding river, and snatches from its murmuring wafted by the wind, muttering as if about to break into verse swollen by the rhythm of the mowing, for as long as the edge remained sharp, and his scythe bit, sheaf upon sheaf.

Shoo, shoo, and whish, and whish, and whish, whish – sheaf upon sheaf in the tall grass.

Then whetted the scythe again, spat on the edge, spat on the whetstone and fondled the blade with it, luring out a terrifying sharpness . . . sometimes . . . da–dadada–dada–dada. Sometimes it seemed to stiffen up. Sometimes it seemed . . .

They were sitting together on a hummock.

They saw the other people heading back home. In the setting sun, shadows defined the shape of the land, ridges, hummocks and all its fissures, chasms.

Do you think God would check out what we were doing if I took you behind the bank here or we lay down somewhere? Do you think He would butt in when no one else can see? and thought: Make secret devotion, and said: If we made love again.

We'll risk it, she said with a gasp, eager.

Her intensity caught him off guard.

Yes, if he is against us. Anyway.

They saw the old man disappear into the house, on the heels of the others.

He looked around first; they felt he was looking towards them, but pretended to be attending to something else. Had the rumour about them reached his part of the district, the farm where the old man had been found a home?

He was a little, slight man, wizened and so shrivelled that his blue veins stood out, his skin shiny in patches, pink with brown blobs, his eyes always running. Like a mountainside brook. He was drawn in the mouth, almost chinless, with a short, sloping forehead, little eyes, a shallow piercing hidden within them.

Later, they thought he had been snooping around them constantly that day.

Come on, he said. Pulled her on to the soft grass towards him when they were concealed in the chasm, which was often their bed during this summer of love . . .

He lay on the heath, weeping. When his horror waned he felt her moving beneath him.

Not the heath, not the earth.

He moved to the rhythm of what he had heard.

Pain, a tune called neither conscience nor anything else, or was it the sound of the fiddle he had heard the simpleton on the riverbank playing? In his mad wisdom.

Another wisdom than that which others made use of, the survivors – in this plenty which was not the gift of God, not from Him who gives good weather when it comes, and good growth in the fields, fish on the tackle, dry weather, and getting home in a blizzard.

Who then? The other one, the unnameable?

The other one, he thought. The fallen angel. Identified with light, but who lived in darkness. But said to live in eternal fire.

The bearer of light . . .

The vicar knitted his brows, said Járnbrá; he didn't like that subject. He never said anything himself. Since he never made any comment of his own, how could he wear that censorious expression? Who did nothing. But somebody had to start things moving. Wasn't it clear that this must not go on in the first place, not to mention any longer? The disgrace. It was an outright scandal. And more than that. A mortal sin. No milder words to describe it. And right in front of everyone's faces.

How can anyone put up with such defiance of the law of God? And of men? Was nothing sacred? And going around the way she did, strutting, that threatening expression which never slipped; defying us all. Almost smirking, just like we were guilty of the outrage. Us. And her and her brother the only normal ones, justified in their perverted act of love. In the hateful lust of their wanton love.

Hadn't she treated him too fondly in public view, in her arrogance, and revolt, against all we have been taught, and is still rightly called a mortal sin, even though capital punishment has been abolished. Didn't such a breach of nature deserve death? Lying on a bed of lust with her own brother.

This was the way Járnbrá muttered on, if only to herself. That

49

woman, old before her time, her life devoid of all rejoicing. It did not even give her contentment to monitor others on God's behalf . . .

Sometimes he feared her when vehemence drove out passion, sometimes he did not recognize her any more. Who is she? Not a sister. Least of all that. She is a mysterious force, a bestial spirit crazed beneath him, snapping at him, biting, scratching like a monster.

He was terrified.

Their lovemaking gnawed at him. But she was too strong. Too natural. What the hell could men criticize them for? The laws of men? What are the laws that forbid them, that can forbid them from enjoying each other? What do we owe to the makers of such laws?

Was it perhaps God?

What has God done for them that entitles him to forbid them from making love?

What God? Scarcely the God of love. No, more likely of hate? In dark depths? Isn't it the very devil who turns against our love?

Sometimes he felt as if she were talking through him . . .

What else did she have? Except the little daughter she had borne to that repulsive man. Who snatched her up like an object he owned. Not even his servant. His animal. Just took her who knew nothing and owned nothing. A waif. Yet he fondled his dog, and rewarded it for favours. What was she but a child? When this man took her like a beast, talking out loud to himself as he did so. And owned her not by taking her there, but by virtue of feeding her. Nor was she spared work even in her pregnancy. Such is the foundation of the society of men who then invoke sacred law to forbid our love . . .

He asked if his suffering would ever ease. Never again. Not that he did not try to resist. Because however often she repeated it, he could not believe it was miraculously natural.

These forces from the depths which have bound them together, who could do nothing but enjoy each other – because she was too strong; yes, was it not her who lured him into becoming her lover? My blood and her blood and . . .

And Járnbrá muttered on. She had even begun to spit in all directions when addressing herself and the Almighty.

And they suffer this, in their own home, the vicar himself. The vicar's wife herself. And he was supposed to be a clergyman. How could he be a clergyman and act that way, just shy and withdrawn. And that little dumpling of his. Like the law of God no longer exists, nor the laws of man. Or nature. Having that for a vicar. Who just looks on blue-eyed; perhaps they might just turn white as snow in all this innocence . . .

There were two of them, cutting turf. Jón wielded the scythe while Saemundur Fridgeir held the rope taut for him. Jón looked at him time and again, Saemundur could tell, and also that he intended to say something, so he avoided looking back at him, giving him the chance to talk. They cut the grass up from the roots. They cut long swaths of turf for drying.

Listen, said Jón.

Saemundur did not answer.

Well, that's to say, said Jón, picking up the scythe and looking at the blade as if examining it; I felt I ought to mention it to you, he said, and bared his teeth; what people are talking about, he said; between you and me like; and had almost reached falsetto when he said the word 'like' and swung it into the air.

Oh. People sure say a lot of things, said Saemundur, about this and that. And the other.

That they do. They do for sure, and Saemundur felt how Jón's greyish eyes darted as he talked and added, panting, while Saemundur avoided looking straight at him: People are saying a few things about you and your sister, and he had begun to lisp.

Oh yes, said Saemundur, hearing his own voice feigning surprise; us, people will talk about anything these days. I thought people had more important things to talk about than small fry like us. Admittedly we are a bit short of nobility around here. But there are plenty of heroes in the Sagas.

He produced a short laugh.

Of course, of course. Tee hee. Indeed, of course. What? Oh, what the hell. You reckon so. But people are saying all the same that there's more going on between you two than brother and sister ought to do, he said, and looked out towards the sea as if waiting to see a ship, and gripped the scythe with both hands.

They were both silent.

Yes, Saemundur snapped; and you think I haven't noticed. There's not much left for people to gossip about these days. But they'd do better worrying about something else. Like how little grass there is yet. And the tough spring. The lambing, all those dead lambs. Wouldn't there be more sense thinking about that instead of peasants like us who stay out of other people's way? And hardly exist.

Well, that's what some people are saying. Among themselves. And it's just as well somebody mentioned it to you yourselves. If you see what I mean. People don't exactly approve of it.

Of what?

Bah, the way you act towards each other. Yes. People think it's more than enough. Sort of. And I've said enough. It's not good for everyone to keep it quiet, where will that get you? Like most people do. If not everybody. And I'm not saying any more.

They'll take offence at anything. If we can't even be friendly towards each other. Without someone sticking his nose into other people's business.

He spoke sharply, as if cutting into the heavy breathing which his companion had released into the momentary silence.

Well, that's the way things are, said Jón; that's all there is to it, and he had cut several more strips of turf. They began trampling on the turf to squeeze the wet from it.

Water seeped from within it as they both trod down.

Somebody had to mention it, said Jón, offering him a pinch of snuff; it's not really fun. Having to bring up what everyone is thinking; and gossiping about among themselves, and spreading all over the district. Because that's more or less what's happening.

It was almost calm. The sun hidden. But a wide view along the plain, the clouds clipping the mountain tops.

The sea was greyish, a glow on the horizon which grew brighter.

A dog was with them, asleep on a hummock. Black, with a white spot on its nose. It sneezed, rose to its feet and shook itself.

They had barely cut enough to fill the saddlebags. The turf they had cut before was beginning to dry out, some of it enough to bind.

They said nothing more. But Saemundur could not fail to notice that Jón would have liked to. Felt him looking over every so often, heard him clear his throat, but did not respond and concentrated instead on finishing his work.

He felt himself steeling in self-defence against this attack, and asked where he had found this grip over his senior. Perhaps it was only becoming brazen, he thought, bitter . . .

She looked out through the farm door, at the moon floating in the still river; and at the dark, single clouds in the blue evening sky. The moon appeared to be just below the surface, with the river flowing over it. She felt she heard someone behind her in the corridor. No one came. She shivered.

She went outside.

She lifted the latch on the church door. The hinges creaked lightly when she walked inside.

He was sitting there on the pew, a narrow bench without a back: her friend, her lover. Brother who is no longer my brother.

My lover.

He was sitting there, hunched forward, and it was too dark anyway to see his face.

As he sat with his head bowed, saying nothing. Motionless.

She sat down beside him, leaned over towards him. And wanted him to kiss her there, in front of God himself. Almighty God. In the house of God. Doing openly what men may not see. Though she had defied men in her love as well.

Hadn't they treated each other fondly in front of the people on the farm? Now the two of them were alone in the house of God. Wasn't it time to put to the test whether God opposed them too and would smite them with lightning, or send a whirlwind to sweep the church into the air, had it been desecrated, had it become the closet of immoral acts, swirling it around in the air like a top, spiralling tighter until He cast it out into the sea. If God were the type some people wanted Him to be, vicious and vindictive, the pedantic angry God of the Old Testament, the God of officials and noblemen and the old deacon on his visitation here with the sheriff, that the old woman talked about when her rheumatism plagued her worst.

She wanted him to be tender towards her. Because she was afraid. She wanted to be allowed to be afraid and small, and snuggle up to him. But she had to be strong, and could not allow herself to let him feel her weakness. It pained her sometimes having to be the strong one all the time, to protect and defend their love.

Now she could see that he had grown taller and stouter since the spring. She pressed herself up against him, and his hidden face was above her, projecting over her. A lock of hair fell over his forehead and stroked the top of her head.

She leaned back away from him for an instant to try to see his face; the dusk in the church was too dark for her to read his expression. But she could tell he was withdrawn and distant from her, felt his eyes were staring although she could not see them to confirm it. She felt that he was somewhere else than with her, though perhaps not with the master of the house who was God, not even with God if He should be plotting to force them apart, where His power was said to be greatest, if He were the type that some people wished to make Him, enemy of this defenceless life; enemy of the weak who had nothing but the obstinacy to demand to be able to love, whatever the commandments and laws of Moses said, and whatever name they called it. Now, in this house, it would be put to the test whether these were laws of man.

Maybe it would also be put to the test whether God existed in another form than as a ready-made instrument of government for those who dominated this society, as it was called.

Her fear grew, and she could barely stand the apprehension that followed, the anguish; she took hold of his arm with what seemed a curious lack of strength, placed it around herself, tried again to snuggle up closer to him. But he only recoiled at her intensity as if in a waking sleep, waking up in a half-stupor, sensing perhaps time and place without responding to either, swayed by a kind of hypnosis, bound by some new paralysing spell; and would perhaps turn to stone if she did not reach him to release him, free him by bringing him under her enchantment anew, unless her magic could influence him and rescue their love. To strengthen his resolve and power to struggle on in their revolt, and defy with her everyone and everything.

She rose to her feet without releasing her hold on him, and when his arm fell limply from her she threw herself against him, and pressed her leg between his clenched knees, pushing between his legs with her thigh; and kissed him violently on the neck, without thought of the mark it would leave, and spread herself with her kisses all over his face; and when she went to kiss his eyelids his eyes were open as if he were ready to look into secret places in dark caverns, or nooks in an awe-inspiring mountain, she touched his eyes delicately with her tongue.

And she felt the taste of her lover's clairvoyant or blind staring eyes, while deep within her resounded the silent shout which bore his name, filling the huge church; and was so painful, so painful – God himself must surely be moved into changing sides, forsaking the group of noblemen and abandoning them to their feeble protests and cries of scandal and disdainful expressions, and coming to show the two of them mercy and forgive them, and permit them what was most sacred to them, whatever anyone said; whatever the people said who were always hanging around him with their pestering and sycophantic addresses, nagging and flattery. In her groping kisses she moved closer to his mouth. But his lips were closed and cold, as if he had no will that she could awaken and guide. No will that she could take into her power, and control.

In this tiny, helpless church in the vastness of the night.

A flame was still alive on one candle on the cloth-covered cabinet behind the railings, beneath the altarpiece, where the chalice was kept, and the cloth for drying it as it was passed on, and the oblates.

And as they were eating, he took bread, and brake it and gave it to them and said, take, eat; this is my body.

An uncomfortable feeling passed through her when she thought of the white, round disc which the clergyman held between his thumb and index finger, and she saw his nails broad and short, corneous, their quicks ragged, the hand of toil, almost dropping what was supposed to be the body of Christ; and he placed it upon her outstretched tongue, dry and tasteless, like a circle cut from a proclamation from the exchequer.

And he took the cup, and when he had given thanks, he gave it to them; and they drank from it. And he said unto them: This is my blood of the new testament, which is shed for many . . .

Then the candlelight seemed to intensify and light up the altarpiece at the far end of this little building. He stood on a bowl and neat arcs of blood sprayed from the wounds in his sides and palms, into the bowl. And the blood splashed halfway down his legs. He stood in the middle of the pool of blood.

An Act of Murder

. . . Where he met farmer Kristján from Stóratunga whose sons had already released the sheep into Seljaland some time before; whereupon he asked Kristján whether he could not shortly leave the corral, to which he replied in the affirmative. Furthermore he mentions having found, in addition to the eight which he had brought from Grjótárgerdi, one of the two sheep which he had expected to find in Svartárkot but had not appeared there, so that in all he had had nine sheep in his charge, while two had been herded in from Svartárkot, owned by Kristján from Stóratunga. He says that he mentioned to Kristján that it would have been better for his stepson Tryggvi to go to Grjótárdalur and attend to the sheep at the end of the pasture, while he went after the others himself in the south, but whereas Kristján was not able to leave immediately, he went ahead with Kristján's two younger sons and the aforementioned eleven sheep, but parted ways with them when they had just passed west of the Vídirker corral, and crossed Sellandsá river and on to the hill called Hjalli, then down east of the cairn and south towards the river at Ytri-Lindir, where he had met Konkordía sitting a short distance from the river; he says that she greeted him but he did not reply, dismounting instead and taking hold of her and placing one of his gloves and his handkerchief over her mouth and nose and holding her down until she suffocated, whereupon he dragged her over in to the river; he says he placed her in the river with her head pointing upstream, although slanting towards the eastern bank, and that the water where he placed her was no deeper than to his calf, not immersing the body completely, although he cannot recall exactly how much

of it protruded above, and he claims not to have considered whether the body would float away from where he placed it or not, having performed the deed at such speed, and in such a frenzy and distraction that he could not have had the presence of mind to prevent it being noticed. None the less he recalls jumping down from the bank, although he is unable to remember on which foot he landed and says that the details of the incident in general are unclear in his mind, for at the same instant he became conscious of having caused the girl's death he had been seized by a feeling of remorse and prayed to God to forgive him that crime.

Conversation at a Place of Rest

We farmers, said the man of the house, we stand together. We are learning that now. The most beautiful feeling is being one for all and all for one. That is the dream.

The light flickered on the wall lamp. The level of the oil in the lamp was so low that the wick would have to be lengthened sooner or later, so that it could reach down to feed the light.

And in the fleeting brightness, shadows moved abroad, assumed monstrous guises, brought encroaching evil spells into this tiny community beneath low eaves, into this penfold of the world of man while lashing rain shed its crazed foam on to the sagging peak above the little farmhouses.

Then the weather grew louder, gusts of wind dashed off at tangents in bursts against the ribbed mountainsides. A grey horse grew darker as it became drenched with the rain on the bank of the lake, did not nibble down at the wet grass but watched instead, completely still, an elf maiden defying the fillies, washing herself in a spring invisible to all others as well. And this eternal wind stroked the marshland firmly, shook cotton grass and cavorted across the meadow on to the banks, ran its moist mouth over stones and soil, boulders and screes alike.

In its determination to reach the lake the river shied from those relentless strokes and arched its back in the current.

In the course of the river through the gully there were yellow and red edges to the cliffs; the rocks mostly ochre or yellow. The brooks had turned white.

A chasm was swollen with yellow and scarlet rockfalls, and sprayed pillars of rock stood guard over it like witnesses brought in from the wilderness as a reminder of the endlessness of time and ask where you had arrived at.

Higher up, there was a plain with a dried-up watercourse, garish and rocky clay, heather around it in a dip of sorts.

A penfold stood out towards the mountain, and rocks had fallen from it leaving a hole.

The traveller was aware of all this while he listened. A guest. And spoke. Images which had greeted his eye earlier in the day lingered in his mind, flickered in his imagination. The wind sang its piece, in accompaniment. Amidst these associations he watched his partner in conversation say: This is stirring up inside us country folk. The thought that we, who have always been so poor and defenceless against merchants and officials, at last we can become so powerful they'll have to begin treating us as if we exist. We see this from the books that the reading circle has searched out and been sending round among us farmers. The best-known phrase of all has been repeated so often that hardly anybody has heard what it really means: In the beginning was the word, and the word was with God. But now the word's come to us, and it'll be our word. It's our turn at last. History teaches us there's no point in resisting when the lower classes rise up and unite behind an oath; wake up to collective action. No power can withstand that, in heaven or on earth. As long as co-operation lasts and the fire of the word stays alive and lasts, as long as our co-operation is not divided. That's what we crofters are starting to turn over in our minds and crow about to each other. And there'll be no turning back.

The traveller saw that face harden, glaring from the bushy eyebrows which looked as if he tugged at them with his hands when he was alone writing odes to the lake and the swan on the crest of a wave, or reading Norwegian authors or Proudhon in Danish. His blue eyes spouted white steel splinters into the millennial darkness of the common people's life, which snuggled unfledged and had gained the hope of a new day.

We farmers had never seen gold before. Never seen money. We never really knew the value of our products. It was all in some strange books kept by the merchant. Now we've seen gold. And we won't be stopped. No more than a shark when there's blood in the sea. Since we started selling our cattle live to the Scottish merchants. But we don't think about gold.

The force of what is to be done, said the magistrate.

Quite, said the farmer; it's a means to an end.

Just as I have always said, said the magistrate.

A means of raising ourselves up and all about us.

The nation, said the magistrate, the country. Strengthening the individual to noble deeds.

The masses. To make the nation see itself as a nation, by joining hands, through co-operation the people will become a nation. Without that, there will never be a nation.

That's the value of gold. But gold is a poor crutch for a limping man. We need strong imaginative and progressive individuals, said the magistrate, men who perceive and understand time, progress in the world about us, and our unique position by harnessing the forces that live in our land, cultivate through technology, create. Men who understand the power of wealth.

But aren't you forgetting the curse of ill-gotten gains? How Sighvatur warned his son Sturla when he was trying to acquire the riches of Kolur the Wealthy?

Yes, then Sturla says if I recall correctly that he knows of other wealth that . . .

Yes, said the farmer, and talked of the other wealth that still greater harm would come of. The wealth of his brother Snorri. So I'd like to go back to the *Saga of Nikulás* and remind you of the merchant that old Sighvatur describes. Who never thought of anything but gold. Thought about gold day and night. And eventually the old man dies. Then his neighbours poured in and couldn't wait to take a look around. Before they opened his trunk they cut the old man open to take a look inside him. They weren't surprised not to find any heart. Then they opened his trunk, and they weren't surprised either to find it full of gold. But they were surprised to see a tiny little human heart there on top of the pile of gold. With smoke rising from it. I don't think, said the farmer, protractedly, rubbing the arched back of his hand tightly with the palm of the other so that his fingers lifted up at each stroke: I don't think it was warmth, but burning cold. And I think most people suffer with gold if they intend it most of all for themselves, instead of enjoying it with others, united in their ideal and human goal, and for the benefit of culture.

Since we're trying to quote each other under the table, I'll recall Sigurdur the Dragon Slayer in the *Saga of the Völsungs*, when the dying dragon warns him of the curse on the gold and he replies, the farmer's partner retorted: All desire wealth until the final day, but all must die once.

And look how that turned out, muttered the farmer; that treasure didn't bring good fortune, nor the force of that which must be done. Quite the opposite, it brought nothing but ill-fortune. It can turn out well if it is used for the benefit of the masses, and collectively. But sooner or later it will lead to ill-fortune when it is given a value of its own, and individuals begin to amass it. They turn into serpents, into dragons, bury it in their dragon's lairs and lie on it, defending it with poison and weapons. Gold must never become gold.

Ásmundur, the magistrate, contemplated the huge hands resting on those kneecaps, the crushed nails like flakes of horn, devoid of all shine, his fingers short and stubby, ingrained soil in his skin, the thick span of his hands, the large veins on their backs, the skin coarse and cracked, his knuckles bluish, and the shiny skin.

Ásmundur thought there might be another face beneath the one turned towards him, in which he might see changes of mood if its weather-beaten mask could be lifted.

What he saw was a broad face, a wide space between deep-set eyes, a nose fairly broad and somewhat flattened, nostrils flared wide, stubble, and a mouth sinking slightly towards the right corner, opening where it was tenser as if to reveal a glimpse of a canine tooth.

There were traces of snuff in his drizzle-grey stubble; occasional runny strings of snot appearing before they were intercepted by his knuckles and sniffed back home. His forehead high and broad, and his hair like tense raven's wings poised for flight above it.

Now he was no longer stooped, this toiler of the soil who stared constantly into his palms, stroking the back of one hand and its knuckles, sometimes right to the fingertips, against the other, never breaking the silence unless forced to. He no longer rocked himself, nor stretched out his toes, but had straightened up in his seat in the posture of an archpriest in a temple, and the living room had expanded to become a draped hall in another story. And this was not only since yesterday, for he glowed with the cold prophetic glitter of tomorrow over rough terrain; not of the solitary traveller, but mobilized towards progress across treacherous paths which the mighty collective vanguard alone can conquer. This moment; in this faith there were gains in sight, in spite of everything.

The word is with us, the farmer said sharply.

That was how the farmer appeared to him. Perhaps I had never seen him before. And he started telling the farmer about various equipment that had begun to come to Iceland to ease the toiling of such men, so they no longer needed to live on obstinacy alone, and dreams.

They no longer had to cut a cross into each hummock with a scythe, carve the earth out from inside and spread the hummocks out one by one with wedges of wood as they had been doing, then beat them down with sledges. Now these old codgers could put their horses to harrows and tear up the land, level it out with horsepower.

With horsepower, break the stagnation of the centuries. Then the dung driven up and tipped on to the bare soil, converting bumpy land rapidly into a flat field. The horses could pull ploughs and harrows and all manner of things; and the tiller of the soil could sit there above it all like a poet, tilting the share so the blades not only cut but tedded as well. And a wooden frame or pole could be pulled across the ground afterwards if it was not already level enough. Transferring the toil from man to his faithful servant, the horse. And the dung, you can grind it in machines, a box with a spiked wheel in the bottom and a handle on the side, and there you have fine ground manure. And when the horses spread it on the fields, you tie a box or sieve up on to the saddlebags. With a hinged bottom, and fixed on to a yoke. Then you just shovel it into the boxes. All there is to it. Nothing more. You just have to make sure you shovel evenly into each side so the boxes don't tilt over, you can see that for yourself. If you can picture all this. And just one flick of the hand to empty the box, instead of the way you toil and trouble today spreading it all yourselves. Yes, my friend, there are so many new things coming to lighten your labours, said the magistrate; and this is nothing compared with what will come after that.

Oh yes, said the farmer, with a hint of impatience; oh yes. But now we farmers have been given a new truth for what we used to think was truth. Everything else is based on it. Co-operation. Instead of niggling and wrangling, looking after number one, trampling over each other and squabbling about boundaries and pastures and meadows the way we've done for a thousand years right back to the Sagas, causing nothing but fun for the devil and trouble for you who are supposed to be our authorities.

There is room to move in the wilderness. Nothing is small there. There is nobility there, said the young official. He felt the force flowing within him, how his spirit had been stimulated by the mountains, by the way the horses quickened when they felt they were heading home to the farm at the end of the lake; which reflected the heaps of cloud frothing over the shoulders of the cliffs, and fell with celestial tides as aery waves in the evening calm over the budding community. Through gaps in the cloud the columns of sunshine with white manes cast light on to the lagoon, making it glitter. The wide dark bay with its rising mountains at the end of the horseshoe of land.

Nobility, said the farmer, but now we're going to breathe in the countryside. Without having to go up the mountainsides to fill our lungs with air. Who goes up into the mountains if he doesn't have to? We're not going to be slaves to senseless toil any more. Levelling out the fields, you say. We're not going to struggle in bondage among the hummocks any more or swagger from one tussock to the next, now we should level the fields. And we'll do that with fraternal co-operation. At last we know who's with us and who's against us. Our force will be invincible. And then we'll dictate the terms instead of letting the merchants and their lackeys dole out our share and grab all the profit from our life's work. Those bastards.

But you mustn't forget the spirit, said the man of authority; what is material progress? he asked; if the spirit loses its wings, its gift of flight?

Spirit, you say, quite right; now it doesn't make a lone flight defying everyone and everything, outside the laws of society, said the farmer. There's no place now for the outlaw's daydreams after he has stolen a sheep to save his life. There's a new spirit now. And we bowed peasants up here at the edge of the world say just the same as the people down in the south of the world: liberty, equality and fraternity.

Did you say something, said the magistrate; he thought he had heard the old woman to his side with her band of wool mutter not to forget the Lord's will. He did not know she was thinking that pride was a fly sent by the devil which he insinuates into the breasts of men to tempt them to the brink, over the cliff and into the abyss. Down to the coals licked by fire in hell. There's more than ideology from the south of the world. Don't you think it would make a difference having a series of steam-driven carriages rushing on tracks from one part of the country to the next in an instant, and tunnels through the mountains? For journeymen going to the fishing plants, for example. Or to make a quick trip into town whatever the weather. And steam-ships to fish in deep water like the English do with their trawlers, and in fact snatch it from under your rowing boats right off the shore. And to carry mail between remote places so the postman doesn't need to risk his life, so the treacherous weather is disarmed. You snatch up phrases from the rest of the world and chew over them with a twinkle in your eyes, and pore over books that have almost nothing to do with the lives you lead, when you're not composing verses, good as they might be in their own right. But practical knowledge is the basis of everything. Knowledge is power. Which will make you free. Ignorance is the worst oppressor of mankind, is the devil. Just think of that, in this starving country where people's wildest dream for centuries was eating until they could take no more. And all that food on the shores that people here still turn their noses up at but is the finest delicacy known in the banqueting halls of kings and aristocracy abroad. And everyone here dropping down from hunger, withering away. Or hunched-up clerics writing poetry in Latin, and farmers mentally composing poems that can be read equally backwards or forwards, with artistry that has no like anywhere in the world, but not knowing how to stick a blade on a scythe without it falling off. And all that fuss and bother with cutting the grass that only ended when you got Scottish scythes that helped you work at triple the speed. You didn't invent them, even with blacksmiths on every farm. And there had to be, with those old scythes you had.

This Laughter, This Laughter

It flared up in his memory while he was sitting there in the dark. He saw his fingers, white in her black hair. Whitening while her hair grew black.

He seemed to be losing them in this hair which was as cool as before. His fingers were shot through with the fire that burned in his heart. She laughed so intensely that he couldn't tell where she was. It was so oppressive, this laughter, so crazed, as if she were vanishing from him into its vehemence. He didn't recognize her.

He didn't know how to act with her naked breasts against his chest, and her legs clasped around his hips and buttocks. Her heels parting his thighs, just beneath his buttocks.

Laughed.

She laughed so much he wanted to weep.

Was she laughing at him in her madness? Black. Bright in the wildness of her eyes. How painful, how painful.

The light of morning spread over their nakedness.

Day flickered aflame again.

The fire in her loins was burning still. He was still afraid. Suddenly he had no longer recognized her in her lust, in the voluptuous climax. She was different, he had never known her, and he feared her.

Feared the voluptuous urge that put the world at her command.

He wanted to flee from her. Far away. At the same time he yearned for her again. To bathe in the same flames. Burn. Burn to ashes, for the breeze to waft away into the glow of day, into the bloody brightness of the first rays.

Whirl up like soil on a slope in the vegetation's last oasis. And the land all eroded. Leaving a brownish cloud in the air, then nothing more. Nothing but the omnipotent wilderness which spares only the bird that knows the way to huddle up and take to wing and soar above everything, in the blueness while it lasts, then flutter on its wings in the ethereal stardust, with its song within, in sparkling dimensions of stars which flow forth with shining signs between them, light year after light year, like a speck in the immeasurability of that which is, and has been, and will be.

One bird in his chest, in the cage in his chest. And this woman who terrified him, and if anything drew strength from his fear.

Stop it, he screamed. She threw herself back and forth beneath him, and around him and over him, away from him and towards him. As if trying to crush him, with her eyes pressed shut.

Stop it, he shouted; stop it, stop laughing.

I can't.

But he wasn't the one who started to cry; she did.

Then she was the one who started to cry.

Not hysterically.

But quietly, almost at peace, almost curiously resigned.

So it's happened then, she says, at last.

Really?

Yes.

What? Happened? What's happened?

What I was afraid would happen.

He waited for her to say.

I'm pregnant.

He recoiled from her.

Pregnant, he said nothing; was it all over then?

Then she gripped his head with both her hands. With her palms on his cheeks and her fingers over his ears and on to his neck, her thumbs on his jugular, which throbbed as it pulsed, she pressed her gums against his collarbone. Then she moved one hand along the back of his head, the nape of his neck, down his back and rubbed it along his spine, moved out to his pelvis, took hold of it, fondled it, stroked his back, softly. Her tears were still flowing. He was moistened by her tears. Afterwards she strewed gentle kisses upon his naked body. Started to lick him as if removing the salt. There's no consolation. Sometimes. Neither for oneself nor others.

And not for oneself even if others can be consoled. But perhaps at the most lulled, calmed.

The Age of Gold

Gold. To create with. And by gold I don't mean what you get paid for selling a few live sheep to Scottish cattlemongers. We have another resource which will never run dry. An endless source of wealth and therefore welfare. The power which lives in our waterfalls and rivers, it is waiting for us to acquire the maturity and wisdom to harness its force and channel the immeasurable power of water into a different course; electrify this country; which we shall never again curse for treating us harshly, but bless from generation to generation for its endless gifts; if we awaken from lethargy and misery and perceive the opportunities, the time of fulfilment. Then flourishing towns will emerge in prosperity and well-being, industry of all sorts powered by electricity; then we shall no longer need to toil for our bread with sweat and tears; we shall eradicate centuries of hunger, lice and suffering. And then we can turn to materializing the qualities of our stock; and become the nation of nations, the tribe of Benjamin will emerge at last then, and the promises will be fulfilled. A spiritual giant of a nation, passing on wisdom to others. A small nation illuminating the world for others; no less than the ancient Athenians who laid the foundation that the entire culture of the West is built upon. The power of waterfalls . . .

It disturbs me, said the farmer's wife, forgetting her shyness and interrupting the flow of his words. She had been standing by the door, her ruddy cheeks ablaze, making sure that the travellers were all served, speaking no more than any of the other people on the farm, who listened, captivated, that our dear old waterfalls should be harnessed. What about their beauty which has warmed our hearts in all this toil? It's not certain that wealth always brings blessings. If

70

everything is to be valued by its usefulness. Don't you think we'll stop noticing the scent of the grass. A price put on all God's gifts. I'm a little afraid that . . .

She suddenly fell silent, felt how everyone was looking at her in surprise for interrupting this eloquent herald of an age of gold when this nation, the humiliated and outcast race of heroes, could rise from the ashes in fulfilment of ancient promises; who surpassed all nations in physical and mental qualities in the Saga age; and the nation's leader had been brought here, a new Freyr of the Valleys; and his countenance ablaze when he spoke. She blushed, smiled all over her face, but most of all with her clear-blue eyes; waved her arms about, as if a tempter were at her nose in the guise of a fly; fell silent with a gentle smile which took a long while to fade.

Then just said softly, as the silence grew longer, as if panicking: It would be a good thing to cultivate woods, like we're doing in the women's association . . .

And the same smile lit up her round face, and she offered the figure of authority another cup of coffee.

Why did Ásmundur suddenly recall the image from the other day of the girl by the waterfall, his swirling thoughts of her life for a thousand years? How her young maiden's hand changed into the claw of a blind witch, her clairvoyant eyes showing the whites. As if the crashing water carried her youth away. And the dreams replaced by visions into hidden worlds, concerning other men's fates.

Yes, that too, said the young nobleman; that's part of it too. We will clothe the land with forests anew. The settlements. From mountain to shore. But the mountains will retain their naked majesty, for centuries. The wilderness. Steel and strengthen our resolve for grand visions and great fate. And we shall live a double life. Progress where men live, and mythology where they do not. And acquire titanic powers in the effort of combining these two natures. The temporal which flies rapidly by; and the eternal and timeless which remains immutable in the depths, and which we have forgotten. Then at last everything within us will resound to the full. And has never managed to develop since the time the greatest literature in the world was written here. It will all return. All of it, he said, intoxicated by the divine inspiration of his vision and the enthusiasm of his audience in the palace, that little farm living room with its flickering light from the coals, as the rain lashed at the window in bursts on the crazed wings of the black wind, which brought that close night.

The Judge's Concerns

Ásmundur was sitting alone in the little room where he was to sleep. It was beneath low eaves with a small window, and the blades of grass trembled outside in the glow from the oil lamp, their green colour turned yellow by the light. A breeze ruffled the thatch intermittently. He was aware of the lake rather than actually seeing it. Because there was no moonlight. But he knew it was long and narrow.

The head of the bed had been pulled right out to allow him to stretch out and not need to sleep half-sitting up like the others. But there was no need to widen it because he had no bedfellow that night. There was a table which constricted that possibility anyway. And on the table, the lamp.

He let his garrulousness from the conversation in the living room wear off: after meeting people in the evening of a mountain journey with a single companion, with the incidents that his surroundings charged his feelings with on the way, sermons from nature. After the clairvoyance which the magic of the land magnified within him, the hypersensitivity to sound of the silent wilderness.

He sat on the edge of the bed and examined everything that awaited him.

His first test ahead.

And relished solitude when he could not sleep in his lodgings. Other people on the farm had retired. Everything so quiet. Except for a strange rushing outside in the boundless silence. And every sound was carried between the susurrus of the breeze on the straws, the grass, the cut fields. Tended with its breath the wakeful edge of the swathe, to strengthen its courage to bud and grow. For all who were waiting, man and animal.

Now that he was alone an apprehensive impatience awoke. He had dipped into the court documents about the murderer, Jón from Raudengismýri by Svartá, which he had copied out when seeking a model for the problem ahead. It was not long ago that Jón had been condemned to death for murder; concluded without more ado. By his father, whose duties he was now dispatching in his absence.

He took out the letter which his father had written, read it in the flickering light.

My dear son,

Everything is well with me. Except that there is nothing but wrangling and endless disputes. Like a contrived ball where the gentleman politely leads his lady a few steps forward then as many back without being able to get his arms around her. This is the way these disputes among the nobility tend to be, and appeal to the fact that the judges are from the same class and will not reveal their base instincts. We are supposed to be a model for the common people, we noblemen. Beelzebubs, as in the folk tale about the parish magistrate who went to church and left his wife at home. And what did the Reverend talk about? she asked when she reclaimed her husband with an affectionate welcome. Oh, he was talking about Beelzebubs. Who are they? she asked. Well, said her husband; they are the noblemen. The nobility? she asked. Oh yes, he said, indeed. Are they people like us? she says. They are supposed to be, my dear Hervör.

Well, without beating about the bush, my dear son, there is a first time for everything. As I write you these lines you are in the grave position which greets every single judge when he is ordered for the first time to handle a difficult case which involves the fate of men and could even determine whether they live or die.

Therefore I would urge you not to let your resolve mellow on hearing tears of suffering, and be on your guard against all devices that could be applied to sway the judge's mind from the duty which he has sworn the Lord of this life he will dispatch, and could make him unmindful of the great responsibility vested in him to

74

maintain the rules and morality which are the fundamental grounds by which human society itself is justified.

Everything depends upon your showing firmness and refusing to allow any connivance or cheap tricks to influence you. You will maintain the correct distance necessary to every judge in order to be able to judge with unswerving logic, independent of everything. You must show firmness from the very start. And forcefulness which never wanes. You must gain the advantage immediately, and must never entertain the thought of laxity. You must tolerate neither stubbornness nor arrogance. Tears must not penetrate your heart any more than the drops falling from the gables into the yard. And you must also be prepared to seek recourse to force which others might consider mercilessness. Threaten people into confession if necessary.

This is what I wanted to urge you to remember, and no wanderings of the mind nor poetical fancies that may lead you to relax. Everything depends upon resolve and steadfastness with the detachment of Christian authority which must not be debased or made obedient to human smallness. Evildoers may be given no quarter; rather, you shall uproot so that the bad grass does not cover the rest of the field.

Know that in this watch of yours you are accompanied by your loving and devoted

Father

Extracts from Documents

. . . Furthermore it shall be stated that the examining magistrate has today, along with seven of those who according to the afore-mentioned letter from the Reverend Jón Thorsteinsson were present when the body of Konkordía Sveinsdóttir was found, examined closely and investigated all the visible evidence where the body of Konkordía Sveinsdóttir was found in the river Svartá, in which respect special consideration was made both of the fact that the riverbank beneath which the body had lain had patently been disturbed so as to leave scratches in the soil and the grass flattened, and of the fact that clear prints of a male left foot could be seen in a lump of mud and sand which had previously fallen from the bank and projected above the surface of the water, approximately three fathoms upstream from where the body was lying when found in the river by the said bank.

He turned from the documents for an instant, stood up and stooped to look out of the window, squinting out into the night, which was now rather too large to be alone in, risking what could insinuate itself into the little room where one could not enlarge oneself by charms or trickery or donning a magic helmet. Such as what? Were there not legions roaming without rest for eternity? All those souls from the accumulated centuries who had been left out when the consecrated vaults where peace reigned were filled, the peace brought by the correct form of valediction, accord with the living to the correct choral accompaniment, farewell. Go thou in peace. But the others whom the thought of the living forced spirit into, forced nourishment of the fancy so they could not rest, these roaming souls, whom the thought of the living drove before them, fleeing over the heaths and banks and boulders of the black night, who descended upon you and this little farm where everyone else was sleeping, and you alone compelled to wake; if only so that the ghost would not approach you in your sleep to snatch from you these papers which told his story as far as could be seen. He was standing at the little table by the window between the narrow beds, resting his knuckles determinedly on the edge, letting them turn white in his solitary game.

Then he continued the game, sat on the bed opposite where he had read his father's letter; sat where had put the letter down and watched his clenched fist, arched tight, slowly straightened out his fingers; and saw the shadow of his hand changing over those papers in the breathing of the light from the tapered lamp. Despite what dwelt outside in the night he continued to tiptoe through the documents he had taken with him on his journey.

... *the court of inquiry was convened again at the same place ... to continue the investigation into the death of Konkordía Sveinsdóttir ... Furthermore the examining magistrate showed the court a box containing the footprint in the mud ...*

... pomm pomm, he exhaled and proceeded ...

... *and one of the two witnesses for the prosecution, the Reverend Jón Thorsteinsson from Halldórsstadir, acknowledged that it was the same box containing the mud and footprint that had been taken at the place where the body was found the same day, and the other witness, Halldór Marteinsson from Bjarnarstadir, who was in the search party when the body was found, acknowledged that he recognized the footprint, that the box contained the same footprint he had seen on the bed of mud in the water at the aforementioned place, and furthermore the examining magistrate showed the court the left shoe worn by Jón Jónsson from Raudengismýri by Svartá on Sunday the thirteenth inst. when Konkordía Sveinsdóttir disappeared. The parish magistrate, Jón Sigurpálsson from Hvarf,* who was present in court, acknowledged this to be the same shoe that he had been given the day before at Raudengismýri by the housefolk of Jón Jónsson of Raudengismýri and his master Jón Sigurdsson.

The examining magistrate urged the witnesses to voice their opinions of the extent to which this shoe corresponded to the footprint seen in the mud, to which they replied that the footprint in the mud bore no small resemblance to the shoe even when dried out. The common characteristic is a larger ball of the foot than we imagine is common among other people.

The court of inquiry was adjourned and the trial began. Next to attend examination was Adalbjörg Káradóttir from Svartárkot, forty-two years of age . . . Under questioning she acknowledged that Konkordía Sveinsdóttir had been pregnant and had told her so in the twentieth week of the summer, mentioning that she would not bear the child until Michaelmastide, and was told by Konkordía on the same occasion that Jón Jónsson, labourer at Raudengismýri, was the father, and understood that she had every hope that Jón Jónsson would acknowledge the child, and heard from her how she had told him of her condition before he left the farm in the recent spring, and recalled Konkordía mentioning that Jón Jónsson did not 'think it was very good', whereupon the witness did not mention the subject to Konkordía until the thirteenth inst. when Jón Jónsson had been there the night before . . . Whereupon she claims to have asked Konkordía: Isn't Jón treating you reasonably now? Which she says Konkordía answered in the affirmative, and they made no further conversation. She alleges that she did not know when Konkordía departed on the aforementioned Sunday, having been serving guests with the other woman on the farm, and indeed claims grounds for supposing that Konkordía did not wish to draw much attention to her departure, since she asked a boy to close the door where she (the witness) and a visiting lady were talking, while she left by the upstairs door to the living room; she was accustomed to be somewhat reticent in the presence of visitors.

The witness says she undressed the body when it was brought home on the sixteenth inst. together with Gudrún Einarsdóttir but did not notice any sand in the clothes except a small amount on the neck, and on the entire front of the body but none at all on the back. She states that she was not able to see anything remarkable on the body, nor any water exuding from it. The witness says that as far as she can accurately estimate Konkordía would have left home on Sunday well towards three o'clock, and in so far as she was acquainted with Konkordía and her normal walking pace she would have taken at least one-and-a-half hours to walk from the farm and to the place were she was found dead in the river Svartá . . . according to which Konkordía would have reached the place where the body was found at approximately one quarter before five.

Next witness to attend was Sigurlaug Jónsdóttir, housewife at Svartárkot, forty-four years of age . . . The witness related how Konkordía was with her for more than five years and she had never noticed her to be anything other than stable of mood, and that she thought her in the best of spirits that summer. She says that Konkordía had implied, although not stated outright, that she was pregnant, by saying that she would not be able to work particularly hard that winter; she says that as far as she could tell she was carefree and in good spirits on the aforementioned Sunday morning, and that shortly after Jón Jónsson had departed she had asked her leave to make a short journey, which had surprised her on account of the high wind and sandstorm, but had not wanted to refuse her since it was a Sunday, imagining that she intended to stroll around the farm in search of firewood, since she was not accustomed to visiting other farms, nor did the witness find out until afterwards that she had changed her clothes. Furthermore she adds as relevant under the circumstances that a girl of eight years who was present said that Konkordía and Jón Jónsson from Raudengismýri had been speaking together in the living room on the aforementioned Sunday, but the subject of their conversation was unknown.

The Wages of Sin

The lad rose up from the woman, raised himself by his arms, naked from her nakedness. He saw her eyes intoxicated by the distance within their proximity. Then he sank back with his head on her stomach, cautiously held her hips, lifted her a fraction, up towards his cheek. Let the hair of her mons tickle his cheek, and knelt with his buttocks raised aloft; she ran her fingers through his hair gently and soothingly.

You who are the fire kindling my body, she whispered; the spring which quenches my burning thirst.

The wind wafted the words to the sea, where a female seal dozed on a rock. No sound was heard from there.

The sun glittered in the grass, the wind whirled, driving the clouds fast: you the young pharaoh. And I am the Egyptian princess, your sister and wife, the progeny of the gods.

When these words reached him, the man held his pen poised above the black ink in its well, and raised the nib; adjourned.

The wages of sin, he thought; revenge wrought on oneself.

He could no longer see those eyes, that pride.

That defiant wordless expression which haunted him.

The Confession

Next to attend the court, in full fettle, was Jón Jónsson from Raudengismýri . . . He said he will be twenty-one years of age on October second proximo.

In accordance with formalities he explained that for the two preceding years he had been a labourer on the farm of Einar Fridriksson at Svartárkot, and had left that abode for Raudengismýri last spring; both these years he said that the deceased, Konkordía Sveinsdóttir, had been at Svartárkot at the same time. He said that immediately during the former year, at haymaking time, she had begun, as it is called, to 'latch on to him', or hint that she desired to obtain his love, and he says that like any other young person he had cautiously avoided these advances, not considering them to be serious, and that the matter had continued in this way until the autumn of the same year when she intensified her efforts to win his love, mentioning it to him on more than one occasion; and still he had shied away, and so it went on until Easter at the end of last winter that he thought of accepting her, although he did not feel himself man enough to bestow upon her the love that he would have felt appropriate; but from the afore-mentioned course of events he admitted that the girl had become pregnant by him about this time. Interrogated further, he stated that the reason he did not feel he could bestow constant love upon this girl was that they were different in temperament, and neither of them of good temper, while on the other hand he did not recall making any matter of her being older, although he did entertain the notion that his parents would not approve of such a match owing to his tender age.

He related that afterwards his sympathy towards the girl had gradually begun to dwindle, and eventually disappeared completely, which had occurred unconsciously and without the woman giving him any cause, until he reached the point of wondering how he could rid himself of her or the relationship with her; but he had never thought of denying that the child was his. He stated that he had mentioned to the girl during the summer, on the latter occasion that he visited Svartárkot at haymaking time, whether she could not agree to – or accept – terminating their relationship thereafter, without having on any previous occasion, directly, promised her marriage. But he said that she had completely refused to entertain the idea and cited a promise of matrimony on his part; which she none the less could not do by rights. Admittedly he had promised to provide her with an abode the following year, if he were able. He said that she had spoken on this point at great length, and that he felt she was doing him an injustice, so that they parted on that occasion in something of a huff.

He admitted that in consequence he had begun to feel within himself bad thoughts and a passion for in some manner ridding himself of her; but he had been unable to see any way or means of so doing other than murdering her; and that this feeling had lingered and been magnified by an unqualified sense that she had originally been the instigator of this relationship between them. On the other hand, he said he had lacked the moral courage either to leave her completely or to think of continuing the relationship.

He said he therefore resolved to murder the woman, in part in pursuance of which he had gone over to Svartárkot on Saturday the twelfth inst., but also in part to look for two sheep which he had left behind the previous spring and were branded with the earmark of farmer Einar Fridriksson.

He admitted that to this end he had arranged, in the living room of the farm on the morning of Sunday the thirteenth inst., to meet the deceased Konkordía somewhere in the area from the byres at Vídirker towards the Ullarfoss waterfall in Svartá, informing

82

her only of his request to meet her at the aforementioned place, to which she readily assented; then he said he had taken his leave of her before departing from Svartárkot, around half past one as he recalled. Then he had tarried a while both inside the farmhouse and in the yard before departing at around two o'clock as he recalled.

Where does such a young rogue come from, the magistrate thought, regretting being unable to reach his father and probe into the problems of a judge in such a case. And he admired the old man's initiative and private ritual in presenting a sparse court in a low-roofed farmhouse with the man's footprint, displaying it to himself the high judge and to the peasants and lads around: the evidence, the murderer's footprint transported across the whole countryside in a box. Now he felt a certain apprehension.

He had a vague feeling of apprehension about the case the following day. It was his turn to be in the same position. To be the judge. The task grew enormous before him that sleepless night as he sat alone in the little room, with no one near him to steel him for the encounter, for the posturing that could relieve the captivity of his soul. Guard him from the spectres of the past. Because it was not merely country ghosts or local spectres that threatened him that moment. Nor fear of the sentence passed on the life of the nation, thinking of this hopeless nation of his nourishing its mind on its monsters, the walking dead which was almost the only thing they all had in common. A poet like Jónas Hallgrímsson was not the common property of the nation. He pondered how different it would have been had Hallgrímsson's poetry managed to unite the nation. Were destitution and ghosts all that this nation had in common? Ancient Sagas, admittedly. But was that not only their heroes, their illusions? It was not Sturla Sighvatsson; he thought to himself: the next time I meet my father I shall ask him if Sturla Sighvatsson, who wanted to possess all of Iceland, was a fool. Not to kill Gissur when he had the chance? Where did Sturla fail as heir apparent? On his pilgrimage to Rome? Seeing the ocean of destitution, herds on their way to hell, or rather already there. Leaving the sparse farms of this country for the pestilent swarms where people thronged in boiling springs of mud, in burning pus. Perhaps. And Sighvatur the wisest man of his age, why did he follow his son to his death? Dreams mean nothing.

There is no turning back. There will never be any turning back, he thought. With the same resolutions as Sturla. Except my father is no Sighvatur. Clever as he might be. That quick, impetuous, flawed genius. Upon whose tongue words play so lightly and frenzied that they lead him into pitfalls with all the more glorious flourishes. And then he bursts forth covered in mud from the pit without losing his dignity, shakes himself like a dog, and continues his divine address crowned with golden-red Olympian clouds. Loquacity.

He could only admire his father, who overplayed his hand time and again in the fiery intoxication of his brilliance. Then picked the cards up again, always certain of protection in the faith that now he would be dealt a better hand than ever before. All those erratic trumps that had gone astray. And was therefore never cleaned out. Rose again after the setbacks which knocked him flat, rampant and noble as if from a drinking bout when the hangover has worn off.

This night of solitude in the little room he felt closer affinity with that royal wastrel of the mind, his superior in wordplay, disarming as words might be. How he grew intoxicated by his eloquence to the brink of danger, even courting disaster, he thought: obsessive relish of words. But when his stupor of words wore off, how pitiful the poor old man could become. Like a bird with such a bad attack of rheumatism in its wing that it is unable to lift itself from what it wants to flee.

But at the same time, however close he was to this man who was his father, he also felt how different he was. In his innermost self he felt the presence of that woman he had had so few opportunities to get to know, his mother. Her arrogance, obstinacy, harsh temper. Her pride cold and powerful. It was his life to possess two natures. With the eternal dilemma of reconciling the two forces he had inherited from his parents who could not live together. And . . .

And no, he returned to the documents of the case that he

had taken with him on his first journey in his father's footsteps.

A judge.

He recalled his old professor from university. Who never tired of saying: Only toughness will do. By evil shall evil be uprooted. This delicate powerhouse who stepped bespectacled out of the Old Testament: an eye for an eye, a tooth for a tooth. Toughness. Softness is for holy men. Who live within some special veil in the midst of mankind. And therefore need to resolve no problems. For them. Not judges. Who have a duty which might be called holy to ensure the justification of human society.

Yes, where did such a lad come from, who without compunction commits such base deeds, the shepherd who while performing this unspeakable crime keeps his flock together?

Has a murderer's footprint ever in the history of man been presented in court in a box? An imprint in mud. Not a fingerprint, a footprint. Has any judge ever allowed himself such a private ritual? For whom else?

Suddenly this shook him off course: Where is my father? he thought, and finally was able to fall asleep.

Morning Inquiry into a
Murderer's Background

While he waited for his breakfast, Ásmundur the magistrate sat in the sitting room and tidied his papers. What he had been re-reading during the night still haunted his mind, in spite of what lay ahead. He was still wondering how people stray into committing deeds which do not permit them to disappear from history. And become ghosts in the national consciousness. Where did he come from? The lad had lived with his parents until the age of twelve, then with various families for a year at a time, sometimes as a journeyman labourer on a farm with his domicile elsewhere. Ásmundur succumbed to the temptation to thumb through the documents he had copied out. This man of twenty owns a few sheep, a saddle and a harness. He has paid some wool to the co-operative society towards the price of the saddle which he had taken on credit, and does not know what it has fetched. His wages for the year so far are still outstanding with the farmer; and then he owns a trunk and a writing desk and 10 krónur in cash, which a debtor had promised to pay in coin in the autumn; while he himself owed four times that amount to his father who had lent him the price of a horse. And he owned some hay and his ewes had given all the milk they could to pay for the fodder, an account that according to the court documents remained unsettled. Nothing else is evident about the lad's origin and circumstances from these papers, and his father is somewhat too far away to be able to describe a murderer's appearance. His deportment, the timbre of his voice, his countenance. So, you are a free poet, Ásmundur said; what sort of murderer would you like in a story?

There was some delay in serving the breakfast. The farmer had gone out somewhere, to keep an eye on how the magistrate's horse was groomed. He had also seen the magistrate with his documents and perhaps felt he needed peace and quiet.

The magistrate thumbed idly through the documents, dwelling in places where he had made marks in the margins. Some kind of aftermath in examining witnesses after everything had been confessed. The farmer's wife from Svartárkot, under questioning, declared herself unable to deny that Konkordía Sveinsdóttir had pursued Jón Jónsson, confirming that his testimony on that subject was correct and not as far as she had noticed exaggerated, and she could not deny being surprised on remarking that Konkordía was pregnant by Jón, considering the advances she had noticed on his part towards the deceased. This was corroborated by the next witness, a girl who had testified before and had spent two years with them at the farm, who stated that Konkordía had pursued Jón Jónsson, and that she had been surprised that any amorous relationship had taken place between them.

Ásmundur heard the farmer's footsteps, rolled up his documents, put them in his case and watched the players in this tragedy evaporate completely. But they had been pale, almost expressionless and largely transparent when they appeared in the light of that morning.

Why did he dwell upon this case? Which was a thing of the past, judged. He thought of the terror resting upon the judge who in this case was his father, and who had to sentence this person to execution. A judge who, in the name of the law and of God, must kill.

He knew he ought rather to focus his thoughts on the terrible case awaiting him to judge. On the repulsive business which he had been destined to immerse himself in, cleanse and enlighten. It was here that he should begin his career as a judge.

The farmer entered, releasing him from these thoughts in an instant.

He addressed the farmer as if in a carefree mood. And immediately after the farmer came his wife with the victuals, smiling and warm with no need to say anything. While the men engaged in light talk on their moment of parting, swapping badinage.

He had already felt the gentle coolness of the morning on his face and hands with the breeze in his hair when he went outside to pass water.

And the day awaited him, whatever business might arise. A new stage, new players in another play, with other chords and urgent messages.

When he mounted his horse the farmer held his hand for a long time and bade him farewell with a few extravagant words. The woman stood at the door which was ajar into the farmhouse, straining and blinking her clear-blue eyes, dumpy with her little children hanging on her skirts; and one leaned its blond head against her stomach, which had borne her husband so many children in that fine home of theirs, delivering them into the harsh world with the security of protection until they had to venture out into the inclement elements. The older children were out in the fields, some in the meadow with the haymakers. Everything here was done in accord, firmly managed with gentle tones about what needed to be said about the work, or with a suggestion as to what ought to be done. The farmer's wife's face was broad, almost round like a full unsilvered moon, where peace reigns and life must surely turn out well, if it possibly can.

The farmer's long handshake was somewhat loose, then two light jerks passed through the fist which was restraining its force, taking care to cause no pain.

Then they rode away. The people in the meadow who were cutting and raking up the hay stopped working and watched with smiles as this singular visitor rode away, and could not deny the impression he had made with his conversation and demeanour.

The horses did not seem eager to leave that farm.

On a Deserted Heath

They were approaching the end of the lake. Then they stopped. They dismounted and sat there in silence, listening to the gentle water coddling stones by the bank. The sun stretched its beams down to the lake, through what remained of the mist. Swans were floating there.

They watched the swans glide across the water in proud, long-necked nobility; ducks and geese sat on the islets. The fleet of swans slowly drove other birds away. A drake led his duck, his blue head fading into green in the sunlight. All was calm until a cob-swan chased a duck and drove it away repeatedly as it settled; whereupon one swan swam between them and told it to calm down, behave itself and not spoil the glorious sunny day. Then it glided on, arching its neck while it sailed as if swallowing something, a fry or perhaps only its thoughts. Then it stopped and remained perfectly silent, waiting for the water around it to become completely still, and pointed down at its own reflection its golden-wedged beak which ended in black, and its eyes two black glistening dots, then thrust its beak into its own image in the water, shattering it, and grabbed a fry.

Young cobs grouped together, traces of yellow on their heads but the grey colour gone, and they glided by, white, arrogantly driving a fleet of ducks before them. Suddenly two cob-swans rose up, puffed up against each other, fighting with their wings and chopping each other with their beaks, whipping up the water and disturbing the whole flock. One was bitten on the wing and seemed to be losing, then unexpectedly drew strength, laid into the other and drove it away, and the fight faded out. And all fell calm again.

Thórdur was silent, thinking about the previous evening in the sitting room of the farmhouse, about the young magistrate's brilliant display and the animated, happy spirit he had kindled around him with his speeches and stories; and he did not mention the people who had drawn him aside and said they had never had such a visitor before. That's what magistrates should be like, toothless old Saeunn had told him, her skin wrinkled like creased leather.

The magistrate feared reaching his destination. It's worth dallying deliberately, he thought. But they had to continue their journey.

Well, he said.

Yes, said Thórdur. Oh yes. Indeed.

They mounted and rode around the glittering end of the lake, and up the heath leading from it.

The sun had been out. Now it had vanished. The sky was grey. And lighter clouds scudded along. There was a cool breeze.

The land was flat, mountains distant. Sometimes there was bare sand, or gravel banks, mossy turf left standing by eroding winds, wisps of couch grass.

They passed the grassy remnants of the walls of a farm.

Tales of hauntings suffered by lone travellers on this heath entered the mind.

Travellers whose bodies had been found with signs of having been murdered in bizarre ways.

And people lived here once, said Ásmundur, and they rode side by side past the ruins; it must have been tough here in the winter snows.

And not so long ago either, said Thórdur; as a magistrate, you must forgive me for speaking ill of the authorities. But I think I ought to risk it after listening to your glorious speeches last night about a better life for all these people. So you lot will have to go on arguing about how to arrange it. Maybe you noticed the farm in the arm of the fjord before we headed up on to the heath. There was quite some action there. Maybe that needs adding to what you were saying about helping each other and your faith in individuals that stand out from the masses and pull them up to better things, progress instead of putting all their trust in social spirit.

Social spirit, said Ásmundur without elaborating, waiting for his companion to continue.

Yes, dear old social spirit, Thórdur said. And, taking his time, he told a story about the farmer who lived with his wife and children by the lagoon, and had been sheriff of the parish. But in the course of a few months he lost his wife and all his children except the three youngest, and in fact they eventually died as well except the little girl of ten who had to take charge of the home and nurse the two younger ones as they wasted away. Social spirit, where was it then? Was everyone ready and willing to lend a helping hand? At least, we know that more powerful people drove him off his land when it was easiest for them in the midst of all his sufferings. The story goes that he managed to keep one shed where the corpse of the youngest child was kept, because of his manhood they say. And just the two of them survived, the father and daughter. With all the powers-that-be against them.

Who was against that farmer? asked Ásmundur; who treated him so roughly?

Who but the authorities? Thórdur answered; led by the district magistrate.

What happened to them? The child, what happened to her?

That farmer never gave way in all his destitution. He never gave up trying to return to the edge of the heath where he had lived; even though the authorities were against him, and everyone who obeys the powerful. And a long drawn-out court case developed about the land that had been taken from him. The court in Copenhagen ruled in his favour.

So he won back his rights, said the magistrate; in the end. It turned out better than it looked.

No, he never won back his rights, answered his companion; the authorities simply avoided obeying the ruling.

The magistrate said nothing, but tightened his grip on the reins. They rode on in silence for a while, until he said suddenly: Listen. What happened to the child? Was she driven from place to place with the old man while he fought his holy war to get back into his croft on the heath? How old did you say she was when they were driven out, taking all their dead with them?

There was a delay before Thórdur replied. It was a time-consuming business sometimes, talking to this companion, who often did not seem to hear when he was spoken to. Sometimes he had even forgotten his own question by the time Thórdur felt ready to answer. Now it was convenient that there was no hurry. There was plenty of time. What awaited him at their destination was not that pleasant. The breeze had cooled. They moved on to a scarp with a low cliff at the top, cut across it some way below that temple of rock, and crossed a low hill. The far end of the ridge sloped away in the other direction, while they reached a heather-covered moor with dwarf birch and shrubs of juniper which muted the beating of the horses' hoofs to almost nothing, when Thórdur said in a low voice: The child, you say. She was brought up on the farm next to yours, as it happens, magistrate. The old man settled there where his sister lived. The little girl started collecting shells from the beach there and all sorts of fossilized old sea plants. And before her eyes she had trolls that had turned to stone in the sea at daybreak while they were splashing on the shore. That was her university, magistrate, because she had a keen eye for things around her, and was dreamy. And she travelled far in her dreams. And became a labourer on a good farm near by, working for a fussy widow who lived well. The young girl and her mistress's son grew fond of each other, and wove their dreams together, and the result was a baby. But this lady of good means intended greater things for her son; and did not give up until she had driven the girl away from her lover and child, and even took her share in an inheritance by snatching the child from her. And she held on tight to all this in the iron grip of her social superiority, gently oppressing her son like everybody else.

It was the magistrate's turn to stay silent again. Until he handed Thórdur the snuffbox from his waistcoat pocket: Isn't it a long time since we had a pinch of snuff, Thórdur?

There were berries here, glimpses of blue among the tussocks where they trotted along.

Do you know the rest of the story? he asked when they had both blown their noses; what happened to the poor girl amidst all this degradation?

Thórdur squinted at the cloud drifting across the grey skies, and answered more quickly than before as if reading out loud from a book: She was torn up again, by the roots. Where did she go? From there she went back to the heath. To her childhood haunts. A little higher up on the heath, in fact. And a new chapter begins. She ends up on a farm where an elderly couple lived with their son. She found a fine husband there. Fit for her. There was no one there to cause a scene if she picked up a book and immersed herself in it. And they didn't stop at reading books at that farm on the heath. They broke out of their isolation with books. Discussed them and analysed them. It wasn't a place where everyone sat in his own corner like some herald of ill-tidings; a poor person was no bringer of doom, there was harmony there, man brought joy to man. And finally her life sprang into bloom, this woman who had to shoulder such heavy burdens from early childhood. They had children up there on the heath, who grew up to be fine and practical because the farmer was a renowned craftsman, and their minds reached maturity in the learned academy of the farmhouse sitting room; where everyone was always striving for self-improvement; and the farmer's wife, this little woman from the edge of the heath, turned her hand to poetry, and even more to study; while her brood of children grew up and gradually flew from the nest. They lived so unbelievably well on the heath that there were even stories about a mysterious chest that they shovelled gold out of. Even about bargains they struck with the hidden people. There was one story about them helping a fairy woman in labour. Doesn't worry me, I like a good story. But these people, they never stopped working, and they cared about the way a job was done too. Everything they did was efficient. And while their minds rang together in the sitting room reading and discussing books, they all had their own jobs to do, like everyone else, and in fact rather more so. And of course the pastures are good on the heath. And plenty of game to hunt. Not just foxes, even though the eldest son is the sharpest fox-hunter in the district and . . .

So it all turned out well, Ásmundur said; everyone was happy in the end, sprang into bloom you say. Everything . . .

The bank, said Thórdur; haven't you heard about the bank?

What?

A remarkable bank grew up on the heath.

A bank?

People started flocking from all around, even from remote districts, to borrow money. There, where they hardly ever saw money except covered in some romantic haze, hidden at the bottom of chests, like something to marvel at in the moonlight, a handful of *spesia*. Or silver buttons as a last resort for warding off ghosts that only silver bullets can kill.

Spesia, said the magistrate. The coins are called *spesia*. *Spes* is Latin, Thórdur.

And means hope, magistrate. But this couple on the heath, now they could lend people money, and were even said to be eager to, and the story goes that people who repaid their loans could borrow more.

That's good proof, said the magistrate Ásmundur; people like that elevate everyone around them. That's the power of the individual.

As long as he does not stand alone, muttered his companion into his black beard with a long grey streak from the left side of his mouth as if a stray moonbeam had landed there.

And have you met this old woman on the heath? Where everything springs to life and flourishes and thrives all around?

I have.

And how did that come about? What was she like?

I don't know whether that's the sort of story you go spreading around. Though I don't mind telling you here. Now. It was when I was a child. One Christmas. Yet another hard winter. That damned sea ice. People were afraid polar bears would start strolling in. The earth frozen solid. We were quite a large family, as you perhaps know. Living on the heath. No one could afford to give us children candles for Christmas. And didn't this good woman come over, it wasn't far away. And she had had a mind to buy candles for all of us, so she just went straight ahead. Brought us candles, one each. You bet that was a

Christmas Eve we'll never forget. What it was like when we lit our candles in the dark in our hovel, lighting up the darkness in the sitting room. And we could even light the passageways with them. Make Christmas there too. Even spread Christmas a tiny way on to the snow, give it a hint of Christmas too. The children were sensible enough to use such wonder sparingly, and still do in fact. And not burn the candles right down, so they could be lit again, the next day; and have Christmas then too, a little one. And my little brother's candle went missing then, when he had been promised to light it, we only found the whole wick from it. The toddler had eaten his candle to keep his hunger at bay. Eaten Christmas instead of bathing himself in its glory. But my eldest brother kept his candle intact. We begged him to light it just for a second. Just for an instant. So we could see. Then he took his candle and lit both ends, and let it burn down.

Dream

They had crossed the river at a wide shallows, leaving piles in the sand on the bed where their horses had placed their prints. They had not gone far from the river when the magistrate began to feel drowsy after the sleepless night before and the tribulations of his soul; and the soothing murmur of the river beyond the lowland and small hill they had crossed, then a trickling stretch of marsh, and they were in a hollow: Let's rest here, said the magistrate; I'm growing sleepy.

They did so. He fell fast asleep, but slept badly.

When he woke up he was sweating, and rubbed his hand across his cheek and said: Sleep is often stormy, said Sturla Sighvatsson.

What is dreamed is better than what is undreamed, as Gissur said, Thórdur retorted; so tell me your dream, magistrate.

I saw a flock of horses rushing over quite a long slope, standing out against the red sky of the setting sun. The horses were dark, standing out from the flooding light, and suddenly I could see beyond the slope out to the sea, which was blue with a burning slick of blood from the half-set sun. One boat approached the slick, rowed by a young man I did not recognize. He looked freckled, with mousy hair. He seemed to be rowing on the same spot for a long time just as he was reaching the horizon on the blue sea, as if a single wave were holding still instead of falling; until he reached the blood-red edge, and I felt someone was missing from the boat, because then I thought there had been a woman in the boat with him, a young woman in a very long dress. But now she wasn't in the boat any more as he paddled the oars on the red and golden and bright glow of the sunset. Then a dark cloud hovered over the horizon and obscured the low, fiery sun, and a cold wind moved across the sea that was completely calm and still blue, clear even though the sky was darkening; and the dark boat moved across the blue bay which seemed to shine in a strange way as if a light were radiating from the depths; and the dark boat drew a shadow that flickered without me being able to tell why. And then flashes started from a fire that was burning I could not tell where. And the boat had turned into a skiff, and this man was sitting in it with a single oar, looking into the depths as if searching for something. Then a wave rose and passed over the calm surface of the sea carrying something that I could not discern at first. And when it reached the boat where the man was sitting with his oar, which seemed curiously long for this country and much more like the sculls I have seen used by oarsmen elsewhere, I saw the lad standing on the prow with his feet apart, sadly stretching out his oar, and I saw it was the long dress that he raised into the air, heavy at first; then it flew up, and at that the young man seemed relieved that no one was wearing it, even though the sadness of his expression did not diminish.

In the dream I felt I knew that I had seen the woman's belly swollen; but I also seemed to know that just before she disappeared in the boat she had been very slender. But the dress flapping on the oar that was raised up to the fresh moonlight bulged as if swollen by a stomach that was maybe nothing but the breeze. And the flashes of fire were over, now the round, pale moon had risen, boding doom I thought as I saw the dark boat gliding into the shadowy bay. And the silver moon glided after it, lighting up the pebbles on the beach, and I saw a cairn appear in the moonbeams that swept after the man when he stepped ashore, and threaded his way, his head bowed, among the pebbles, but he seemed to avoid the cairn as if shying from something inside it. I could hear the vague howling of a pained animal, or a baby; and then the man's image faded, and the beach, when the horses returned with such violence that they drove everything else out of the way. The leader seemed by far the largest, getting so much in the way of the others that they slipped my attention, although I knew they were still there, and I heard hoofs thundering with such intensity that all other noise was drowned out by their pounding; I watched the steed rushing in the moonlight, marble, and silver sparked from it against the pale moon. And for all I could see it was a winged steed, and it rose and soared into the cloudless sky; but never went so high that it could not touch the ground with its shiny hoofs if it stretched out its legs; but it kept them pressed up against its chest and loins, its mane spread wide and its tail erect. This went on over an ever-changing landscape, and beneath the horse passed mountains and valleys and white glaciers and hot springs giving off light steam, dark plains and peaks bathed in light, bellowing rivers in chasms that screamed through narrows to pierce their way through the rock, and the steed glided around peaks on newly sprouted wings, alone except for an eagle at the highest cliff examining the ledges in search of a perch to settle for its nest, then gliding on mental images over wide valleys, seeing from the air the rivers moving at an incredibly slow pace over the land, and its eagle-eyed sight noticed farms and ruins grown over with turf where no one lives any more, except transparent spectres slouching like clouds of steam over grass-covered meadows.

This seemed to be going on all the while I followed the steed in flight. And the thought entered my mind that as I glided over this vast land and its wealth of untold tales, that I was at one with the flying horse, that it was me, and I it, and that we were a centaur with a twin nature, a winged steed and a child of the earth, bound and free at once.

Then suddenly this flight came to an end on the bank of a stream with shallow mud and everything so calm. Even the water running so slowly, so incredibly slowly. And a woman seemed to be lying in the water staring with blue, ever-bluer eyes into the firmament, and tiny bluebells on the bank, forget-me-nots.

And then a man came, I did not know whether he was the same one who had been rowing the boat; he appeared there and sat down on the woman's stomach which just protruded from the surface of the water, slowly making himself comfortable, and began rowing with his palms and fingers pressed together, broad fingers with the nails cut straight across and horn-like, as if suitable for claws. He rowed on in the shallow stream, crossed where it rippled over the mud, and a black dog with a white patch on its forehead and one of its ears ran alongside, excruciatingly slowly even though it was running, beside the stream, the white patch around its eye like a monocle.

The man rowed along on his throne on the woman's swollen belly, dragging her along the bottom of the stream, and her long hair billowed out in the current. He leaned his head back, rolled his eyes and screwed up his pallid face, and sang: Higher, My Lord, unto thee – at the top of his voice, while the sheep began to pour forward and flowed like milky brooks down the slopes. Then the woman's head rose up from the water while he was rowing, her eyes open and still growing bluer, and her mouth open with black sand in the corners, between her teeth in places. When he realized this the man reached behind his back and held her head under the water without even looking over his shoulder. And I saw his knuckles whitening, and blood spurting from beneath the nails to leave a thin trail along the stream which faded into the pale-green reindeer moss by the bank.

And then I woke up. Thórdur, do you know what my dream means?

Thórdur was in no hurry to answer. He chewed a long straw all the way to the head. Tossed it away and said: Dreams mean nothing, said Sturla Sighvatsson.

The Journey Continues

They gathered up their food and put it back in the saddlebag, which Thórdur tied up. He stood by the horse's crupper, rubbing a finger across his nostrils to stop the brown trickle of snuff, holding his red handkerchief in his fist and looking with concern at Ásmundur.

I don't think it would do us any harm to have a dram, companion, said the magistrate, stroking his thumb and index finger over his impressive moustache, firmly, and its curled ends; so you'll have to give me the bag again.

He took a fine silver measure out of the flap pocket of his wide-collared waterproof riding jacket, and poured out a dram for Thórdur so brimful that it called for a steady hand, and Thórdur emptied the measure into his mouth, held the mouthful for a moment under his tongue, stretched out his gullet and swallowed, his Adam's apple jerking as he consigned it to his depths.

After two glasses each, they leapt on to horseback and continued their journey.

They were replete, too, and travelled so slowly at first that they hardly seemed to inch forward.

The weather stayed dry.

I didn't quite finish the story, magistrate, Thórdur said slowly, stroking his chin with long probing fingers on to his left cheek, right up to his eyes, speaking slowly with prolonged pauses between his words; since I've said too much already, and more than too much. So it's maybe right to take the story further and tell what happened to the blossom of this great woman's family.

Really? said the magistrate; I'd like to hear that.

They rode on side by side, and the horses seemed to cock their ears too and wait for the tale with their riders, plodding on so as to cause him no disturbance.

Yes, said Thórdur; yes. The latter like a philosophical conclusion. As if he had reached a conclusion for himself after long contemplation of the subject. The second yes was in a deeper pitch, almost a cello. Was that all? The magistrate and the horses waited. There was no sound but for the quiet plodding as they made their slow progress, the land was mostly soft, sand or mud, sometimes patches of grass, the occasional clash of a horseshoe against stone. One cloud stood out whiter than the rest and drifted across the sky, stretched until it frayed apart.

Yes, said Thórdur; they were all promising children up there on the heath, hard to see which was the most promising, and they grew up to adulthood well, all of them. But one was sent off to be educated. Somehow he must have been thought more promising than the others. He even went abroad to study, and then he returned and was welcomed with open arms, adored by everybody, the learned one, as he had been when he was a child on the heath where the bank was that we were talking about. A farmer and a teacher. To cut a long story short, he found a suitable bride. They had taken a liking to each other, and seemed a good match. And soon the wedding day arrived. He was just like the rest of those people, sparing no expense if there was a celebration to be held. There was plenty of meat from a cow that had been slaughtered, along with some sheep, and neither food nor drink were lacking. Plenty of spirits had been brought in, even cognac. But there was just one thing. There was no trout. And the bridegroom wasn't pleased at that. So he chose a local man that he wanted to go with him. He was called in and they left together to cast the net. His companion held one end on the bank, while the bridegroom took off his shoes and socks and rolled up his trousers since there were no waders to be had. And he started to wade out holding the other end and went as far as he could. He knew the technique well and was considered a first-rate huntsman with a rifle or what have you, whether he was fishing in lakes and rivers, shooting seals or culling seal cubs. He was also a dab hand at trapping foxes if he needed to as well, although he was not as renowned for it; his brother was better, one of the best in the country in fact. Anyway. They were doing this the way they should and everything was in order, no need to go into detail since everyone knows how it is done; I hardly need to tell you, magistrate, you are the poet after all. Not me. They combed the lake with the net, the bridegroom wading and his companion on the bank holding the other end. The net was growing heavier and they were sure there was enough for the banqueting table; there was never any doubt about that with men like them at work. Then the bridegroom's companion saw him sink up to his knees. He sank slowly, and then he was up to his chest. Up to his chin. He had stepped into quicksand. And it went on sucking him down until he disappeared. And you know the way people sometimes gain redoubled strength at such times, so the companion tugged with all his extra might at his end of the net, and it snapped right next to the bridegroom who went down holding just a strand.

And then he was gone. And the man had to bring the tragic news home. On the way he saw a group of people riding along in high spirits, and he saw more parties on horseback. It was the guests on their way to the joyous occasion when the greatest people in the district were to be married. And he arrived and the joyful celebration turned to sorrow, and the world wept. The fiancée who had been waiting at home for her beloved had to be confined to bed. She yearned so passionately for him to be found so that she could at least have his grave to tend and look after for the rest of her life; but it was a forlorn hope that the depths would ever give him back, and she was overpowered by her grief. In the spring the river changed its course, moved to one side, and the man came back up where it had been, completely intact apart from being a corpse; the sand had kept him preserved quite undamaged and he wasn't eaten away or whittled down or rotten even after lying there that long.

Then they quickened their horses' pace and a distance developed between them for a while as the magistrate went ahead engrossed in his own contemplations. The land was deserted, barren, with sand and mud terraces in places. Not a living creature in sight, neither sheep nor birds. He was troubled by the wilderness which reawakened his fear. He slowed down to wait for Thórdur, glad not to be travelling alone over that dead land, and thought about the things that haunt solitary travellers there when dusk falls; and even in daylight, when the weather was like this, not to mention when it was bad or even doubtful.

Wherever it might appear from. Woken from a guilty mind, a crime that no one knows but you, or from popular tales, restless souls roaming in search of vengeance against anyone they could collar. All that superfluity of the dead that this nation carries with it, generation upon generation, for centuries. People who have frozen to death on such sands, spirits smothered or crippled in the destitution and mercilessness of human life. Infants exposed at birth, begotten in illicit love. He felt here how weak a defence reason would offer against an approaching ghost. Perhaps it was not absolute when you started accusing your own thoughts and sought sanctuary in dividing your personality. The breeze was beginning to ruffle the sand and toss it into the eyes, nose and mouth.

A yellow-brown column of smoke moved across the ridge ahead of them.

The Vicarage

It was dusk by the time they arrived at the farm; their horses were relieved. He thought he discerned some kind of movement when they went along the path to the farmhouse, but it was too dark to be sure. The vicar stood in the yard with his young wife, quite a tall man and gannet-like, thin of face with a black shadow of stubble around his mouth, cheeks and long chin, even on his long neck. Somewhat hunched, and his nose long with a wart on it; his forehead on the narrow side, but high; and his hair smooth except for the wave in it and his receding hairline, black and somewhat greasy. He cocked his head slightly as if braced ready for a gust of wind, holding his hands in front of him with the palms cupped together, clasped with the fingers curling tightly around the backs of his hands, instead of interlocked; and his thumbs crossed in the manner of Franciscan monks, as if he had adopted the custom after his ordination, to conceal his young age.

The weather was calm.

His wife was short and plump, freckled, blue-eyed and shy; they were married the previous year, and she took over the keys to the pantry from a housekeeper who left in a huff.

She had plaited her hair into a bun. She blushed slightly when she shook the magistrate's hand, after he had greeted his old classmate; the two had not met since they left school.

The men needed to bow their heads to pass through the doorway into the farmhouse. He had not been there since he was a boy preparing for school with the old vicar, and had not needed to bow his head when he went in then. He recalled the time without joy, having left there in a terrible state, ill after catching a chill. He was in such a

104

bad state that his aunt took him to her farm elsewhere in the district, and nursed him back to health. A shiver ran through him at the thought, the memory of his stay there long ago; when he remembered how small and helpless he often felt, lonely with the old people who ran this farm then, so few, silent, gloomy; with the dark ages howling from every nook and cranny; spectres whispering in the passageways and out on the roof. And monsters on the beach, weird beasts in the crevices and among the tussocks.

And there was no one for him to tell how stiff and introverted his terror made him, especially when he was sent after dark to the byre down by the sea. Or on some other errand down to the shore.

There was much to fear in those days, besides the devil himself whom you always had to be on your guard against and show good manners to prevent him gaining a grip on you. One thing was never to empty your mind, because the devil might see the chance of taking control. And then the forces of good which want to help would have been poorly placed to conquer the power of evil, since it had long been an open question which was the stronger in that timeless struggle of forces. This he had learned from the old blind woman on the farm who never said anything straight out, seeing more than other people see anyway. She never tired of teaching him to beware of the devil, that untiring carrion beast. Signs of the cross and crucifixes could be of use although they were not infallible, the old woman would say out of her darkness, heaving a sigh, and snuffling if she had chanced upon a grain of snuff. And if she was deprived of snuff for long she grew crotchety and made do with cursing and fussing, occasionally spitting into the air when apparitions of bad spirits assailed her. She had many stories to tell but took a special delight in the terrifying tale of Brandur the ghost from the farm at Skálar, whom she had learned about in her own district and had often seen, and whenever she did someone invariably came over from Skálar. She was unable to determine whether the ghost had been forced to walk abroad during the exorcism of a dead old man called Árni Chalice, who had been fairly insignificant while he lived, or was the awoken ghost of a ship's cook found on the beach after a Dutch ship sank with all its crew on board, and who some say had been raised while still warm, and so powerful that he could talk to men. Those who performed the deed had joined forces to take vengeance on an enemy and enlisted the services of a well-versed practitioner called Árbjartur. And when the old woman went into the corner to describe her favourite ghost Skála-Brandur and his deeds of terror, she grew animated as if Árbjartur himself had been present there to raise her too from her cold decrepitude, and her blind eyes began to blaze. She hissed when she described Árbjartur's retort to the request: I don't know whether I can handle an adult ghost, but I feel confident about a lad; and she stretched out the hissing between her withered gums right up to the trap door in the ceiling.

Sometimes he enjoyed the old woman's tales as much as anyone else; but something remained of them when he was alone, and affected him. Then he would be afraid to be by himself. And they preyed on him in particular when he was sent down to the sea front, and assailed him by the byre. He had no one to confess this to and could not ask to be excused going there, even when dusk was falling.

When they entered the vicar's farmhouse, most of the farm workers were in the sitting room. An elderly man was twining a horse rope and eyed the visitors askance.

The women were twining wool, and looked up to see the visitors. All except a young woman, whose jet-black hair fell over her cheeks and hid her face, as she sat with a spindle in her hand, spinning with her head bowed. And she remained unmoved by the stirring of people around her, and seemed to focus past the spindle on to something still; and no one could imagine what it could be.

Over Punch

The wonder of the soil, you say, yes, it glitters and grows whole, you said that too, didn't you? In the poem. What exactly did you mean? How can a poet take such liberties, poet though he might be? In this valley of tears, said the Reverend Stefán, his paleness yielding to the glow of punch in his cheeks, the red blotches on his forehead growing sharper; tell me that. It is my lot to splash back and forth through these floods of pain, these waters of wretchedness, if I may borrow your idiom, old schoolfellow; washed up on this shore of death from magnificent foreign halls, after your schooling in life in the bowers. You are no longer there, dear friend of whom this nation expects so much. Perhaps not the nation which sees only the nobleman in you, much rather we who feel we know or suspect the powers you possess. The poet. But it is my task to try to console those forlorn people. That is rather different. Your poetry doesn't work then. Those people prefer to plod along in their own monotonous themes, not to mention the complex sport of rhymed verse. Once we learned about Sisyphus continually rolling his rock up the slope. Was always somewhere on the side, never reached the edge. That is where we part ways. You react angrily to this wretchedness, see it in the illusions of time yet to come. What do you know? Who are a poet, and have an escape behind you, or before you. Who can flee to fairer shores, as they say. Didn't one of you say that somewhere? You guardians of the illusion. The sacred illusion. Which is blessed, and blessed over again. And this man of God seemed to be someone else, perhaps turning transparent in the glow from the lamp with its light trembling beneath the glass. And would soon be seized by divine intoxication: this sacred illusion.

It is for other people, said the poet, lighting a cigar; other people.

Was he hiding behind the cloud? While it was his move. He offered the vicar a cigar which the man of God accepted, and accepted a light too.

You do not know the price we pay for it; that you cannot know. Obviously not. How could you? No. To be able to carry light into other people's lives. You surely don't think it costs nothing? Just handed over with no visible payment? I think not. We do not have the grace of lethargy to grant us mercy. Or the faith you deal in. Trade in, you might say of some. Not of you, old friend, he said, although he had never before got to know that reserved childhood school companion of his. The Church's elixir of mercy, all that. Oh no.

The Reverend Stefán breathed on to his tumbler, ran his finger over the cloud it created. He sank back slightly in his seat, stretched out his mouth, jutted out his chin with his eyelids lowered, and trembled; and his long eyelashes, almost feminine, cast a shadow, like crow's feet below his eyes over his sunken cheeks, his eyeballs showing vaguely like fruit in a tight gourd, a herb. You are too lofty by half. You wade on inconsiderately in poetic intoxication. Up in the golden clouds in the frenzy of your inspiration, and know precious little about human life in the Bible's much quoted vale of tears. Which is precisely here.

So tell me another thing, vicar, the magistrate said; do you know any greater pleasure than fucking a woman?

Are you talking of heaven or hell? said the vicar, and slumped his head forward on to the table. He gave no sound; but spasms passed through him which he tried to repress.

At that point his glass fell, spilling over his hair and hands.

You're impossible to drink with, you bastard, muttered the magistrate.

But at the same time he thought of the considerable difference in their stamina, which was to a large extent his own fault. He knew that behind this rather too thin wall the wife was waiting for her husband, this weak man of God with his hidden gifts, who was responsible for souls, and she terrified at what the drink would do to him and possibly dangerous conversation with that old school companion of his who had never been a companion anyway; now the light of the land appeared, confounding all proportion; disrupting what had to be accepted here, treading down straws, smothering with his entire manner and reputation his little brother at the northernmost of all oceans.

Scourged; and could see nothing before him in his intolerance towards all he felt to be small but was perhaps the lifeline for survival here, for not falling victim to the hazards that lay so heavily over everything that tried to live. And incited him to break off his pacts and rise up to action which his meekness had protected him from, and was now to be condoned for.

No, Ásmundur thought later.

No, he said. Was he imagining things? Had he imagined to himself that the Reverend Stefán had slumped his head down on to the table, and knocked over his glass of toddy, spilling it over his hair and hands?

That the drink had gone straight to his head, was that his imagination? Fiction.

That the drink had gone so much to this godforsaken wretch of a parson's head that he had become incapable when their conversation reached that point. Or had he justified his own part through the memory's automatic tendency to present things favourably? When he searched within himself on the subject he was not sure which it was.

A Further Confession
by the Murderer Jón

. . . He said that he rode to meet the herd being driven just ahead of him from Svartárkot to the Vídirker corral, and that Jón from Sigrídarhóll and Illugi from Svartárkot and Sigtryggur from Thröngadalur were in that party . . . Then he rode with them for some way. Then he went ahead of them out to the Vídirker corral, whence he left for Grjótárgerdi to meet Sigurpáll from Halldórsstadir; who had been sent to gather up the sheep owned by the farmers on the western side of the river for the Vídirker corral and had taken seven sheep from Raudengismýri which he intended to return there, and he asked Sigurpáll to help him sort them out of the flock where he had gone past Grjótá to the west of Grjótárgerdi, which he had done, since the sheep were marked, and then he drove the sheep south to the Vídirker corral, at which moment the flock from Svartárkot which he had ridden with had reached the corral, where he met farmer Sigtryggur from Thröngadalur whom he had intended to accompany over the river and whose sons had already released the sheep into Seljaland some time before; whereupon he asked Sigtryggur whether he could not shortly leave the corral, to which he replied in the affirmative.

Furthermore he mentioned having found, in addition to the eight which he had brought from Grjótárgerdi, one of the two sheep which he had expected to find in Svartárkot but had not appeared there, so that in all he had had nine sheep in his charge, while two had been gathered in from Svartárkot, owned by Sigtryggur from Thröngadalur. He said he mentioned to Sigtryggur that it would have been better for his stepson to go to Grjótárdalur and attend to the sheep at the end of the pasture, while he went after the others himself in the south. But on Sigtryggur not being able to leave immediately, he went ahead with Sigtryggur's two younger sons and the aforementioned eleven sheep. He parted ways with them when they had just passed west of the Vídirker corral, and crossed Sellandsá river and on to the hill called Hjalli, then down east of the cairn and south towards the river at Ytri-Lindir.

Where he had met Konkordía sitting a short distance from the river; he said she greeted him.

But he did not reply.

He dismounted instead, taking hold of her. Placing one of his gloves and his handkerchief over her mouth and nose. And holding her down until she suffocated. Whereupon he dragged her over into the river.

He said he placed her in the river with her head pointing upstream. Although slanting towards the eastern bank. And that the water where he placed her was no deeper than to his calf. Not immersing the body completely.

Although he could not recall exactly how much of it protruded above. And he claimed not to have wondered whether the body would float away from where he placed it or not.

Having performed the deed at such speed, and in such a frenzy and distraction that he could not have had the presence of mind to prevent it being noticed.

None the less he recalled jumping down from the bank, although he is unable to remember on which foot he landed. And said that the details of the incident in general were unclear in his mind, for at the same instant he became conscious of having caused the girl's death he had been seized by a feeling of remorse and prayed to God to forgive him that crime.

The examining magistrate mentioned that the testimony of the accused appeared in this respect to be honest and without concealment.

Furthermore, he was shown in court the aforementioned box containing the footprint, and said he could not counter in any way that it was the print of his own foot.

Although on the above grounds he could not recall very clearly how he stepped down from the bank.

He said he had then immediately ridden away alongside Svartá to the north, and a short distance from it east of Ullarfoss, and out towards the ford known as Melpallsvad, where he had seen the three sons of farmer Sigtryggur Ásláksson from Thröngadalur driving the sheep a short distance away and admitted taking what he believes to be a white sheep one winter old, which was on the bank close to the ford, and pulling it to the river . . .

The magistrate put down the papers, stretched himself out flat. The next day he would need to be well rested, and feel comfortable in the difficult task awaiting him when he would begin examining the witnesses.

He had let it suffice to make arrangements for preventing the brother and sister from meeting each other.

The Hearing

The magistrate decided to examine the old woman Járnbrá first. He was repulsed by this gossiping old woman who burned to be able to tell all she knew and turn out all she had collected for the detriment and deprecation of others. She was small and seemed as if she wanted to spit but had to restrain herself in the room, closed her eyes frequently and almost gasped for breath when she began talking. Her face was small with little eyes and a sharp nose, and dark wrinkles around her mouth which was sunken and almost toothless. She's some sub-Arctic breed of viper, the magistrate thought, as he sat cold and imposing in his seat, still not entirely free from the influence of the punch they had drunk the night before. He let it suffice to get her started with dry and concise questions, since she needed little encouragement.

The court officials paid little attention to what was going on, bowed their heads and appeared remote, although also as if they were in some way guilty. One of them, Thórdur, took the opportunity to gaze out of the window, as if afraid that his horse was bolting out of the meadow. The other, the district doctor, held a tattered snuffbox with an ornate, looping inscription on the lid, reading his name over and again.

The old woman rambled on, described the weather and the husbandry; gave detailed accounts of irrelevant events and hinted at all manner of gossip spread from one farm to the next that concerned people other than the accused. The magistrate sometimes had to usher her back from this tittle-tattle, recording only the details relevant to the case, while the old woman chattered away in her zeal with occasional gasps for breath. She had long waited for the chance to speak her mind. Related how she had often seen the brother sitting with his sister on his lap. Yes, she said; yes, she had often seen them kiss, she said, nodding her head, falling silent momentarily and pressing together her fleshless lips which reduced her mouth almost to a tiny dot. Her hair was thin under her shawl and greying blond, and she scratched herself at length with her little finger. The magistrate asked if she had seen anything particular take place between them which she felt to be related to a criminal act between them. Then she said she simply could not keep such a thing to herself, especially before your worship, an official and magistrate, that she had not been able to avoid noticing that the relationship between the half-brother and half-sister was quite different in character from what you would expect between so closely related people, and I really must say that I felt it unseemly to watch.

When the magistrate repeated his earlier question as to whether she had seen anything particular which could be interpreted as a criminal act the old woman answered that perhaps there was no single particular incident; yet saying this with such a tone of voice and bearing that it could just as easily be construed as a positive answer to the magistrate's question, although he recorded her statement as it was made, but abridged from her ramblings. It was not rare, she said; for me to see Saemundur sitting with his sister on his lap, she repeated as if uncertain that the magistrate had heard; and further-more I saw them lying in bed together on the Sabbath.

The magistrate asked whether they had been undressed. No, they were in fact fully dressed but that's all the same to me, she said. Was it in the evening or at night? the magistrate asked. No, in fact it was the middle of the day. Then the magistrate asked if it had occurred in such a way as to embarrass her more than other demonstrations of affection between them. No, she said taking a lengthy breath. Then, blowing the air back out with a sigh, that she was terribly upset by seeing it all the same, that she must say.

The doctor took an inconspicuous pinch of snuff from the box with the ornate lettering on the lid. Then Thórdur blew his nose protractedly and stopped looking for his horse. The doctor gave a start. A gull squawked greedily outside, down by the river, which wove its course a short distance from the farmhouse. A shadow passed over the meadow, headed up the mountainside, and disappeared out of sight from the window by the gables.

Járnbrá went on. The magistrate recorded little of it. None the less, some statements by other people from the farm tended in the same direction, which he recorded. And my husband, she said; Jón, who also works on the farm here, and knows what he's talking about, he was outraged to see them. Brother and sister treating each other like that, he says there's no disputing that it's not lawful. And I said the same to the dear vicar's wife, the old woman said, scratching her scraggy hair; I've been telling her over and again and never heard her say she was happy with their behaviour.

The magistrate asked whether she had mentioned it to the vicar. Our vicar? Oh no. I thought it was quite enough mentioning it to the vicar's wife.

But did you see any sign that Sólveig Súsanna was pregnant?

I didn't think there was any hiding the fact. And nor did anyone else I've spoken to. I thought it was obvious. As far as I could tell she got fatter and fatter, then suddenly it vanished. I wasn't the only one to think that was a remarkable change, and not the sort of thing that happens overnight.

Did you raise the subject with the brother and sister?

Oh no. Dear me, no. Not me. But I understand from the housekeeper and you can ask her yourself, your worship, that she mentioned it to Sólveig, but I don't know how she reacted. I didn't think it was any of my business interfering even though I didn't like it going on in front of my eyes. That was the job of the master and mistress of the house, God bless them and preserve their souls.

The magistrate had grown tired of the old woman's ramblings and the time had come to give her a rest. She wanted to say more but he dismissed her, and next he called up the young housekeeper. She had curly strawberry-blond hair, blue eyes and red cheeks, and was distressed at being called before his worship, stared into her lap and scratched and pinched the tips of her fingers and said in a low voice that she had often seen the half-brother and half-sister embracing and kissing and treating each other in such a way that she could not have helped feeling shocked. Then she fell silent and stared down at the floor, pigeon-toed in her seat with her rolled-down socks and stitched sheepskin shoes.

Have you ever seen the brother and sister in bed together?

Yes, the young woman said, and fell silent.

Well, said the magistrate; do you intend to keep quiet about that, he said brashly, impatiently.

Yes, she had seen them lying together in Sólveig's bed at night, up in the attic above the sitting room. She said that Sólveig was undressed.

And Saemundur?

She was not prepared to verify that.

Did you see them moving from one bed to another?

No, she said she had woken up beside her husband, who was a labourer there, and slept with the other farmworkers in the sitting room. They were right beside Sólveig's bed. And I always fell asleep before they left.

What about the child, said the magistrate; Sólveig's daughter? Did you notice that the child was restless or perhaps cried when they were in bed together?

No, she replied: I never noticed that. The child's only four, she whispered.

I know that. But do you know anything else?

Once I heard the child say something. To do with that business.

Speak out then, said the magistrate, frowning.

In fact I heard the child say once, during weaning time for the lambs: uncle sleeps in my bed.

Have you mentioned this to anyone else?

Mainly my husband, she said, her forehead covered with red blotches. Yes and Járnbrá and her husband Jón. Often really. And the vicar's wife. They were all shocked like us.

Have you heard anyone else mention that they noticed the couple sleeping together?

Yes, my husband. Just like me. Many times. And the vicar's wife one night. I was awake. She needed to go down the stairs from her bedroom. And they were in bed together yet again.

Do you know how the vicar's wife reacted?

I know that she was upset about it happening in her home.

Did you see Sólveig growing fatter?

Yes.

And how did you interpret that?

I thought – , she said and fell silent.

Well, what did you think then, say your piece.

That she was pregnant.

On with the story. Did she continue to grow fatter?

It changed suddenly.

Really.

Yes, she was ill for part of the day.

Did she go to bed?

She was dressed. She lay in bed a while.

How long?

Well, two or three hours I think.

But dressed?

Yes, yes.

Did you mention this to anyone else?

Yes.

And what was their opinion?

They thought the same as we did.

We who?

My husband and I.

What then?

Well, really, that she was pregnant by her half-brother. And had got rid of it, the woman said in an almost inaudibly low voice.

Did you ever mention it to the brother and sister?

Yes, twice. Sólveig started talking about it. The first time was when Sólveig's daughter, Áróra, told her mother that the vicar's wife and I had been talking about love between brother and sister, and the vicar's wife told her to tell her mother that it wasn't allowed. So

Sólveig told me that there was no need to listen to what the child was babbling about, but I could not help saying I did not like the way they were behaving. The other time she was saying how she noticed quite well that she was being spared the hard jobs. It was quite unnecessary. She felt people thought she was pregnant. She was terribly sad and said that one child for the authorities to support was quite enough.

Now the magistrate adjourned the hearing; he was hungry, and the food was on the table. He dined with the vicar in the study, and they said little. He felt repulsed, was upset by having to deal with this. The people he had been interrogating, he felt them trivial. Remote from him. So that is my nation, he thought, feeling repulsion.

The vicar cleared his throat several times as if about to say something. His eyes were brighter than before. As if his glance boded doom, the magistrate thought.

He saw a face appear at the window.

A Face at the Window

He was standing in the meadow swinging his scythe. The grass was wet after a night of rain. There was more rain in the air, overcast. He had not been able to see her all day. He had never seen anyone he disliked more than this magistrate. Although he had only seen him from a distance, a cold air emanated from this remote, haughty man who hardly greeted anyone except the farmer and his wife, but was like a god from a splendid pantheon with lightning itself in his quiver. And conceivably no quarter would be spared. No refuge in indifference, no defence in the country being forgotten, too paltry to remember the people in this rural district, hunting down its sins and crimes, as the righteous called them. Now he could no longer derive strength from her. At this moment he stood alone.

He wielded the scythe on the long grass, with a regular motion. There was a chill within him which he could not rid himself of by cutting the grass. He recalled the time as a young boy when he parted with his mother, and he scarcely remembered his father. However, they had supported him for the first years, most often separately to prevent him being taken into official care. He had earned his own living from the age of ten, and moved from farm to farm. That was his world. He knew no other. From an early age he felt himself alone in the world.

He felt the fresh scent in the air but could not relate it to himself. He tried to swing the scythe more rapidly but felt no warmth keeping the chill at bay. It had often been cold, too, watching over the ewes when there was no shelter to be had in the little hut, because he had to move with his flock; shivering nights when the whole earth was bathed in dew, and the ewes shying from him and running through the chasm, fleeing from the sheepdog over the river; and the dog returning soaking wet and shaking itself in front of him, pretending to have done enough, and disobeying his order to go back down to the gully and fetch the sheep; rainy days when his whole existence was a dreary valley of tears, and no mollifying force anywhere; and he was wet, and could tell from the tide when the fog cleared for an instant that it was too soon to bring the ewes back to the milking pen, and he would be scolded by the milkmaids for not staying with the ewes longer so that they gave more milk; alone, small and cold, and thinking that nobody cared if he would never ever be warm again; that they would curse him if he fell to his death off the cliff or drowned in the river without bringing the sheep back home first. And the dampness dripped from every clutch of heather and every blade of grass, and the water welled up out of his shoes. The fog exaggerated all the drizzle and made it seem alien, and everything was blown up to monstrous proportions, and a host of images hovered about with fateful warnings, waiting in ambush for him: piles of straw became grotesque cliffs with trolls' faces, menacing; and birds shot up from nowhere and whisked forebodingly past; and a towering monster approached with its huge prey in its mouth; and fortunately did not notice him, until a man drew closer with his dog; and it turned out to be only a vixen with a scrap of stockfish in its mouth.

When he had finished cutting his patch he set off home. Here he had felt best and strengthened. Until he met love. He could not resist stopping to look indoors. At just that moment the magistrate looked up and saw a face at the window.

Jón the Farmhand;
and Another Disquisition at Night

When Jón, Járnbrá's husband, appeared before the court he was not afraid to speak. He said he had often talked to the other people on the farm, and also to the half-brother and half-sister who had mentioned on their own initiative the rumours about them, and said they were sheer gossip. But it wouldn't leave me in peace, he said; so there you go. And I even spoke about it to our vicar. He did nothing about it. I was in the habit of answering for them. There were so many people from the farm who broached the subject with me. No, I don't remember them all. There were so many. But I could not help seeing so much of them that I simply stopped taking their side.

The magistrate thought the farmhand was boastful even if he was not garrulous, and even that a grin crossed his podgy face with its huge jaws and sloping forehead and receding hairline. He confirmed most of what had already been said. But now it was late in the day, with evening drawing near.

The magistrate adjourned further examination of witnesses until the following day, and saved the defendants until later.

After making the appropriate arrangements he dined with the vicar and intended to take an early night so as to be in good form when he needed it most. He went out into the yard and urinated, watching the moon for a while swimming in its gossamer veil of clouds. It looked almost circular in the mist. The weather was calm and little could be heard but for the murmuring of the river, as if from a freshly awoken distance.

He went into the farmhouse, closed the door quietly behind him, and hoped that no one would be awoken by the creaking of the stairs.

He had his hand on the handle of his bedroom door when he heard someone whispering to him in the dark.

He gave a start at such a sound in the darkened, silent farmhouse where he did not expect anything indoors to rend the quiet, excepted newly begun snoring, and maybe rustling. He thought he was alone and felt a chill run through him like cold breath down his neck.

He stood still holding the handle, which was made of copper and salvaged from a shipwreck.

Did anyone miss the copper from the ship? Cocking his ears, he thought he heard the murmur of the sea. Perhaps it was the rush of the river, or the wind stirring on the turfed roof, night singing through blades of grass. He felt sweat pouring from his forehead. A pang of fear at what dwelt in the dark, from the loneliness of his childhood. Which he had never managed to repress completely, neither at urban establishments of learning nor through the cultivation of rationality, nor detached mockery of the subject and joking, exaggerated tales to raise a laugh at evening gatherings; when night came and he was alone, those defences gave way and he was exposed.

Then he heard the whisper a second time, and now he could discern what it was saying.

Now I've seen that side to your character, he heard whispered in the dark. A tiny glow emanated from the lamp by the door post from inside the spare room. But he could not see who was talking. Whether he was transparent, or a disguised ghost, in a brown jumper or a shiny breastplate. Who had sent this visitation?

Why? He was unable to move. The terror pounded in the dark. Outside, inside, in his ears.

Then he felt a cold, dry hand, for an instant, on the back of his hand, and the moment he snatched his sweaty palm from the door handle the other hand retreated as quickly. He held his breath, and heard short heavy breathing in the darkness, deathly tense.

An image darted through his mind of how the round moon had rocked in the silver mist, and he remembered how his own shadow had shrunk on the porch in the yard, and remained behind huddled up when he had gone inside the farmhouse. Then the hand touched his shoulder, and the voice whispered: It's only me.

What? he started, hearing the word himself.

Don't you need a drink? the voice said in the dark, and the hand pinned him down.

Now I have seen the judge at work. And the hand disappeared from his shoulder and opened the door, and in the trembling light from the peat he saw the gangling vicar, almost unreal in the moonlight as if he had induced it himself for his own salvation. May I offer you a wee drop? I think we could both do with it. It's been a difficult day. And worse is yet to come.

You haven't spoken to the accused, said the vicar, accepting a cigar from the magistrate. Ásmundur watched his face flare up when he lit the cigar for his old schoolfellow, and felt again how he had never got to know him. Perhaps had not felt enough respect for him to talk to him, did not think it was worth the bother, until they sat drinking together the night before. Although he remembered him clearly from those distant days at school.

Yes, you are a judge, said the vicar. I have never been able to imagine what that side of your character could be like. All the time I have been expecting you to clear up the case. Judge it.

The magistrate puffed smoke towards the moon outside, chasing the wisps with his flat hand, suddenly tearing the weft with his fingers outstretched. One does one's duty.

And to whom does one have a duty? To what?

They clinked their glasses, making them jingle like little silver bells about to peal.

What, the magistrate said, and silently watched the vicar's still shadow on the wall, so large it seemed to tower over them both. Then it trembled slightly with the spluttering of the light in the lantern, from the little flame nourished by a snow-white wick of cotton grass.

Yes what? said the vicar; to life?

Yes, to life. To make life liveable. For society to be able to thrive. For it not to be poisoned by ill deeds. For a civilized society to be maintained.

You, the individualist. You who believe in the power of the individual. But hate his weakness. The weak and the small, don't you ever think about them? Don't you ever wonder how the criminal feels? What he feels within? His yearning for life. His dreams. Shipwrecked in his yearning. Hopes that struggle against hopelessness. You who are a poet.

Here I have another role to perform.

How can you be both at once? A poet with a duty to understand all that tries to live. And the awe-inspiring judge who shuts himself off to whatever fails to accord with the paragraphs of our artificial laws.

Who says a poet should understand anyone and everyone? Everything? Do you think a poet should be a pastor of souls? Should he don your guise? Console and heal? Tolerate what is forbidden? Even taboo? No, the poet is a creator. Understanding is for the rest of the people. What he has created. And creation is his divine vocation. Nothing else. Only that which he can use is important. Then he is a poet. Fulfilling civic duty is quite another matter. In anything one undertakes. To dispatch one's duty beyond reproach. And do so in such a way as never to disturb the poet. Support the poet but leave him in peace.

I beg to differ, said the pastor of souls; I see a poet quite differently. As someone who loves life so intensely that he is incapable of judgment. And feels his weakness, when he is strongest. Because then he is most true. It is not up to him to pass judgment. His role is to try with all his might to understand, try to cause no one harm.

Yet you send your worker to watch over a fox's den and uproot the family that lives there in harmony. As far as I can tell the accused is your arm and instrument in that respect. I have heard he is matched only by young Arnór from Múlaberg in keeping foxes at bay in this part of the country. How do you reconcile that with what you are teaching me or pretending to preach? And you go fishing with your farm workers. Don't you feel the satisfaction of hunting when you make a good catch? Don't you feel the hunter's joy? Don't you feel glee when the line jerks and you begin to haul it in? I know how happy and excited you feel when you bring the fish aboard. I have no

124

doubt you can imagine how the den-watcher feels when he has caught the fox and his good lady, and killed the cubs. Surely you acknowledge the familiar combination. Of ferocity and the cathartic joy of killing. There are instances of it everywhere. The pride of getting the better of a worthy opponent, the thirst for vengeance on finding a pile of bones or whole limbs left by a scavenger. You have seen live sheep just as I have, with their noses bitten to shreds and eaten off by that fierce, cunning animal that has killed the lamb and taken it home to its den to feed its own. Isn't all life like that? Why should man be an exception? An eye for an eye – you would do better preaching that from your own book: a tooth for a tooth. It is impossible to give quarter to any force of destruction that threatens the whole. The well-being of mankind.

He paused to hear how the vicar would reply. But nothing was forthcoming from him, he just twiddled his thumbs, leaning forward.

The fox snatches little lambs to feed its cubs. While the vixen hardly moves an inch from them and licks their blind eyes, their snouts, their backsides as a laxative. I'm told there is scarcely any other animal that shows such care for its offspring. How do you explain that this same creature, the fox, attacks its own offspring and kills them?

That's only when it is afraid, terrified, crazed by fear. Might it not be to save the offspring from an even worse fate? I have that from a fox-hunter who told me, happy and proud, how he had found a plan for catching the male when he had already killed the vixen. He took two of the cubs and tied them up in different places to lure the father into range with their howling. The fox was so cautious and in fact was well aware of the danger, and didn't come for the next two nights. The third night he approached to fetch his young whose mother had been killed. The hunter had hung out there, poorly dressed in lashing rain, hadn't slept a wink with his few provisions all wet and un-appetizing, kept warm only by his gleeful urge to hunt and shoot the fox. He kills the parent and puts down poison for the cubs in the den if he cannot catch them, and is overwhelmed by joy, full of the glory of nature which he loves and the delight of living there in the uninhabited wilderness which he has made habitable for himself, by learning the ways of nature; he knows enough to entrust himself to nature and cannot lose his way or die even in weather that would not spare other people.

So there you see, ferocity, there is ferocity everywhere. Isn't it the guiding principle in being able to live at all? That applies to everything. You cannot deny ferocity as a force in the service of life. You cannot . . .

I know, said the vicar. We are weak and discordant within ourselves. We cannot live without destroying some living thing. But it should not please us, but sadden us instead. Needing to make that sacrifice against our better judgment, in order to exist. You can talk about it academically. You are not a farmer. In the autumn you have no need to slaughter sheep that you know and love. But a home needs providing for. And you must not provide so well for them that there is no hope of having enough food left for them to survive through the winter and last until the spring. We farmers know that. But we cannot avoid it. You put the most beautiful of flowers to the scythe. But not with any happiness. It is definitely painful.

But the joy of hunting. Don't you feel the joy of hunting? Sometimes? Are you a saint then, said the magistrate, donning a smirk.

We are very imperfect. The good that I would – you know that verse – or the bad, we are complex. And it is not painless, trying not to dissolve into one's opposites. My soul does not feel joy. But we have to live this life, its injustice has to be accepted to a certain extent. Avoid it as you might like to. And do good in accordance with one's conscience and yearnings, to the utmost of one's abilities. But you, he said; what about you? Are you a hunter?

I can't be bothered. I never try shooting a rifle. I can hardly be bothered to cast for fish. My joy of hunting is contained in the verse I manage to write. In poetry. I also acknowledge the thrill of the hunt that I think the academic feels. Immersed in ancient lore, piecing together fragments of fact, speculating where the sources run dry or digging up new ones to shed light on what was already known.

Understanding things in such a way as to be able to create. No, I take no enjoyment in destroying life like the hunter.

Yes, you do not destroy life. But all the same you pry into the secrets of the dead, as a poet. And what about the living? Do you spare their secrets? You who pass judgment. No, you destroy no life. Judge not, that ye be not judged.

They smoked in silence for a while, seldom sipping their drinks. The contents of the bottle diminished slightly as it stood there on the table bathed in the merging glow of the tender light from the lamp which brought life with its inchoate shining and the pale silver of the moon which will never be fully extinguished.

We grow and grow, said the magistrate; because we will never be completely satisfied with ourselves.

Seek and ye shall find, the vicar said sadly.

Something other than you seek? asked the magistrate; seek and ye shall find that there is something yet unfound.

Dream: Largo

Watercoloured glass bells stained with red and blue roses pealed like ice like icicles when struck together like cones, and broke and the splinters of glass stuck into the backs of both his hands which were lacerated as he tried to protect his face from the gold-melting tones with hands that the brightness struck out searching beams of light or the silver shock of the moon if he broke forth rending strips of cloud with the hue of hell, and a scarcely silver any more rather a white moon he put himself in where he approached a cuneiform row of windows in a niche beneath a belfry, which formed a high gable window on this large hall the like of which he had never seen, and glass bells smashed one after the other when the clapper of the heart touched them, spraying rapid splinters the caravan of horses stormed along after casting off their bags or pulled their packsaddles like scuffed shreds on the heaps of sharp rocks on the stony paths on the hill ah he hears her scream ah where she lay unable to dodge their iron-shod hoofs ah her ah louder ah stop he says to the old long-bearded god who posed as perpetually youthful and the gigantic deity with his quiverful of thunderbolts hidden under the cowl he had wrapped around himself, and the splinters from the bells smashed stuck into the soft brown ochre earth in this shower white-maned by the deathly light of peril, and slid into lakes and stood there as poisoned needles or shafts.

Again he hears the beating of hoofs clattering on the rocks thundering on the blue ice the grey yet softening on scattered stretches of snow you must never touch me again look haven't we done enough see eh if you could touch that soft hair again the moon would have got there first suddenly it had waxed yes and see the horses are waiting turned away from the wind on the ridge baptized new ah whiter snow and dawdle hairy shaggy under violet-swollen clouds whizzing close far though from this silent image, which suddenly stands completely still quiet with a deafening howl still far constantly threatening this shrill note so spread out on the fearful brink of song but flies astray through space while the image latches the eye to a moment's peace and saves saved those who could not lose their sight blind would hear that note those notes seemingly stirring awake, a twinkle in the shaggy horses' eyes which move not life respite from death which watches in the timeless vastness on plains on mountains on the false blue ice over the sea of white peaks so dark blue as almost to seem blackening flight through the air harder harder ah faster . . . until breaking loose, until slackening, until extinguished . . .

And everything continues outside it; and nothing is void, except that which ceases to exist. Its substance transferred to something else, used for something else – something quite else.

Enough?

Destroy?

When the earth shook, said the old farmer whose his wrinkled face was carved all over with indecipherable letters, his eyes watering with a hint of blue; shook, then the trembling broke the ice on the bay ice on the sea like a thin shell so think of the deep, suddenly, and in an instant the bay had all turned wide yes the ice in tiny flakes on the sea the ice that had been covering everything as far as you could see from land in the freezing fog there day after day. We were starting to think that those big, ponderous polar bears would come, but still so swift in their hunger no not wolves, never heard the like of it before, oh no they are somewhere else . . . then suddenly all the ice had broken, yes about those bea–

Huge jewels frozen dew in multicoloured drops lodged between strands of twined horsehair rope twisted around shrubs laid in the heather hung on a hook in the chasm wall low down by the ferns to point into a hole perhaps show a trapped lamb; here were no trees, no mountains any longer, no longer the lake under ice, no clattering of hoofs, the ridge vanished with the horses that had stood facing away from the wind in a dip; occasional jingling in the wind or a passing rush, scattering the green drops of rays over the glittering pack ice, the thawing snow in a sunlit hollow so the woman was able to dip her toes she pressed them into fur-seamed sheepskin shoes and the black sheepskin she had donned and the dark underhair twinkling beneath the shag making the light arouse blue sparks there and he who was not a moon lacked the might of the moon did not touch the skin let alone her black hair. Let alone that. His heart clutched the melancholy of the violin to prevent the image exploding how distant now the autumn heather with its colours. There was no red, no yellow, the moon was full again, leaning as it edged its way through the bright night sky, and the stars boded infinity, timelessness.

Then trumpets sounded (for this inescapable day had come, dooms-day, dies irae) yellow and blue horses were drawn by fawn bridles with glittering bits shaggy as before with glossy-black nostrils almost blue, drawn on their bellies across the steel-grey ice, trying to scratch it with resisting hoofs, over the clear white snowdrifts, with a crushed red rose or pink in one nostril or both. But the high steeples split with hopeless violence, he himself hung from the clapper in the huge bell that swung slowly too slowly from its balk in the exposed belfry that was left when the rest fell away and crumbled in the rubble on the pavement the great flags in the mound of rocks where she stood at the top of the elfin castle of rocks a dog narrowly escaped the falling wreckage himself he was ready to try to kick himself free with his feet if the clapper came too close to the shiny orb of the bell-casing crushing him as it emitted a dull ring. Far below him he saw some mice playing on the floor in the light of three tall white candles, and a blue one almost burned down, which were standing in a gigantic candleholder, in a row.

He remembered the horses as he hung there the vicar he had seen standing at the door with his long arms aloft, blessing, before the towers exploded, he was puzzled at how he had been carried to where he was now.

Had he flown in the explosion? Been shot into the air? And swung slowly. Slowly . . .

Until he stood by the side of the sea, the razed grass yellow and pale in the glow of the moon, and the heavy crashing of the sea against the skerries, spraying over the rocks on the beach, he was unaware of any footprints in the black sand between the boulders, between the pebbles between the washed-up strips of seaweed below the seaboard; a bird glided tardily.

No boat.

No ship.

No light of man. No snow. No horses sheltering from the wind on the frosted meadow by the unlit farmhouse. Just a few redpolls and thrushes hopping on the pink solid turf beneath the houses empty of men.

And the sound grew heavier in the crashing of the sea and . . .

And what now? He thought he could hear her voice whispering. From where he did not know.

When it grew light he was still standing there on the beach, watching the swollen sea. The weather, which had whipped up the ocean, had calmed; white ripples were rolling all over the sea.

The horizon narrow, defined by a cream rim from the purple bank of cloud with foaming fronts slowly growing.

The big copper bells rolled about on the sea wall, sometimes tossed so far they reached the corpses of birds which lay in the snow-drifts, or were sucked in the outwash beneath these heavy bells when they fell calm. The clappers had been smoothed by the rolling, scratched the casing of the bells or fell against the metal with a ghostly resonance in the raging sea, as if singing the dead birds away from this world.

Nothing abroad.

Except a woman. Barefoot in the smell of seaweed, shells pouring over the arches of her feet, barnacles around her ankles, like trinkets guarding lost eyes as they dissolved.

She was naked, her breasts heavy with milk; and swung her head as if wanting to shake off something she could not tolerate, and dragging in her tracks a bloody veil which stained the waves groping towards her, and took her vague shadow, and tore it up. She paid no heed when the dead birds floated around her feet.

No light. No boat at sea.

Not a bird in the air.

Only heaps of dead birds on the beach, rolling in the inwash of the tide, and tossed about in the waves beyond.

Then I woke up and did not know where I was.

I felt a vague post-recollection of what I had dreamed when the tide seemed to dry up on the floor and be sucked out of the door; and then I gradually began to realize where I was and why. I do not know whether it happened slowly, or in a flash.

Second Day

For most of the day the examination of witnesses was along much the same lines as the previous day, confirming what had already been testified. More people had often seen the half-brother and half-sister in bed together. A farmhand the same age as the vicar, twenty-seven, answered the magistrate's question as to whether he recalled having seen Saemundur Fridgeir leave his own bed for the bed of his illicit lover.

Yes, says the witness; I did see him late one night leaving his bed in his underwear for Sólveig Súsanna's bed.

Do you know how long he stayed there?

Yes, I do, I know that. I was awake while they were in bed together. I reckon it was some two hours. Yes, I was awake all the time. Until I saw Saemundur Fridgeir go back to his bed.

Did you mention it to them, complain about it?

I can't say that. I don't talk to the people on the farm much anyway, only about idle things if it's not about work. Then it's largely my wife. Though I know the vicar's wife saw the couple in bed together. Oh no, I've never mentioned it to the vicar. What? Did I ever hear about any other man involved with Sólveig? Not since I came here last year.

In other respects he corroborated what his wife had said. Adding that he had heard stories or known the rumour suggesting that the woman was pregnant; and noticed that people tended to assume that it was the work of her half-brother.

Now the judge felt it was not right to spare the master and mistress of the house any more, and called up the Reverend Stefán. The man of God could not entirely disclaim that, shortly after the two had been together at his house, he had noticed their unbeseeming

133

attentions to each other; but added: I did not really pay much attention to it. I felt their attentions were more like what sometimes takes place between close relatives, rather than bearing witness to carnal lust, although I cannot deny since I am asked, that I thought it somewhat indecorous, one might say, and rather unpleasant to watch.

Did the witness mention it to the workers on his farm?

The Reverend Stefán was not very prompt in replying, and was ill at ease in his seat like a guest in the room, feeling rather out of place: Well, that would be when Jón, my farmhand, mentioned out of the blue that he thought the poor woman was unnaturally plump, I don't remember exactly when and . . .

And how did the witness react? the judge retorted, although more softly than usual.

Well, I don't have much of an eye for that sort of thing and didn't pay any particular attention to it, perhaps.

But the witness perhaps said something when the subject was broached.

Yes, said the vicar; yes, I suppose I did. I did tell Jón my opinion that then it would just emerge when the time was ripe, if she were pregnant.

But what did the witness himself think? Didn't the witness examine the matter more closely? If he had not already noticed it himself. Perhaps it is not completely impossible to ignore such a thing. When it is obvious.

Yes, I did have a vague feeling that she was rather plump in a way that was not exactly normal. But as I said, I don't know much about that sort of thing. Childless, and as good as newly-wed to boot.

Did the witness never try to investigate the matter once suspicions had been aroused?

Yes, I was travelling with our doctor who is sitting here, and he can confirm that I asked him whether such plumpness among women could not only be caused by the woman being pregnant, or that there could possibly be another explanation, and the doctor said yes.

Did the witness notice that the aforementioned plumpness increased in the course of time?

I did not notice.

Did the witness not notice anything suspicious? Nothing at all? Did the witness not think she became thin again rather suddenly?

Well, I cannot deny it entirely.

Then the magistrate began grilling his old schoolfellow who was far from animated in his replies. Had he never seen the half-brother and half-sister do anything that in his opinion was unlawful?

Nothing that I could state unequivocally.

Nothing?

Well, admittedly, when my wife went to fetch me some water one night she told me that she had seen them lying in bed together that night.

Didn't the witness act on the matter?

Well, I had one frank talk with Saemundur, he said, stroking the tablecloth firmly, with quite long strokes with his fingertips, watching the back of his hand.

Oh yes? said the magistrate.

Yes, said the vicar; when I felt various people were beginning to be shocked at the brother and sister, I spoke a few serious words to the effect that he should stop shocking them by showing such affection for his sister, and not give the others grounds for attacking them or creating an argument; that sort of thing can be interpreted in all manner of ways, and it would be quite infelicitous, and ought to be unnecessary to . . .

The magistrate felt this speech was rather on the long side, and wanted to know how the young man had reacted, whether he had remonstrated.

No. Really and admittedly not exactly directly, as it were, oh no, he did not absolutely deny that he had done so and cuddled his sister. But he said it had all been innocent. So that was the end of that conversation.

But has the subject never been raised with people outside the farm other than the doctor?

Yes, in fact, that could be said. With our sheriff. But it was nothing in particular, hardly worth mentioning. Except our sheriff, I heard from him that Saemundur here was supposed to have said something that led Bjartmar Sigurláksson, the farmhand at Beyla, to believe that he acknowledged the child Sólveig was pregnant with to be his own. But I cannot affirm nor recall too clearly what words were used nor am I sure that it was our good sheriff rather than anyone else from another farm.

The vicar recalled or had a notion that he had heard Arnór Björnsson the shipbuilder from Múlaberg mention that he and Bjarni Ásláksen from Sydra-Hóll had agreed that there could be no avoiding lodging a charge with the magistrate, with the rumour so widespread in the district and even starting to spread beyond it. He said the rumour would not be laid to rest, the vicar said, stretching out his speech to postpone the magistrate's questions, which were beginning to shower down upon him; not when it's gone this far, Arnór said. There's no avoiding it, it's everywhere. Although nobody says it out loud . . .

When, asked the magistrate, tired by his long-windedness.

Ah, sighed the vicar and furtively wiped the sweat from his brow; when?

Yes, when?

Well, I think it was after our sheriff who in fact spoke of it to me, well, he had lodged a charge with the magistrate by then . . .

In consultation with the witness then?

Well, what can one do? Consultation, consent? What do you think one can do? I did not say no. When does one say yes?

Has the witness heard the accused admit that the woman was pregnant?

I have a vague recollection . . .

Can't the witness remember . . .

. . . that Saemundur had been asked at the next farm here to the east . . .

Can't the witness clarify this? Asked by whom . . .

. . . by farmer Sigmundur if Sólveig were not with child and . . .

Really? said the magistrate; and what did he reply?

That if that were the case, he knew whose work it would be.

Oh yes, and what was that supposed to mean?

Well, it was supposed to mean that the person who asked could have inferred from Saemundur that it was the work of someone other than him. And in fact I remember, as the magistrate perhaps feels worth pointing out since we are talking about what could be called gossip, that their mother, who was at Múlaberg here in the district around the time, some time last year, was said to have reproached her children not to shock people by showing their affection for each other in that way.

Where did the vicar hear that?

I don't have the vaguest recollection. But I definitely didn't hear that until some time in the summer. I remember it now that we come to mention it, well, it does just come to mind when we go back over everything that happened.

And isn't there anything else that can be remembered? said the magistrate coldly. His companion and court official Thórdur thought he saw him smirk.

Well, how should I put it, there's perhaps a chance that there is. I don't remember too well. But there was someone who said . . .

Who?

I expect it was the sheriff who said . . .

What? Said what . . .

Well, he had heard hints that Saemundur and the lady of the house here at Sel, as they call it over there to the west, that they had been talking together, and the subject arose of his sister being pregnant, and he had begun as they say jokingly guessing who the father might be, and named various people, including young Arnór from Múlaberg whom he had recently been fox-hunting with. And in the version of the story I heard, if I am not getting it confused, he is supposed to have said something along these lines, as if he were joking: that people would maybe blame him for it himself . . .

And didn't the story include her reply as well? said the magistrate tetchily.

Yes, she is supposed to have said that no one would dare, or probably not.

Well then, I shall ask the witness formally whether he has heard any other male mentioned as being involved with Sólveig Súsanna other than her half-brother Saemundur Fridgeir, that is to say after they were both staying here at the farm, and I point out that I shall record the answer before the witness leaves the court, and allow that to suffice for the moment.

I do not recall having done so, and do not bring to mind anyone else who could elucidate the matter. Should the magistrate request an oath . . .

We shall see, we shall see.

In the doorway he met his wife who had now been called before the court. They exchanged glances briefly, his head bowed, she small and looking up towards him. The magistrate was impatient to conclude this part of the proceedings; and the two court officials on either side of him, and the empty chair for her. She was apprehensive, and did not make contact with her husband, who stumbled embarrassedly out and stood on the top step on the unfloored corridor, casting occasional glances over his shoulder towards her; released the door so that it yielded on its hinge and closed shut between them.

And the hearing began.

While the Vicar's Wife Was Waiting Outside, and the Interrogation That Followed

She expected no mercy from this arrogant man who had now spent two nights sitting drinking with her husband. Her dread grew, not least while the Reverend Stefán was before the court. What could he have answered? Now the subject they had so long kept silent about, had not even discussed among themselves, had been broached for them.

She fumbled with the tablecloth, moved it until she could see she had set it crooked. Tugged it immediately back, almost knocking over the lamp that stood there. The lantern glass fell on to the table, but in her anxiety she still managed to catch it before it crashed to the floor. She saw the shadow of the chair by the window wax and wane as the cloud parted from the sun, and another sailed slowly in front of it. She heard the breeze at the window, and saw the same effect happening to the shadow of the grass on the roof outside, waxing and waning by turns. She heard the dog bark in the distance, sounding as if it came from the riverbank. She also heard the bull bellow where it was tied in its stall. She heard the cow answer from the meadow. She sat down on the chair, forgetting the lamp in her hands, sat there open-mouthed with her face slack and a dulled look in her eyes as if trying to imagine what it was like to be pregnant.

How should she know?

Then she heard the loud cries of Sólveig's child Áróra Anníasdóttir. Probably in the pantry, she thought, knowing that old Járnbrá was there sooty-faced in front of the stove in sweltering smoke, muttering and spitting over the pots, rapidly blinking her tiny, spiteful eyes, seeing nothing unusual to stimulate her curiosity because of the smoke in them. She puffed, hissed occasionally as if to ward off something no one else could see.

The child's sobs carried along the corridor into the little room panelled with the wood that had drifted up on the beach the previous year. It was as if she had never seen some of the knots before. It was as if she had never sat there empty-handed looking around her own room. She crossed her hands over the stomach which had never swelled with new life, snuffling, and started picking one nostril with a stubby finger with its small nail. She saw Saemundur afar, working in the meadow. She knew Jón was watching over Sólveig in the spare room; unable to leave it unaccompanied. She felt painfully aware of her tender age.

The child's crying had become intermittent. Perhaps she was more aware of than actually heard its sobbing in the little room. She felt she ought to go and tend to the child. But there was a terror within her which she felt ashamed of. When did anybody talk to that child?

The examination dragged on in the parlour farther along the corridor. Oh, how could she occupy herself? She could not stave off the thought of birth. The child that was sacrificed. Human sacrifice. Perhaps it had been born live. It was too awful a thought to pursue. And yet she could not keep it at bay. The thought gnawed her that they could have adopted the child. Brought it up as their own. But they held back. Why hadn't they found someone to confess to its paternity? Costing him nothing? As if it could not have been arranged at no expense, with some journeyman labourer in the district? And they could even have paid someone to do so. They had been married for a whole year.

She gave a start when the door opened, and her husband appeared, his head bowed, heavy-browed; and tried to see his eyes, but he turned his face aside. She could not make contact with him, the next thing she knew she was sitting facing this impressive judge who had descended from the clouds to upset everything they floated along on from one day to the next. She could see the recorder's hand with its finger so perfectly straight on the shaft of the pen, and a slight hump on the nib where it was inserted into the shaft, and it was like a bird waiting for prey in the air over the inkwell. A raven, she thought. That prankish bird of carrion. That hoarse denizen of hell that feels most at home among the dead. She imagined someone else talking within her in this thought. No, she said to herself while hearing the magistrate read out some preamble to his recorder before beginning to examine her. She imagined a raven moving in on a sheep, over a dead lamb, to peck out its eyes, black as night above a white sheep in the snowland of autumn, not a speck on it. Completely white apart from this black bird, this bird that was said to know that which has yet to come to pass, and boded misfortune.

There was great resonance in the voice which she would have preferred not to have had to listen to.

Have you been aware of unseemly displays of affection between the two here accused?

She heard herself whisper yes, cleared her throat and said yes in what she felt was rather too loud a voice for this little room. Too loud for herself, although she was answering a booming voice. But that voice was from a completely different place and did not belong in this room. She lived here and was not accustomed to raising her voice. It was the blockage in her throat that caused it.

She hastened to add: I have only once, she said; seen them lying in bed together. She was surprised at hearing herself talk so much. And he, Saemundur, he was wearing his shirt. Although they were both in the same bed and . . .

Her face grew hot, she was short of breath and said 'and' three times.

Has the present witness not heard her housefolk mention that they have been aware of anything in their opinion particularly criminal in the behaviour of the brother and sister?

Not that I remember.

Nothing in particular?

Well, perhaps slightly now I come to think of it. Yes, it was er Kristín er and her husband Vigfús who both work on the farm here. They were saying some time, I can't remember when, she said . . .

Would the witness please speak up.

Well, they were saying they had noticed that the brother and sister slept together.

And is that all?

Well, once I asked our shepherdess Marsibal from Beyla whether she thought or might think Sólveig was pregnant. I think it was after people started saying that Sólveig was not fat any more.

Yes, and what did the shepherdess say?

Well, she said it was such a long time since she had seen her that even though there might be some grounds for this talk of her being pregnant she was quite incapable of seeing any sign from her figure, and hadn't been able to see it before anyway.

Well well. Is that all there was to it?

Well, the shepherdess was saying something about a strange look on her face.

But what about the present witness, didn't she see anything?

The vicar's wife's answer was inaudible, so the magistrate raised his voice: Not a single thing?

Maybe. Yes, a little sort of abnormal swelling quite a while ago.

And did it grow, or what?

Yes, it sort of did.

Did the present witness feel it suggested that the woman might be pregnant?

Yes, she whispered.

And did the present witness see the swelling suddenly go down? Well? Or what? Well?

Yes, sort of.

And can the present witness recall with somewhat greater precision the course of these events?

Pardon?

Can the present witness state in more detail what happened? Whether she was ill, or confined to bed for an unusually long period, perhaps unfit for work, something like that.

I don't know.

You don't know? What?

Well, she was ill for part of the day, a couple of hours. Around that time. When she seemed to change.

Was the present witness aware of the accused Sólveig spending an abnormally long time outside in the evening around that time?

Not that I noticed or can remember, she said, adding in a hurried voice; with the sort of work she was doing it was not unusual for her to come in for bed later than other people on the farm, yes, and then she often stayed in the forequarters by herself. That was quite normal.

And in other respects nothing in particular that the present witness would like to state?

No.

She was relieved when the judge adjourned the hearing. She hurried out, flushed and sweating, absolutely avoiding looking at the judge and the court officials, and the dog was waiting for her in the corridor when she opened the door, its tail curled, and looked at her in expectation. She did not know where her husband might be, and anyway she needed to be alone to try to make contact with herself.

The Prisoner

She had never seen such a man before, this young woman who had hardly left the parish where she was born. What did she know about what lies beyond the mountains? First there were ever rising hills, one after the other, beginning with a long, gradual slope. Rose, until they became a mountain ridge, a plateau. She had never been in that direction. And the land that began on the other side of the mountain ended at the Arctic Ocean itself.

The ocean of ice, no land beyond that ocean, apart from a single island. Just an ocean that flowed into the sky itself.

She had never ascended those slopes. She had travelled through the countryside with all the mountains beyond her. And then this man arrived like an emissary of the Almighty, to judge her. Over the mountains, if not down from the heavens. He came from other countries where there were cities. Where did he come from? She had scarcely given a thought to the existence of these cities, and had never even been into the local town.

Such a man she had never seen. Except perhaps the King on the vicar's photograph in the parlour. Yes, perhaps the picture of Jón Sigurdsson too. But he was quite different. So sunny and pure.

Yet he reminded her even more of the man on the wall beside the vicar's writing table with his mouth buried in his beard, and the eyes that burned day and night in the vicar's little study. Those eyes that burned, eroding as if the fire were consuming itself, yet as if they could see far beyond the farmhouse, across the meadow and past the river, perhaps over the mountains and the moors. He was much more akin to that one. The King did not burn.

Sometimes when she was dusting the photograph of the King she had been surprised that the King himself did not have better eyes. But was still a King. He was terribly dull-looking, as if he were just like other men; except that he had plenty to eat. Like the merchant. Didn't he ever dream? Perhaps he had spent too long waking over his subjects, and was growing bored; since there were so many people between him and them, and all sorts of complaints and bother.

She had seen that fearful man come riding in at dusk. Yet she felt there was some glow about him when she thought of him now, like the flicker of will-o'-the-wisp.

Disdainfully she contemplated the guard who had been assigned to her. The poor thing, really she pitied him in her contempt. They would not break her. No one would break her. When she thought of the interrogation ahead, all fear seemed to vanish from her; she grew cold. They would not break her. First when she thought about that man, how different he was from all other men, she felt her pulse racing; but the threat aroused her pride and scorn.

She felt herself seem to grow at the thought of duelling with this emissary of the gods. And to put to the test which side God was on in that struggle. And if He was on the side of the powerful, she would fight on regardless. She felt no fear any more. It seemed to be behind her. She felt the guard avoiding looking straight at her; he wanted to say something to her. They remained silent. She sat on the edge of the bed in this little room where she was kept, rigid, and stared in front of her, her cold hands in her lap, slightly pigeon-toed in her ragged clothes. She thought of her daughter, whom she had undoubtedly neglected; she was not particularly fond of her, and perhaps had never been. At that moment she remembered how unimpressed she had been when the newborn baby was laid in her arms. It was as if she had nothing particular to do with that child. It had been forced into her body, and could not be retracted. She had tried to make herself love that child later, but seldom felt any relation to it. Now the child had followed her for four years. It was at this moment that she missed it. Perhaps it was more self-accusation than a sense of loss.

The child had never been close to her. It followed her like a second shadow. Which disappeared in certain types of light, revived and turned around her, obliged to do so, without being close to her. Yet she had borne it in torment, screaming and thrashing about like an entrapped animal, like a fox unable to escape. Unable to gnaw through the limb that was caught in the snare.

Try as she might, she could no longer remember the feeling of it growing within her, and could not remember whether it was her anguish or her emptiness which was greater when she discovered she was pregnant by the man who had taken her, impervious to her inclination or desire. Perhaps most of all ignorance, helplessness, destitution. Not regarding herself as her own property. Repressing her feelings, not knowing her inclinations until too late, even less how to apply them. That came later. Being aware of her body, filling with the pride born of obstinacy, nourishing herself by challenging everyone and everything, and demanding her rights. And perceiving the power her nature possessed.

And a second time she had felt a living being stir within her, and grow. But that life must never be born. It had been judged. It was the great human sacrifice. Her position was more difficult than Abraham's when God himself demanded that he sacrifice his son Isaac. Which everyone learns without comment or explanation. Supposed to understand and accept. And God spake to Abraham and demanded of his servant. That he proved his loyalty. Take now thy son, thine only son Isaac, whom thou lovest, and get thee into the land of Moriah; and offer him there for a burnt offering upon one of the mountains which I will tell thee of. And Abraham bound Isaac his son, and laid him on the altar upon the wood. And Abraham stretched forth his hand, and took the knife to slay his son. And the angel of the Lord called unto him out of heaven, and said, Abraham, Abraham: and he said, Here am I. And he said, Lay not thine hand upon the lad, neither do thou any thing unto him: for now I know that thou fearest God, seeing thou hast not withheld thy son, thine only son from me. And the Lord sent Abraham a ram caught in a thicket by his horns, for a burnt offering in the stead of his son.

What had the Lord offered her but the most painful of courses? To conceal her birth. The concord of their love stated that the fruit was poisonous to them and itself. It carried death. She had borne in her womb the angel of death. They both knew that heavy as the punishment would be if the deed came to light, the burden would be even heavier upon the one who bore no responsibility itself. Their child would be branded by what is called a crime. By what others saw as the most deadly of sins, their love. It had always been clear to them that this sacrifice could never be fled. It was a wretched enough life to be housed in the power of strangers, without bearing a cardinal sin on a child's shoulders.

Its life would be hell. Our life has been bad enough, and its life would be so much the worse. For its own sake, it had to be exposed at birth. They would bring the law to bear upon us if it lived, they could prove it as they pleased, and make our guilt devolve upon it.

She was aware of someone else in the byre. She heard another sound mingling with the squirting from the cows' udders into the pail. There was something in the darkness, beyond the confined light from the lamp hanging on the rafter. A chill ran through her when she thought of ghosts and poltergeists. The cow was uneasy, aware of something impure. It had been milked almost dry. Then a hand grabbed her shoulder, and a hoarse voice said: What do you say, my little girl; you're growing up now. You're quite big enough to be kind to a poor old man like me.

She spun round on the milking stool without dislodging the hand from her shoulder, and a lock of hair fell over her eye, and she narrowed her eyes at her master who was standing up close to her with one hand on his crotch as if fondling himself.

She was rigid with fear, although it was not a ghost.

She was ice cold, paralysed.

Hee, hee, said the farmer, using the hand from his crotch to block a brown drip from his nostril. Ho ho, he said; ho ho, wheezing with short breaths.

He snatched her up from the stool and placed both hands on her newly sprouted breasts, which she had been examining at night when no one could see her. She had no one to ask.

147

He held her breasts, which vanished in his huge paws. Although not a large and gangling man, he had big feet and hands, but short arms and legs, and was skinny. He had a bushy moustache, and the stubble of his beard reached up to his eyes. One was half closed, its light-brown pupil scarcely visible, but the other seemed to be trying to look over whoever he was talking to, as if he expected a bird to come and peck out the eyes of that person, or of a lamb behind him.

What did he want of her?

Listen, my little pretty, he said, as if talking to someone else. He was not in the habit of addressing her. She had sometimes been aware of him following her with one eye when she entered the sitting room. But she was not sure. She had never seen him looking at her. Nobody spoke very much on that farm. And he pulled her towards him, pressing her chin against his shoulder, where his jumper was unbuttoned.

She was so afraid that the next thing she knew she was lying on the straw, and him on top of her. Had she done something wrong? For what was he punishing her?

And the next thing she knew, his fumbling hands were touching her bare flesh. And he was struggling to undo her underclothes. He had pulled up her skirt, as if intending to pull it over her head and kill her.

He tore down her garterbelt and her woollen stockings fell loose around her legs, and he thrust her legs apart with his knees and ripped down her woollen knickers, and had one hand between her legs and the other fumbling to unbutton his flies. And when they opened she saw his lanky member straightening up; had never seen a male member before, and scarcely knew the difference between male and female genitals. She was shaking and trembling and heard the man muttering, all right, all right, my little pretty. My little pretty, my little pretty. Easy does it. Easy does it. It's all right. That's right, that's right. And she snuffled and whimpered from fear from terror in trembling and the man spread her wide and grasped his barely erect member, and thrust it with a wheeze inside her and she hardly felt it until afterwards; except she felt it suddenly stiffen within her and thrash about for a while, and she felt a piercing pain within her like something bursting or ripping, as if she were rent asunder, burst into shreds and knew nothing until she came to her senses lying alone there in the byre, and the cow as close as it could come to surprise, looking towards her, chewing with dry, withered hay hanging out of the sides of its mouth, without lowing, and the sheep hunched together in their pen, unaccustomed to events of that sort. She was naked from her stomach to her knees, and bloody and alone; and her weeping magnified the animals' tension as they pressed towards the far end of the building. And the wind blew in heavy gusts outside; there was no movement to be heard from overhead, from the sitting room above her.

The horse looked at her sadly from its stall, and did not reach for the hay from its manger.

Gradually she became accustomed to the man visiting her on such an errand. He was generally quick to conclude it. Yet she could never grow accustomed to it. She tried to overcome her repulsion. Vacate herself while it swept over her. Her master swept over her. She had no idea that she owned herself.

As the winter passed by she began feeling peculiar, continuously nauseous and as if she were ill. But far from wasting away. She was growing fatter, and she sported a stomach quite unexampled during the lean years up to then.

Then she grew aware of whisperings among the gloomy people on the farm, and the farmhand continually smirking when he met her. Nobody said anything to her.

One day the old dean arrived and was sitting talking to her master in the sitting room. The other people had been sent to work elsewhere.

As he was taking his leave, the dean said: Well, well, poor thing.

He stroked her cheek, so gently she could hardly feel it, with his soft fingers worn thin by age.

Then she was sent to stay on another farm, where her child was born.

It was never close to her. That child, she did not feel it was hers. That she had borne it with sweat and tears, thrashing about as if something was being torn from inside her, that hung on a cord tied to her, foaming out of her bowels in the midwife's hands; the midwife had been ferried over two wide rivers.

And then the midwife cut the umbilical cord and tied it in a knot, without leaving her free from that shadow of hers.

Aren't I allowed to have some water to drink, she said, standing up huffily and sweeping past the guard, who jumped from his seat, and followed her like a faithful dog.

Confession to a Crime

How old is the accused?

Now he was no longer named Saemundur Fridgeir. Now he was called the accused; and nothing else, after his right name had been duly recorded, for the first time in his own presence. He stood before the man of authority. He was twenty-four years old. But just who was he as he stood there under his inhuman burden? Just like any other lad.

He avoided looking at the judge's terrible expression, but found the sharp eyes beneath that frowning brow piercing him. He was immediately afraid of not being able to conceal anything from those cold eyes; he felt them ripping away his defences, his armour, burning all over with the infernal glow of eyes that were scarcely human, he thought. He had never stood in such a frost as at this moment, burning all over, fearful that he would begin trembling. He's only a man, he thought, trying to repeat her words; remember, he's only a man. Be strong in the divine name of our love. Who can assail us then? You should just quibble and wrangle. Don't let yourself be led along. Think of our love and shout within yourself yes and with the yes of our love resounding through you, close yourself around our love. Hunch yourself up and imagine you have escaped into a shell where you can survive, and do not let yourself be tempted out, for then it is all over. And say nothing, and if you do say something, then say only no. Try to lie mainly by silence, and with sparing words if they cannot be avoided. Just keep yourself to what we have talked about so often. Nothing happened. Nothing.

He had rehearsed this time and again with her, by himself out on the heath, with his dog down by the river, up on the mountain with the sheep, or a stone on the edge of the gully, standing on the brink above the precipice where the river beat its way through the rock, wound its way foaming and spraying and spitting on to the sides, having nothing but rocks to answer its shouts and pounding with echoes alone. And poised between life and death, balancing, he had also rehearsed the last time how to face human power, and fight for what was most painful to them, and everything.

But it was a different matter when it had reached the point of standing in front of the bailiff of the Almighty, who was documented as such, and be spoken to in the formal plural like a vicar, addressed as the accused. It left him so confounded that he found no way to make the thought of love strengthen him, instead the word used here was crime, and how on earth could he begin to deny the threatening power with which this word filled the room, and its orthodoxy, and its superior force sanctioned by law, and replace it with another, however true that had seemed at certain times, if only as something to hold on to, even a straw to clutch at in this game in this terrible room, which excluded all other worlds, forbade all other life than that justified here. In the action taking place here.

It was as if the room had become a building apart, with everything around it destroyed, all vegetation, and no matter how he thought he could no longer make contact with anything beyond this cell of judgment and torture.

He was standing, stooped, flushed and sweating. The people he knew, they seemed to be other people and he did not know them. He knew of them, but did not know them any more. A single will reigned here, and his life depended upon staying firm and resisting.

From a vast distance he heard those awful probing dangerous questions, and knew that he had to give his all to avoid the pitfalls, to see where the trap was stretched wide to catch him.

Gradually he began to realize that he was being asked questions he had to react to in what would look a natural way. And then he heard the question: Have you ever by yourself or in the sight of others done anything with your sister that could be considered scandalous?

Not at all. What could that be?

Are you sure?

I don't know what that could be.

Scandalous in your eyes.

Definitely not.

Or likely to be scandalous to others?

Out of the question.

Nothing in the slightest?

I don't understand.

You don't understand what?

What I am being asked.

Does the accused not understand anything that is said to him?

I thought I did. Generally speaking, he said, and felt himself growing brazen in his obstinacy at last.

This is no place for obstructiveness, said the judge, tapping the end of the bent index finger of his left hand with the flat of the other.

The accused made no reply, awaited the next sally, and suddenly felt that he would be able to establish a grip and pull himself up from the brink and ward off the attacks in this encounter, where he felt his position was so precarious that there was everything to win. He heard the irritation in the man of authority's voice, and grew stronger. So he is just a man.

Has the accused never heard anyone mention that . . .

What? he brashly interrupted his opponent's impatient words, and he felt glee at his impertinence and was about to say: Like what then, but held his horses.

Wait for the question, will you.

He stared in front of him at the magistrate's hands, which were clenched on the table now, and saw the recorder lift the pen with his straight finger resting on the shaft and lower the nib slowly into the inkwell, as if his fingers were stiff with cold.

Have you never heard anyone that you have spoken to mention feeling anything scandalous in the behaviour of you and your sister towards each other?

He remained silent, saw the pen emerge and scratch the question into the book while the magistrate waited for him to finish, cocking his head as if to point with his nose the course that the pen was to flow across the paper, and the magistrate's well-trimmed moustache hid his upper lip like a hairy step placed on the lower one, and his chin long and fine although steadfast, and his expression sharp over his long face, with his curved eyebrows, his nose straight but not high, his high forehead, his hair short and thick, and his ears rather small, the lobes rigid rather than loose. Although he had never before seen such a fine figure of a man, he felt no fear.

I don't know who could have felt that.

Nobody raised the subject?

Not that I remember.

No one?

No.

Really. No one at all?

Well . . .

Well what?

Not anyone I have talked to.

So perhaps somebody that you have not talked to?

Well, I . . .

Perhaps you know more about the thoughts of people who never say what they are thinking?

I mean . . .

Yes, would the accused please say what he means.

Yes, it could . . .

Could what? Could it possibly be that someone mentioned the matter to you?

No. No, not really.

Then unreally perhaps.

No, not sort of like that . . .

Well, how about showing what ought to be seen? Perhaps the truth might be seen then. If it is not too much to ask.

Well, it could be that someone said something.

Yes, I wonder if it couldn't. And said what then? What I was asking about?

What? said the accused, trying to gain his foothold again.

Have you perhaps forgotten the subject under discussion? Do you perhaps not have the faintest idea about anything? You are present in court. And we would like the truth with no digressions.

Yes, but I . . .

Yes, it is unnecessary to delay the course of justice with digressions. But I shall repeat the question. Has the accused never heard anyone mention feeling anything scandalous in the behav–

No one that I have spoken to . . .

Really?

No. I mean, well, perhaps some people have said they have heard about other people feeling it was scandalous for . . .

Oh yes. Indeed. More than one perhaps?

Yes. Several.

Who, how many?

I don't really remember.

Some of them you do.

Well, I only really remember the master of the house.

Indeed.

Yes, he mentioned something of that sort once but I don't really remember anything about it.

Will you try to remember something substantial? What did the vicar say? Don't you even remember what the master of the house himself said? Are you a complete idiot?

Yes, I mean no. He said that I showed too much affection towards my sister.

And was shocked by it?

Yes, he said he thought it was shocking.

Let it be recorded that the vicar said he was shocked by the affection you showed for your own sister.

The accused could hardly be heard as he said: Yes. And repeated in an even lower voice: Yes.

Did the accused mention to his sister Sólveig that their behaviour towards each other was considered shocking?

No.

Never that it was considered shocking.

No, he said, no, never. In a low voice.

155

Then I shall ask formally and remind the accused of perjury and warn him and point out to him to take notice of where he is and who is above us all and sees all, has he been to bed with his sister?

Silence.

Well?

No. No. No.

I shall ask again . . .

No.

Neither by day nor night? Now I urge the accused to take notice of what he is saying.

I would never think of going to bed with Sólveig with the idea of caressing her. No. Only in a way that would not seem unnatural for a brother and a sister, sort of.

Now I should like to point out to the accused that they have been seen in bed together. Testimonies have been recorded in this register which prove that.

Prove? Prove what? said the accused in a low voice, trying to regain his obstinacy, and steel himself: Who says what? You can always bank on gossip. Who . . .

There is documented testimony here that . . .

Well, there could have been once, yes. I remember one time if that makes any difference, if the idea is to record everything that doesn't matter anyway and isn't anything in the slightest. There could have been one time late at night when I lay down beside my sister in her bed, and I was in fact fully dressed then, and as far as I knew everyone in the sitting room was asleep, and . . .

Did you take lengthy advantage of that warmth?

Er, warmth. I wasn't cold. After all, I was fully dressed. How was I supposed to have been cold then?

I am asking whether you stayed there for long in a place which was not natural for you to be, under these circumstances . . .

Natural? What's more natural than lying down beside the people you feel closest to, there's nothing unnatural about that. My own sister. I can't understand how that can be made to look suspicious. Is there anything unnatural about that? My sister? Fully dressed as well.

And in fact I had no reason to mention this if it was not innocent. As far as I knew everybody was asleep.

Will you answer the question instead of trying to lead us off the track, enjoyable as it might be to roam around with you in sheer digression and evasiveness. Just answer. Straight out. Did you lie there for long in that bed?

No. Oh no. I don't think you could call it that. And who is supposed to have known? At least I left by the time people usually wake up.

Aha. Indeed. So you are claiming that it was all in innocence. But still you go creeping into her bed when you think everybody is asleep. And crawl back out with your tail between your legs before the others are supposed to wake. Why such furtiveness if everything is supposed to be as pure and white as you pretend, my lad? That's the main thing. But there's something in the records. They weren't all asleep. It's written here, clear as day. And much more besides. And the only course for you is to admit to your crime immediately. And now you will tell me whether you didn't get into her bed a good few times and not that well dressed either according to what other people have testified and corroborated thoroughly, my good man. Didn't you get into her bed more often?

Well, if I think hard I do remember getting into her bed once a long time before. Sometime in the spring. Just for a rest. A quick rest. When I was watching the sheep. I don't know what could have been more innocent . . .

And dressed in your Sunday best, of course . . .

Admittedly not. In fact I expect the magistrate knows that people like us don't own Sunday best.

All right, were you wearing all your togs? Fully dressed? And maybe with your cap pulled down over your eyes and ears as well? And why not over your nose too to keep out the stench of you and your sister, the stink of kith and kin together in their pit of filth, eh? The smell of the blood you share? Why don't you answer? You haven't got your cap over your mouth now. Or have the accused's lips perhaps frozen over in the midsummer drizzle? So, perhaps you were fully dressed. That's not what the witnesses say who saw you and heard you creeping around for the delight of the devil and the despair of the Lord God Almighty.

No, perhaps not.

So, how were you then? Running around stark naked?

No, I think I might have been wearing my underpants.

Well, well, now we are getting somewhere. Did you maybe always take to your feet the moment you thought everybody was asleep? Rushing back and forth the whole night long?

No. Definitely not. No no.

What else?

Nothing else. There was no more. Than that. Just those two times.

All right, let that suffice for now. Though I feel you should confess more quickly. I fail to see the point of delaying the case. That is a great deception, a miscalculation. But on those two occasions you had carnal relations with your half-sister?

No. No. Nooo, he exhaled. No. No. No.

Perhaps we should turn to another matter then. Perhaps it is expecting too much of your senses for you to have noticed the fact that your sister grew fatter.

No, I saw that she was getting fatter in the spring.

And did you think that was quite normal?

No, I didn't think it was quite normal.

And did you see it continuing afterwards?

No, I didn't. But I did notice that it suddenly disappeared in the summer.

You have perhaps heard other men mentioned as involved with your half-sister, or what?

Yes, I have. I have heard other men mentioned. Yes, yes, I have.

Oh yes. Example?

Yes the, er, farmer in Beyla told me about a local man here, that people were talking about him and Sólveig together. Yes, and the wife of the farmer at Múlaberg, she had heard about someone else.

We are not prepared to chase around after those two names any more than after any other fabrication. To what do you attribute the aforementioned fatness which you state that even you of all persons had noticed?

Well, she told me it was from illness. She said she had been to our doctor who is sitting here and can confirm that, and also that I fetched some medicine from him. That was in the late summer.

All right. Now it's about time to start telling the truth. You've spent enough time rambling on and delaying the proceedings. That is enough. Can't you see how inconsistent you are? And contradicting yourself, if only because you denied earlier that you had ever been to bed with her, and why should you have denied that when it was all so innocent, and now you are prepared to admit that you got into bed with her over and over again.

No, I . . .

Be quiet. Now you are only going to speak to tell the truth. When did you first lie with your sister?

The lad started to weep. He wept silently, and tried to hide the fact and covered his eyes with one hand, holding on to his jumper with the other, with white knuckles, and shook.

And are you going to cry now in your brazenness, the magistrate said impatiently; when did you first have intercourse with your sister?

The lad wept.

Well, we shall go about this gently if you conceal nothing, said the magistrate; when did you first live at the same home?

It was just under two years ago, said the lad.

A little louder. You can't be heard.

A little less than two years ago. When she came here to work.

And when did lustful thoughts begin to awaken?

Shortly after she arrived I began to feel my feelings towards her were different from what is maybe completely natural between brother and sister.

And whose initiative was it? Or how did it begin?

Oh, the lad sighed; really it was her who began to show me greater fondness than I would say seemed quite proper to me. And gradually the feeling began to stir within me, I can't really phrase it like the magistrate, but it might be what you called lustful thoughts. But I was horrified. I was horrified that it was happening to me. And then it was about a year ago, he braced himself, then continued; well, about a year ago it happened between us, first, and then afterwards more often and over and again, right up until when my sister told me in the summer that she was pregnant by me. And then we were together much more often, much more often. Until she suddenly told me she had had the baby. She said it happened in the byre here on the farm in the middle of the day, and she said she had put it in her chest in the room, in the little room, under the porch, will you bury it, bury it. You've got to bury it. I promised to do so. I promised straight away.

Alive? Did she say whether it had been a live birth, the magistrate interjected into the snivelling, sobbing man's frenzied speech; say whether the child was a live birth, he said slowly and surprisingly gently, if his companion and court official Thórdur was not mistaken.

There was silence in the little room. But for the pen scratching the paper. And the lad snivelling while his weeping died down, and ended in a sob; finally like a hiccup.

Now the magistrate took his time. He had caught his prey. What remained was to dress the catch. He had not even tried to prompt an answer to the last question.

One of the court officials took a pinch of snuff from his box. Without offering the other. It was as if he shied away from drawing attention to himself at this sad moment. Although he seemed to be wondering whether to hand the box to him, perhaps even to the man who was confessing to his crime. But he put the box in his pocket. It was the doctor. Here he was merely a witness to tragic events. Had no other role to perform. He blew his nose on the corner of his red handkerchief, inconspicuously. He had finished recording what had been said, ending with the words 'live birth'.

Well, said the magistrate then, slowly and unaggressively, as if there was time enough, everything had slowed down; did the woman mention whether the child had been a live birth?

I think so, probably.

Did she say that?

I think so because I saw its head was bruised.

When did you see that?

Sólveig went down to the room with me. Where the chest was. Showed me where the child was.

And . . .

I took the child and carried it out in my coat to the edge of the sea.

Alone?

Yes, alone.

And then . . .

And buried it near the sheep pen.

How was it covered up? Was it covered up?

There was a shawl around it.

A shawl? said the magistrate slowly, pensively, a sound carried in from outside and merged with the word in his expression; he listened for something else as the word was being spoken; a shawl, he repeated, almost crooning.

Yes, from woven cloth, said the lad; that my sister had.

Are you quite aware of and able to recognize the place where you buried the child?

Yes. I'm sure I would recognize it. Quite sure I would recognize it.

Everything was calm now. The record was made without haste. The questions became sparser.

Of course, I must ask whether you have continued to go to bed with your sister, said the judge without glaring at his victim, now he had started to scrutinize him when he looked at him, and no longer applied his grand manner.

Yes, but only three times. But at long intervals; but we didn't do anything like that.

Does the accused mean that he did not commit carnal relations with . . .

No, nothing like that happened. Well, I mean, sort of.

Nothing?

Nothing.

All right. I think we should stop here for the day, said the judge; that will suffice. An unequivocal confession that you have committed incest with your half-sister, and abetted in disposing of the child to which she secretly gave birth, I shall record that. Do you have any comment to make upon that? Then it shall be written down. It will not be retracted. And we adjourn the rest of the hearing until tomorrow.

When the judge had read out the records and been through them twice he asked the accused to confirm that all he had confessed was correctly recorded.

Then the judge made arrangements for the detention of the guilty parties who were initially put into custody at their home and the master of the house, the vicar, was assigned in consultation with the judge to ensure that it would be as convenient as the arrangement of the house would permit, until another place of custody could be found for them, either separately or together. The pronouncement was read to the accused, and the accused female ordered to appear before the court for the first time to hear the pronouncement before her trial began.

The Pronouncement Is Made

She said nothing.

She stood there sharp and proud, challenging those who might govern either heaven or on earth.

She appeared so fragile, yet would not be broken; strong. No one can manage her any more. Who could manage her any more?

There was no mistaking the fact. From the moment she had entered the room and stepped boldly over the threshold. Then she had wiped away the withered hand of the old woman who followed her in, and reached out towards her; she brushed her away with a swift movement of her hand, as if a mouse had darted out from a half-open drawer and settled on her shoulder in its confusion.

She rushed in through the low doorway with a whisking sound, and stood with her head held high before the court. Silent.

When she looked towards the young man, he was stooping, staring at his toes as if expecting the mouse to run past. If she was startled, she concealed the fact, cocked her head to one side, tossed back her black locks. And her eyes were dark and hard in their blackness when she stepped out boldly before her judge, and his assistants. Who until now had been ordinary men like those found in rural parts, and perhaps still were though they had been led into this role in the service of justice.

The magistrate read out to her the formal pronouncement, which referred to the cause in the unequivocal confession by the accused. The details of the confession were not stated, only the direction in which it pointed.

The magistrate held the court register in both hands and grasped his fingers tightly upon the cover as he read, and darted his eyes up towards the woman, whom he had never seen before.

The woman stared straight ahead, as if standing in a huge, wide timber hall, and the echoes from other halls could be heard. Unless it was the hall of a cliff, with the language of dwarfs from gullies and holes between rocks, and time completely altered from what it had been. Centuries converged, snatches of language from past ages resounded again, and moved into new tales, or material for new tales if there were time, if something lay ahead.

The magistrate strove to constrain himself in the mantle of his office. He had never seen this woman. Yet it was as if he had seen her at some time, somewhere. Where? Probably nowhere. Yet there was something he recognized in her deathly pale dignity. Which he recognized, knew, felt he understood in some manner; had never seen before.

Was it from a dream, was it from a poem? Was it something he had tried to compose and perhaps never managed, not until he saw her standing before him, and knew that his power could no longer extend to her?

Jason, he thought; Medea standing before Jason, wreaking vengeance. Dealing him the blow. Vengeance which is never absolved and has killed their children. Why was he thinking of Medea in the flash when their eyes met, and perceived that his power would never extend to this woman?

Medea, the princess seized from her paternal home, and forced to roam fatherless through the world with her lover, who failed her when put to the test, betrayed her, betrayed their love, and chose another woman and another kingdom. And baited the animal that dwelt within the depths of his lover, the wild beast that eats its offspring, when there is no escape.

Why did this cross his mind? When his eyes sank into the dark depths which dwelt within those facing him, and all else on this stage vanished.

Everything, the little room, the chairs, the table, the ink and pen, these manual labourers who rocked in their seats and hesitated to cough or blow their noses, the young vicar in his embarrassment and hesitancy, the lad somewhat younger who had confessed to a crime and condemned them both, alone, hunched up and outcast; the shadows outside rippling over the meadow, and the clouds scudding across the sky; the sunshine on the green grass, glittering on the brook which fed the river; the two dogs fighting outside, everything but this woman standing in the omnipotence of her fate; a vision opened up for him into what he had never seen in another person, never suspected except within himself when he stood face to face with death, once, a long time before. It was perhaps not such a very long time ago.

Those eyes were not black. Perhaps they were brown, streaky. Perhaps they were green. And stared out of the vast distance of a dark forest; encountered him inescapably. First he was sucked into the whirlpool, swept deeper inside, into her, or himself. Both, he thought later, as if they had become one at that moment in the unspeakable wealth of destitution, at the end of the corridor of despair, of anguish, where nothing remains but the human being itself in the highest light of its misery, the core of dropped masks; the guise dashed away.

He knew of nothing else, only this woman, and was shaken by the thought that he desired her, then tried to break free; but her eyes transfixed him, ensnared him.

It was she who had won, the one who had lost everything.

She was free, nothing could restrain her. No prison could contain her. The magistrate shook himself free of this grip, out of this piercing embrace; he started away, tried to reach land on the bank behind him; snatched the shaft of the pen as if intending to write something. The moment had passed.

He declared the court in session.

He stayed behind on his own when the others had left. He sat down by the window and looked out, and tried to reawaken the land to receive yet another outlaw, from the desert.

The dogs had stopped fighting, lay crouched on their paws in the sun, while a warm breeze wafted the aroma of grass somewhere. And the cloud had cleared, leaving only strands behind; which dissolved.

165

After the Confession

It rushed forward. The horse galloped and galloped. Its head bathed in the glow of fire; but its body struck by the blue waves of light that flooded over the earth, and dashed against the wall of cliff, and were reflected back.

The image of the galloping horse followed him perpetually, startled by his hypersensitivity, driven away by the rushing that coursed through his veins, whether his eyes were open or closed.

In the steel-blue at the top of the mountains the reddish sunset was reflected; blue shadows snuggled up below to a naked stone, and opened it and rendered caresses soft and warm and easy to visualize, managed to stop; linger.

And the grey moss waited, dry, thirsting for dew in the promise of the night which waited and was awaited.

The horse rushed into the shrubland, stroked by leafy branches, birch, rushed on, bathed in sap which merged with its sweat, and its trail curved through low brushwood from which an occasional tree protruded, with occasional branches suddenly descending to return it or stop it. But it was accompanied by a glow or ray of light which no longer searched for its head as it once had, bounced in time with it as it darted onwards.

Until it halted in its tracks.

And stood completely still, and dusk had fallen, but it was bright enough to see the trail across the plains; the black mountain ridges, chasms like gaping mouths with water sporting deceptive smiles, offering silver in their depths if the moon soon appeared; silver from the depths, silver into the depths.

And the moon was invited. Offered. Waited.

And the moon sported a dark cloud whose edges glowed.

While the horse stood completely still.

Why was it standing like that? Had it been listening for whispering voices beyond the mountains?

The whispering reached the man. Those enchanting voices, extending so far in time. And stretching far over the land.

From where?

Sedentary in the flowing water. Those voices. Did he need the water to flow to perceive that babbling, hear speech again?

Again?

He lay on his back in the moss, so soft; which invited him to rest there with open eyes, and see the moon appear, the odd clouds whisked away lined with silver, as if they were breathed through the air, before his sight; and when he closed his eyes it grew bright, and became broad daylight.

And in this flowing glow the coruscant obverses of clouds were swept along and past; so he tried to press his eyes shut and make it dark. Then sea-blue specks fell spitting and exploding, becoming a purple comet (as if the moon were consumed by poisoned fire that would never be extinguished again), and this erupting body blazed (with the vague hint of its provenance unforgotten); until it transformed into a charred sienna and mud-yellow orb, rent and rocked, enclosed by purple fire; and sea-blue flashes in the dim starry depths.

Then relaxed again, and the flood of light was ochre with rare blue-grey dark spots, and a blue-black net, as if sketched over with pencil.

He opened his eyes suddenly; and everything was new in the world.

He looked at the sky which had come into being at that instant; no whispering voices any more, since before.

No point of reference. How could he comprehend those voices from the waterfall, no, from the river, from countless streams, from a single stream, while the waterfall knocked heavily on to the rock?

How could he comprehend what was being said to him?

Those voices: what message did they proffer him?

The moon lit everything. Where do you want to go? Who did you want to be?

He walked down to the river. Descended a low part of the gully which offered a gap to reach the riverbank. Sat down there in the grass, with angelica nearby; watched the eddies around the rocks.

And tossed a buttercup out, watched it spin around, be dashed, until it broke free from the rock, and floated away.

The Scream

Everything was quiet now. Day was drawing to a close. It was still bright into the night. Most of the people in the house got little done. Everybody gradually gathered in the sitting room. The accused was kept there with a man to watch over him. The clergyman and his wife were in their room. The magistrate in the spare room. He did not feel composed enough to deal with the documents he had intended to. He was trying to settle down to Nietzsche.

One day when Zarathustra crossed the large bridge he was surrounded by cripples and beggars, and one of the cripples spake to him thus: Behold Zarathustra! The common people too learn from you and acquire faith in your teachings: but one thing is still lacking before they can believe in you entirely – you still have to convince us cripples! Here before you is a goodly selection and verily an unappreciated opportunity! You can make the blind see and the lame run; and you could in fact lighten a little the burden of those who carry too much on their backs: that I feel would be the right way to have cripples believe in Zarathustra!

He held the book at a distance with his finger between the pages, listening to the quietness after the conflicts. Although he was not relaxed, it was pleasant to rest in silence. About to read Zarathustra's answer, he paused for a moment and listened to nothing, then read on how Zarathustra had answered the man as follows:

If a cripple's hump is removed, his spirit is removed as well – such are the teachings of the common people. And when the blind man has his eyesight restored he sees too many ugly things happening on Earth; and he curses the bestower of sight. And he who makes the lame man run does him great injury: because as soon as he is able to run, his sins lead him astray – such are the teachings of the common people about the handicapped. And why shouldn't Zarathustra be able to learn from the common people, since the common people can learn from Zarathustra?

He got no further with Nietzsche. A scream burst forth, so piercing that he had never heard so much lie behind and be conveyed by a single sound.

What Lies Behind a Single Scream

The magistrate started up from his chair, unable to move from the spot while the scream pierced him, and stood as if impaled by a human-sized needle of ice from head to toe down and deep into the decorative floorboards of the spare room, through them into the foster earth itself. A Hadean spear that pierced him so sharply that it nailed him to the floor, paralysed, and sent coursing through his Lethean veins this scream which pierced him right to his fingertips his toes the roots of his hair so they shot out sparks; is this what it's like to die? asked his sober consciousness in its bondage, rooted to the spot.

And what was it in comparison to feel his pelvis dislocated and the infernal burning of deathly frost in his skin all over his body, and mentally see his pink countenance reflected with eyes stretched wide enough to burst, and the anaemic image of himself?

He had no idea how long the scream lasted, the scream the like of which he had never experienced before. And he hardly had any notion of where he was when the bottomless pit opened before him at that instant.

Was the moment he came to his senses when the book about the *Übermensch* dropped out of his hands, and plunged to earth, and formed a gable by his toes like a sheep-gathering party's abandoned mountain hut, or a sheep-cote after the shepherd has frozen to death in a blizzard and now lies abed on the ice beneath linen of snow?

The next thing he knew he had thrown back the door and the sitting room was there in front of him like a flash before his eyes, everybody half standing up from the beds there or crouching absurdly by their looms, or sitting with stiffly plaited horsehair and loose strands hanging from their hands on to their laps, and even the nodding old woman struck dumb, and the clergyman in the doorway to his room clutching the frame to act as a support for the woman behind him so they wouldn't both fall or be dashed to the ground by the blades of this darting scream which lit up the entire house.

He grasped the woman and heard himself shout: Nobody move! Keep still! Still. Here. I . . .

And then he was down below, with the scream out circling the edges of the cliffs; and into the sitting room a violent, spasmic howling came from the little room under the flooring beneath them all. They had all stayed behind in the sitting room as he had ordered, he who had ruled that she be confined below, the unflinching murderess of her child who had been found guilty of incest with her own brother.

He could scarcely have hesitated in front of the door for long under such extreme circumstances; but vaguely recollected later having thought at the door how relaxed she had been when she retired to the room, how collected, and he recalled feeling that such self-control scarcely boded well, such dauntless calm. And he barely had time to think at all, although he felt afterwards this was why he had not seen reason to have her change her clothes or order a close search of her underclothing, neither as had seemed fit under the circumstances nor in accordance with the custom he knew to pertain in such cases in Iceland, when people are first remanded in custody at farms. And on being put into that special room, moreover, she had asked for the bed to be made, saying she wanted to lie down and rest. This was agreed to by the responsible party, the judge. And so it was done presently, and then she went to bed. Later on he was also to remember resting his hand on the doorknob for what could hardly have been more than an instant, and the thought must have flashed through his mind that it was he himself and no one else who checked the pockets of the accused, and had taken away any objects he thought she could conceivably use to inflict harm upon herself. Nothing had been found on the person of the accused woman apart from a large key which was confiscated. The woman was crying in a frenzy that most resembled an epileptic fit. And her helpless guard was trying to restrain her as she thrashed around on her bed, groping and writhing, trying to stop her injuring herself if she were to bang her head against the bedpost or bruise herself on the side or shoot out on to the dirt floor which had been trodden down into solid flags.

I thought it was the despair she felt, the magistrate later told the clergyman when they were sitting together that evening, the two of them alone; I thought perhaps it was partly from sorrow at having her child taken away.

Do you want your child back? he asked in desperation, beside the writhing, deranged woman.

Do you want to have you child back with you? he said as she thrashed around in unrelenting sobs and spasms.

He had no idea how to react to such madness, such unrestrained misery. He caught himself repeating these words like some charm that healed no one and by no means alleviated his own troubles. No words passed between him and his faithful companion Thórdur who had taken turns with Jón the farm labourer in guarding the woman, and this resourceful traveller had no idea how to react either, to say nothing of dealing with the situation. So the two men stood there over one woman, realizing their inadequacy and the power of despair and sorrow, like the weather when it prevails over the land, and there was nothing to be done but huddle up like a bird on ice-covered ground while the storm rages and does its will.

Gradually, perhaps over a long period, how could you tell, the sounds started to calm down, and the agent of all executive power here finally had the sense to go off and call a doctor. It was as if a sort of slumber came to the woman, perhaps sleep passing over her.

Then the magistrate rushed out in a panic and called out ferociously to fetch a doctor, but not from too far away.

Later he did not know precisely what he had done next, perhaps given orders and taken them back in succession, since bedlam reigned back in the sitting room. He couldn't remember clearly afterwards. But he did remember turning back to the woman in the little room under the flooring.

As far as he could see, Sól– no the accused had expired. Or was in some death-like state.

He rushed out to the doorway and called: Isn't there anyone there?

Then he turned back to the woman and saw no sign of life. Her lips were blue and her face like polished stone, marble. Or perhaps hardened wax. Only the whites of her eyes were visible. No breathing.

He shot back to the doorway and called: Listen! Come here. Someone. And they were crowding at the door where he was fussing around her and the guard had been driven back against the wall, redundant. Nobody knew any method for trying to resuscitate the woman, apart from sprinkling her with water, which the clergyman's wife had fetched in a bowl, and he put some drops on to her forehead and chest, and so did the clergyman's wife. It failed to revive her. Everybody crammed in the doorway vying for a look inside the room; while the magistrate applied the water to the lifeless woman with the assistance of the clergyman's wife, and the clergyman stood dithering near by. One of the crowd was the young man, her lover, her brother, and he made no noise, and his guard went about his duties, clutching the back of his shirt to prevent him fleeing to the mountains or the river or the sea. Or beyond the reach of the law, like Grettir the Strong.

The old woman was nodding like a bird caught in a fox's mouth; and she gave a reed-like whistle; and was muttering something and seemed to be saying that's the way it looks, that's the way it looks, and hissed to herself: He above obeyed the word; fear not the Lord; the scourge was handed out; her punishment was mete. The robber on the cross knew that, the old woman said softly, whether or not anyone else was listening; unless the only one who listened was she who gave no sign of doing so, nor that life was within her.

The congregation stood there, bowed, and crowded at the door on this stage where no one knew what had happened.

And waited for the doctor.

Sitting Together at Night

They sat in silence, these two men, unable to avoid the encroachment of the night so menacingly heavy and dark, and the blackness from its outer space drifted into their consciousness; it swam through their veins, pressed on their hearts. That night. Two men. How could they protect themselves?

The vicar thumbed through the holy book; he looked at the man of authority and saw his deep state of shock; he had no expectation of dignity at hand, no defence in his masks, nor escape in arrogance and pride. They had never been friends, he thought now. But when he arrived at the farm to act as judge here in this little world of ours, with the land and the trolls and the stimulation of his journey, he acted towards me as if something had happened between us that linked us together. From those remote school years, those years at a school a vast distance away, although it was long ago that we were both young. And at school. Classmates, what does that mean? Scarcely an accord for life, scarcely binding by life-long pledges, least of all a blood oath. We never let our blood flow together, never let our company meet. Can I remember us talking together then? He the unanimously elected leader, bestowing in abundance; I a shy boy, a solitary figure living in my aunt's home, where meals were taken in silence and grace was always said. Yet he treats me as though we are friends. And intends me to sit by his side when he judges. Judge not, that ye be not judged. How can I judge those entrusted to my care? My tragedy is not being able to reach the people I am supposed to serve, thought the vicar. Poor, destitute people. Yet this man and I have nothing in common; this man who came over the mountains with his horses and companion, with two horses in train; leading the

175

reins of the devil who sat with a crosier and a sickle, brandishing those weapons over his shoulder invisible to all but perhaps the clairvoyant old woman who has been spitting in all directions for three days on end, cursing and fussing, sooty-faced with puffy red eyelids and bloodshot eyes. Perhaps I have never liked him, admire him as I might. Perhaps. I have never considered it before. Not until now when I feel pain for him, and my aversion has disappeared. Now that his spells are broken, his wand smashed. And he still cannot find the poet within himself, blocked by the judge's terrible deeds. Poetry will be his means to grace when he has walked in the darkness without discovering the glow of a light. Then poetry will light his way. Perhaps. He thought, yes that is true.

Then he began to read as if to himself: from the Book of Job, where Job himself says:

How hast thou helped him that is without power? how savest thou the arm that hath no strength? How hast thou counselled him that hath no wisdom? and how hast thou plentifully declared the thing as it is? To whom hast thou uttered words? and whose spirit came from thee?

He paused for an instant, then quoted Job again:

Dead things are formed!

The vicar paused for a moment again before proceeding, and saw the sad countenance of the magistrate in bowed profile against the window and darkness of the night, his breath disturbing the candlelight. He repeated the words:

Dead things are formed from under the waters, and the inhabitants thereof. Hell is naked before him, and destruction hath no covering. He stretcheth out the north over the empty place, and hangeth the earth upon nothing. He bindeth up the waters in his thick clouds; and the cloud is not rent under them. He holdeth back the face of his throne, and spreadeth his cloud upon it.

At that point the rim of the moon appeared in a tussle of clouds above the mountain, and the murmuring of the river flowed over their silence, no wind. While the moon tried to squeeze its light through the tease of clouds they remained silent, until it waned anew; the vicar began reading again, as if following that struggle:

He hath compassed the waters with bounds, until the day and night come to an end.

He saw the pained expression of the broken man who had plunged from the summit of authority, found no support in his distress, pretended not to see what he saw, now you are in pain. And read out raising his voice from the low pitch of before, as if no longer thinking of those who might be asleep, and read forthrightly:

The pillars of heaven tremble and are astonished at his reproof. He divideth the sea with his power, and by his understanding he smiteth through the proud.

They remained silent, until the judge turned his face to the window, as if staring out to where the moon had disappeared and nothing was to be seen in the blackness.

Read on, he said; read on, he said, placing a finger on the window-pane, idly scratching the glass. And the vicar lowered his voice again: read, and his voice had grown darker, coloured by the night:

By his spirit he hath garnished the heavens; his hand hath formed the crooked serpent. Lo, these are parts of his ways – he paused over the last words, looked up over the book, watched the man probing nothing but the black void of the night, repeated the words: *parts of his ways* – let those words hang suspended in the unbridged air between them. Then he quoted from memory the passage that followed, staring straight at the flame of the candle: *but how little a portion is heard of him? but the thunder of his power* – he took a good pause before completing the quotation: *who can understand?*

Hand me the book please, my friend. He searched for a while, unhurried, paused, moved on. Then he closed his eyes and with them shut began to read from the passage before him in the mighty book.

Remember now thy Creator in the days of thy youth, while the evil days come not – he paused, took a deep breath and held it, with his mouth open while he restrained himself, opened his eyes and read with the book close to his face – *while the evil days come not, nor the years draw nigh, when thou shalt say, I have no pleasure in them* – he rubbed his eyes, pretended to wrinkle his brow and press his forehead where it met his nose, and proceeded – *While the sun, or the light, or the moon, or the stars, be not darkened, nor the clouds return after the rain: In the day when the keepers of the house shall tremble, and the strong men shall bow themselves, and the grinders cease because they are few, and those that look out of the windows be darkened* – he seemed to steel himself, his voice rising in the quiet of the night – *And the doors shall be shut in the streets, when the sound of the grinding is low, and he shall rise up at the voice of the bird* – and then the vicar said, as the magistrate's voice boomed louder: *and all the daughters of musick shall be brought low.*

Then there was silence. What sounds dwell in this night of this land so near to the ocean without end, except in eternal ice?

The magistrate stroked his hair which was too short for him to push over his forehead and stave off this total silence. Yet which was not that; for he heard the vicar's short, irregular breathing, seemingly impatient or an embarrassed hesitation in such irregularity. He could even hear himself breathing. And he even felt he could discern the murmuring of the river, even the fleeing breeze from the sea; or was it just a rush of wind? So low it could scarcely be heard. Perhaps just in his mind, so he resumed reading:

Also when they shall be afraid of that which is high, and fears shall be in the way, and the almond tree shall flourish, and the grasshopper shall be a burden, and desire shall fail – and then he handed the vicar the book which he thought he recognized from long ago, and the man of God took it with both hands as if being handed a child for baptism, watched the open pages sprouting in the lamplight; which blessed his hands too, and flickered across the lower half of his face and his long neck, and moved the shadow of his jaws; but his eyes were in the shadow of their brows, and lay there deep and hidden; and his voice was like a stream after the restrained turbulence which dwelt in the man of authority's repressed tones: *because man goeth to his long home, and the mourners go about the streets: Or ever the silver cord be loosed, or the golden bowl be broken, or the pitcher be broken at the fountain, or the wheel broken at the cistern. Then shall the dust return to the earth as it was: and the spirit shall return unto God who gave it.*

The magistrate could hardly be heard as he muttered what was written in the book in the vicar's hands: *Vanity of vanities, saith the preacher; all is vanity.*

Recorded in the Register

The district doctor appeared before the court and submitted for the record a report concerning the events of the previous day.

Yesterday evening, he said, the farmhand from Kaldbakur had called on him at Sjávarland with a message that the accused Sólveig Súsanna Jónsdóttir had been taken ill and was making noises. The messenger was unable to give any further description but brought a message from the acting chief of police that the doctor come immediately to visit the patient.

He said that he acted immediately after gathering up such medicine as he considered necessary, and arrived at Kaldbakur and entered the room where the accused lay. He said that he concluded from various signs of death which he examined on the spot that she was deceased, from a cause most closely resembling tetanus.

He said he none the less proceeded immediately to make such attempts to revive her as he thought possible, with the help of those present, but in spite of repeated attempts of that kind he was unable to detect any sign of life. He said that, together with the acting chief of police and Thórdur Níelsson who had been watching over the patient, he had searched her room for what could possibly have been applied to cause her death. The search revealed a phial containing traces of white powder inside a small ball of wool beside the bed where the accused had been lying since retiring that evening.

Then he said that on first impressions the powder appeared to him to be strychnine. Particularly with reference to the cramps which appeared to have accompanied her death.

Finally he said he was none the less reluctant to pronounce any final verdict on the matter but reserved judgment until proposed forensic examination of the powder, and the post mortem.

Afterwards, the judge saw reason to add that two men had been appointed to watch over the corpse for the entire night, with strict orders to see whether they did not notice any sign of life, whereupon they were immediately to wake the doctor, who did not leave Kaldbakur that night.

Thereafter the record states that in the morning the acting chief of police had requested the doctor to pronounce whether death had not taken place. After a careful examination he declared that in his opinion she was dead.

The judge had had this recorded in a state of some distress, examining the witness in such a way as to need to repeat the question on occasion. Sometimes the doctor did not hear the judge's question. At other times it seemed unclear to him, or rather more in the nature of a comment, which in his opinion was irrelevant. He was surprised considering the man involved. Yet at the same time he thought it unnecessary to wonder at the magistrate's obvious state of shock. His steadfastness and concentration were gone. Seldom had he seen such a great and sudden change in a man.

The change was all the more striking in that this man was customarily an imposing and dominant figure. Now it was a different man who sat presiding over the court, insecure and hesitant. The doctor noticed sharp spasms, especially at the shoulders which he appeared to be restraining, a twitching of the face, particularly around the mouth, and repeated blinking. Yet it cannot be certain, he thought, that this will be reflected in the record as well, and when it was read out the points of the matter, as far as he could tell, were all dutifully recorded. He was then allowed to leave the court after testifying that the record was correct.

But he tarried at the farm for a while, without realizing why.

Next to appear before the court was the Reverend Stefán Arinbjarnarson, who as the circumstances required submitted a statement for the record that immediately after the pronouncement which had been delivered in the court the previous day he had, in consultation with the judge, arranged custody whereby the accused, Saemundur Fridgeir, would be confined to the sitting room and his half-sister in a room separated by a partition at the northern end of the building; both under the guard of adult males.

The vicar was tired after a night spent awake with the man of authority, who feared being alone. It was not only lack of sleep; he felt drained. While feeling that he would have liked to possess greater power to strengthen the young man in his distress, he also now felt sympathy towards the other who sat, broken, presiding over the court. He also perceived his torment, now that he was facing a human problem and had been dealt a harsh blow. Although it could be called self-inflicted punishment or hubris, it was not for him to find words to describe it. It was for him, if he could, to find words that could heal. Or mollify in some other way the trials of the suffering.

That was his work. Perhaps he had not chosen it from vocation. But by nature he was dutiful. He was sorely pained at not having strength to bestow on the weak. At lacking a message. Perhaps lacking anything to give to others. He was pained at being shy and hesitant, even at such a moment.

When the formalities had been fulfilled, the record read and its correctness testified to and he was allowed to leave the court, he remained sitting still as if wishing to say something.

There was silence in the room.

When the silence had lasted long enough, the vicar felt that the farmers who were present as witnesses were staring at him askance, furtively up from their hairy brows, examining him enquiringly. He did not look back at them in his isolation, and stared at his palms in turn as if perusing his corns.

Finally the magistrate made a move and said: Thank you. The witness may leave the court, he repeated without looking at him, nor the others, and had cleared his throat twice before speaking.

Next before the court was Thórdur Níelsson. In his testimony he stated that he had taken turns with Jón Snaebjarnarson, the farmhand from Kaldbakur, in watching over Sólveig Jónsdóttir, and had not noticed her do anything that could have inflicted harm upon herself.

He said that he noticed she had fallen into a slumber after she stopped making a noise. It seemed to resemble a faint. His testimony stated that the judge had entered the room at that moment to watch over the patient and felt, like him, that she was dead. He mentioned, under questioning, that he had assisted the doctor in attempting to revive her but had not noticed any sign of life. Finally he mentioned that he had sat watch over the corpse during the night but not noticed any sign of life. He said he was unable to state anything further concerning the matter and left the court on completion of the due formalities. The other guard was not called before the court, since he was tending the sheep.

Now it was convenient that the doctor had tarried on the farm since he was recalled and urged to conduct immediate forensic examination of the powder, and a post mortem, and the judge also urged him to be on the alert during the post mortem to any evidence of pregnancy, or visible signs of an abortion having been performed. Furthermore, the judge requested the presence of the doctor during the search for the body of a child by the shore the same day and, if such were found, to conduct an autopsy in his presence.

This was recorded.

Finally, the register stated: Concerning custody of the accused Saemundur Fridgeir Björnsson, it shall be recorded that after the probability was established that Sólveig Súsanna Jónsdóttir had committed suicide by poisoning herself, he was made to change his clothes in the presence of the doctor and the judge, and a close guard was mounted to prevent him from inflicting harm upon himself.

Since it was becoming late in the day, it was decided to make an immediate search by the shore, because the sheriff had arrived and was ready to attend.

The gloomy men rocked themselves out of their seats and made ready to go down to the sea.

By the Sea

The sea was not swollen. No gloomy clouds overhead, weighed down with fate. No black bank of cloud on the horizon, growing and boding doom at the rim of the ocean.

Enough of that.

It was a calm day, a slight breeze, fairly warm. A light mist in the air, overcast. By the shore the men were standing silently in a little group with their spades. They did not need to look around the area.

All right, where?

No answer. The farmers avoided looking directly at the repressed young man. They were not haughty.

All right, said the magistrate; we shall wait.

The beating of the waves seemed to have a soporific effect. Two purple sandpipers ran across the beach. Went right to the edge and ran back from the breaking wave on the smooth compacted sand where a stone sat, and a track from the last time it had been moved. And on the bank where they were standing the blades of grass relished the warmth of the breeze. There was a domesticated ewe by the sheep pen with its two lambs, one black and the other white, and both had grown well so far during the summer.

We're not going to wait for ever, the magistrate said; tell us where to start digging young man. Here?

No, said the lad, his head bowed, and the breeze chanced to waft that word towards the magistrate, not away into the great beyond.

Oh? said the magistrate; not here? But this is where you told us in court, you said so in your confession all the same. Weren't you telling the truth?

Not really.

184

Where then?

There.

There where?

Just over there. There in the sheep pen.

The sheep pen also stood by the edge of the sea, and the band of confederates headed there, bound by the evil deed committed in this vast land and the smallness and helplessness of the nation that inhabited it; a few men in a dispersed group on the seaboard, at the outermost coast of an endless ocean.

When they reached the sheep pen they went in through a gap where the rock wall around it had crumbled, and just as they were about to look inside a ewe with one white lamb and one black one burst out towards them, straight into them in its commotion, the lambs close behind, and skidded away from them and fled through the gap in the wall, and rushed up to the heath above the estuary in their fear of man, the husband of the earth.

Inside, the young man pointed to where they should dig and they did not need to go deep, the body was discovered where he had told them, buried around two feet in the earth. The doctor supervised the operation, and it was carefully dug up according to his orders.

Two of them carried the bundle between them like an unbroken egg. Outside the wall they unravelled the shawl.

The woman had owned that shawl, but had never danced with it herself.

Before them was the body of a baby that had not been laid in a manger but buried in the dirt of a sheep pen. No star lit the way to it. Indeed, no one knew whether it had been living at birth.

No one?

A detailed examination was made of the body. The doctor said what should go on to the record and the judge asked occasional questions. That bruise on the head. What does that signify?

They worked silently, speaking only when they really needed, then the day was done, and at the doctor's request the examination was postponed until after the Sabbath, to be resumed on the second day, on the Monday morning as soon as it was light.

Perfectly Natural

The hearing continued in the same room of the church farm Kaldbakur by the sea at the bottom of the fjord. After a preamble, the recorder noted that the accused had appeared before the court in full fettle and been shown the corpse, and asked repeatedly whether he had not noticed blood or other wounds to the baby when his half-sister gave it to him to bury. Then he was finally told that his sister had passed away; perhaps the judge had not noticed that he had been one of the witnesses when she was found dead in the room beneath the porch. At least, he saw no sign of shock from him; and indeed he did not appear fully conscious of himself, and stood stiff and remote and deathly pale with staring eyes in front of his judge, and answered his questions in a monotonous voice like a sleepwalker. He had to be asked repeatedly until his answer corroborated what he had confessed during the trial, that he had only seen bruises on the baby's head.

Where?

On the part not covered by the shawl that the body was wrapped in.

And where was that?

The forehead, and face.

How did he carry the body to the sea?

He had carried it in his coat. Then the coat was examined. There were no signs that blood had flowed on to it.

Has the coat been washed since?

No.

Then he was repeatedly asked in detail whether he thought, in accordance with his earlier statement, that the child had perhaps been killed after it was born.

He said he thought that was the case.

On what grounds does the accused reach that conclusion?

I would have thought it was perfectly natural.

I would like to remind the accused very firmly to watch what he is saying, said the magistrate almost gently; do not confess to anything which you have not done. But neither should you conceal any of the truth, so that it may be revealed in full, without evasion. Nor augment it in any way. We cannot avoid discussing the matter further. Had you perhaps discussed what should be done when the time of the child's birth arrived?

The accused admitted that he and his half-sister had agreed to try as far as they were able to conceal the birth of the child.

And even at the price of killing the child? said the magistrate wearily.

Yes, he answered, inhaling the word rather than breathing it out.

To prevent the birth being known? said the judge.

Yes, exhaling, lightly.

Then we cannot avoid asking the accused further how long previously he had resolved upon that course. Can you name a date for us to add to the record?

Silence.

Perhaps just before the birth?

No.

Earlier?

Yes, earlier.

How much earlier? A month?

Possibly two months before. No, earlier, I think.

Shall we say more than two months before the birth?

Yes.

You and your half-sister agreed upon this then?

Yes. More or less.

And was this resolution kept? All the time? Right up until the deed was done?

You could say so.

Record that.

Yes. More or less yes.

What does the accused mean by phrasing it like that? the judge said cautiously; did it ever occur to the accused at some time during the intervening period to abandon his resolution?

No.

Never?

No.

Was the subject ever raised between you and your half-sister?

No.

But you did discuss this resolution on other occasions?

Yes.

Often?

Yes, more often than that. Often.

Did the thought never occur to you when your sister told you about the baby, did it never occur to you to tell anyone what had happened, even abandon the plan to conceal the birth at any price, even at the price of the child's life?

No.

Pardon? Let me hear. Speak up a little.

That no was slightly lower, and was recorded.

Shadows of Clouds

Shadows of grey clouds crawled over the land, flowing blue across the black sand; then headed up the slopes, moving aside for the occasional spectre passing by.

But oh! how the days passed. Scarcely the sound of weather against the windowpane, scarcely still a song through the blades of grass which will soon be straw, yellow. Such befalls us all, eventually. Now it was quiet.

The day of rest.

The beating of a hammer against an anvil. Someone sharpening a scythe.

The bell in the steeple began to make itself heard. Helplessly, the ringing headed for the mountain, tried to extend itself but reached only a short distance out to sea; a gull cawed back at it, borne on the wing of the wind over rippling waves, wave upon wave fell crunching with its foaming petticoat, am I not mistaken or did the bell in the gatehouse answer? I do not know.

Funeral peals.

Towards the mountain headed the sound of the bell, century upon century, seeking sounds from mountain spirits or elves, as if the river bore it against its own current right into the narrow valley, to its innermost roots.

But this bell also peals to the world of men, calling people to church.

The congregation whispered outside the church and fell silent. The vicar and his wife were approaching. Everyone fell silent, and contemplated the magistrate as he walked into the church, not haughtily. Even when the doctor passed, they remained silent. They even chastized their dogs when they leaped at each other in the joy of meeting again.

Then they drifted slowly into the church, first the women almost in a single group in traditional dress, the sound of their footsteps muted by their sheepskin shoes, and the occasional male drifting in with them, sitting down by himself on the male side while the women's pews were filled; some needed to share a pinch of snuff outside, others had a wad to chew, and others still needed to smoke and ask about the haymaking and catch up on other news, before they sauntered into the house of God; and soon the male pews were full too, the officials in the front row, Beelzebubs with the magistrate himself and King's delegate at their head.

The leader of the choir blew his nose so loudly that it resounded around the church and he made two attempts to reach the note, reaching it in the end with his huge groping paw, delivering it with a splendid growl in a voice like a stalactite, and crooned the opening of the hymn in solo. And the congregation tagged along afterwards, grudgingly accompanying the leader's rumblings and answering them, to create a chant astride a single tune between them, with stray voices on either side.

The leader of the choir was a large man, bald with a peeling scalp and a carbuncle on his long nose. His forehead was domed with a scar on the top, and his eyebrows shaggy; his eyes pure as sweet choice bilberries. His mouth broad and spacious for his great deep voice to break out within and boom around the church, and the lower part of his face large with wide jaws; and beneath them flowed a long straggly beard where he could have hidden all his three grandsons from their vindictive mother, his daughter. He had long arms and held a hymnbook in one, using the other to clear a path for the song with his spread, knurled fingers. Sometimes he raised his shoulders and puffed up his chest and jerked back his neck, rolling his head as if to budge his way over a stiff crest in the notes.

When the churchwarden helped the vicar into his robes he noticed him trembling. Yes, he's a young man, the poor fellow. Our dear vicar, thought the churchwarden, and brought him his robes. He wanted to rest a hand on his shoulder but did not think it was seemly. The vicar went out in front of the altar, and knelt down at the railings.

The altarpiece confronted his sinless eyes. The wound in the side still bled, the arcs of blood were still neat and tidy, gushing from the wounded side and palms, into the goblet as our Saviour Christ stood amidst the crowd, blood pouring over his thighs. His eyes were tired and anguished at our sins and wickedness and the loneliness of a man who becomes a saviour. How forsaken, how completely forsaken. A soldier was still drying the blood from his spear, forsaken too in the role assigned to him. As if he had been forgotten in the painting after his role was completed. He did not have the sense to rush back home to the comfort of his family who awaited him in the sanctity of the home, the children waiting for him to play with them, can't we stay up until Dad gets home? And the wife weary and fatigued, it's a tough job being a soldier in a faraway country, even though his family can go with him; it is difficult to feel the hatred of the people and the subservience and obsequiousness of those who laugh along, then return home after obeying orders and answer the children's questions, and look into their eyes, or stroke their cheeks and hair when they are asleep, and you arrive. He should have got himself away by then, out of the picture. Admittedly he took care not to be splashed with the blood that gushed incessantly into the goblet from the wounds of the man who had risen from the cross the previous night. So were just the two of them left, when the festivities were finished and the carousing of the masses was over?

The vicar's taking an unusually long time over prayers today, a young woman whispered to her elderly mother. The old woman merely nodded several times, stared at the back of the vicar's head and rocked, had she seen something? The sun slipped in through the window, a curiously white glow zigzagging like the glint of a saw blade on to the top of the vicar's head, and moved down on to his neck when he bowed his head lower and could take his eyes off the blood orgy on the altarpiece.

Meek and racked I kneel at the Cross and its root;
My Lord watched over me while I was asleep;
With penitent tears I kiss the Saviour's foot
Rejoicing that my doomed soul He gave hope.

The leader of the choir stretched out his neck, threw his head back, closed his eyes, tightened his gigantic grip upon the little black hymnbook and packed the bellowing back into his mighty frame. And the congregation's disjointed song faded out at the words: 'Rejoicing that my doomed soul He gave hope'. The vicar stood silently in the pulpit, his head bowed as if beseeching the Lord for help, to grant him words, bestow grace upon him, to speak into their hearts, inspiration. Not to speak tongues, not to enchant, just a few simple words to bring someone grace, light someone the way in this terrible darkness which beset his heart, besieged his soul.

A few words, he thought; and with thy spirit.

He began slowly, softly, indeterminately; hesitantly: Before I read the sermon for today I would like to say one thing even though it is not in accordance with the rites: God is love.

He looked around the church as if searching for something which perhaps was with everyone sitting there, perhaps for something that was not there. But searching it out none the less. Inside the church. Then he said carefully, as if sounding out their reaction: God is love. He asks nothing. Except one thing, are you whole? There was a close silence broken only by a cough. Someone sneezed after trying to hold it back. He looked around at the indecipherable faces, the white walls, the black heaps of dead flies in the windows that even the choir-leader's bellowing had left undisturbed, scarcely budged the freshly fallen pot-bellied flies that lay on their backs with shiny wings beneath them, their feet pointing to heaven. He felt he needed to add something before beginning to read the lesson to the congregation.

What? What could he say? My God, give me words with thy spirit. Give me words, my Almighty God:

God is not vindictive. No. God is love, he said; God is . . .

He paused as if expecting to hear something. Then he said: Is.

He clutched the rim of the pulpit with both hands, and composed himself, then gritted his teeth. And said in a low voice: The lesson for today is from the Epistle of Paul the Apostle to the Romans, chapter eight, verses twelve to seventeen.

A New Life

The woman.

As noon approached she began to feel nauseous, and started to feel pains. That morning she had repeatedly stopped, rested the palms of both hands on the straight rake, its teeth by her toes as if it were a slender shoot that would suddenly sprout leaves and attract small birds.

She dried the sweat from her face with the corner of her scarf. It was a cold sweat. She was sweaty all over, shot through with a chill.

When she felt the pains disappear she said ow and said she was surely falling ill.

I think I have to go and lie down.

Yes, just go and lie down, dear.

She walked home.

There was no one at home. She was alone in the farmhouse, and lay down on the bed, hot and cold by turns. The sun warmed every-thing, everyone was working as hard as they could in the crackling dry weather. Outside in the meadow. And she could hear the men whetting their scythes. That whishing sound of the whetstone as it sharpened caressing blades, and she thought for an instant between her labour pains how they whitened, and felt she could see how sharper they were for tossing aside the glowing straw, the grass flourisheth and it is gone, as the Bible says of the days of man.

What a state I must be in; she heaved when the next contraction struck, and tried to bear it, although she thought no one but the dog could hear. Everyone was outside in the haymaking. And her little daughter playing with the lamb. The black domesticated one that followed the child.

She crammed the pillow into her mouth when the pain was at its most intense. Bit it. Had the sense not to bite her lips to the point of making them bleed, and held her tongue.

Then at last she felt the moment had arrived. She was giving birth.

She wrapped her arms tight around her stomach and staggered, bent double, down the stairs, her thighs and knees pressed tight together, her calves tense, pigeon-toed and trippingly, rolled her awesome weight from her heels on to the tips of her toes and tried to sew her genitals together, lock her womb shut, and crawled along the dark passageway, groping her way from wall to wall in nothing but dirt, knowing that now she must use all her strength to escape from human sight, and away from the eyes of God, though she barely thought so with nothing to do but hold out until no one could see her, and get away before the birth drops, bursts forth, that which no one must know, no one see, become alone and invisible, hidden from them all, with no help to have and no mercy, and no grace and never any consolation, without thinking this, without knowing it.

She reached a hole among the rocks, there could be a fox here, there could be a den here if the farm were abandoned, if there were no farm, no people. But it was shallow, and she squatted over the hole. Bent completely double, remembering, despite her pain, despite the frenzy that enveloped her, never to bite herself to the point of making herself bleed, nor scratch. And when it broke from its moorings, perhaps the wait had not been as long as she had thought, and when it came and slid out of her, she straightened up, and her birth dropped out of her, into the hole, stirring dust from the bottom, fine ashen powder into a cloud of dust, when that tiny, unremarkable lump plopped on to the porous bottom of the hole, thumped down there with a mute sound, causing ghostly echoes in her benumbed, crazed mind.

How could she have imagined how long her loss of memory would last? For a while she seemed unaware of what had happened, nor the way she had reached the hole. She could see the farmhouse if she did not stoop, and there was no one there. Some distance away she could see some people. At a vast distance. And knew nothing. Not who she was herself, less why she was here, not to mention anything else. Else?

Such as what? She felt something hanging down between her legs. A slimy thread. And with a deathly chill her sober sense awakened, thought; her feelings benumbed, perhaps dead, murdered.

And knew what remained. What had to be done. She took the slippery cord that hung out of her, wound it up and knotted it. It had torn with the jerk of her birth falling down from her. And after dealing with it, she felt it slip back inside her.

She threw herself down, tearing up grass and earth, in a chilled frenzy, tossing it over that strange object that lay within her reach inside the hole, still as the grave. Had it made any sound? Except the thud when it landed in the pile of dust.

Perhaps she had fallen asleep in her bed. It was almost evening. She had to return to that place. Conceal it better. Their life depended upon it.

She took the baby's body out of the hole and wrapped it in the rose-patterned shawl she had been given long ago. Probably on the birth of her first child which lived. Which she was never allowed to see. And did not know whether was still alive. And perhaps no longer wondered whether it was still alive.

She carried it in the shawl into a shed, and put it into her brother's trunk, where he kept his fox poison. Locked it, and put the key back into her apron pocket.

Lay down on her bed in the sitting room, and pulled the blanket over her head; lay there with her eyes open, dry.

Completely dry, staring into the dark sky of her blanket.

The Lesson and the Sermon

Therefore, brethren, we are debtors, not to the flesh, to live after the flesh. For if ye live after the flesh, ye shall die: but if ye through the Spirit do mortify the deeds of the body, ye shall live. For as many as are led by the Spirit of God, they are the sons of God. For ye have not received the spirit of bondage again to fear; but ye have received the Spirit of adoption, whereby we cry, Abba, Father. The Spirit itself beareth witness with our spirit, that we are the children of God: and if children, then heirs; heirs of God, and joint-heirs with Christ; if so be that we may suffer with him, that we may be also glorified together.

More song, freely rendered.

The text of the sermon was from the Gospel According to St Matthew, chapter seven, verses fifteen to twenty-three:

Beware of false prophets, which come to you in sheep's clothing, but inwardly they are ravening wolves. Ye shall know them by their fruits. Do men gather grapes of thorns, or figs of thistles? Even so every good tree bringeth forth good fruit; but a corrupt tree bringeth forth evil fruit. A good tree cannot bring forth evil fruit, neither can a corrupt tree bring forth good fruit. Every tree that bringeth not forth good fruit is hewn down, and cast into the fire. Wherefore by their fruits ye shall know them. Not every one that saith unto me, Lord, Lord, shall enter into the kingdom of heaven; but he that doeth the will of my Father which is in heaven. Many will say to me in that day, Lord, Lord, have we not prophesied in thy name? and in thy name have cast out devils? and in thy name done many wonderful works? And then will I profess unto them, I never knew you: depart from me, ye that work iniquity.

This is the text of today's sermon. Beware of false prophets. And I say unto you, my beloved congregation: Beware of those who desire to deceive you, work wonders before you, or corrupt you with embellishments and fanciful things, or divert you from the righteousness which dwells uncorrupted in your hearts, if you manage to listen for that voice, namely the voice of God in your breasts. As the Lord's commandment says, thou shalt love thy neighbour. Thou shalt love thy neighbour as thyself. But how, with what sort of love? In what way should you and may you love your neighbours? And in what manner and on what terms should you love others and relinquish yourselves?

A good tree, the Evangelist says, a good tree cannot bring forth corrupt fruit. Can we permit ourselves to dispute the word of God as spoken through the mouth of the Evangelist? Without doing so, let us imagine there are circumstances under which even the good tree could bear fruit which society considers evil and rotten. Although we shall remind ourselves that this is not in itself the word of God. For God is love, and God is life, and loves all life. And while the Evangelist phrases it thus, let us, in order to understand what the Scripture is intended to tell us, always remember and never sway from, and give ever a place in our hearts, and let our hearts and our minds be one at all time: God is love. And when we pronounce our judgments, howsoever we base them upon the laws of this country and the accord on which we have built our society, nation or whatever name we give to it, let us none the less not rejoice in our hearts at the fate of those on whom such judgments are pronounced, but remember instead that there is one above us who sees all, equally that which we wish to conceal and reveal to no one, that which enters our minds; he sees all and there is no place of concealment from him, not in the darkest of caves, not in a locked room, nowhere. And he is love. We shall remember this when we call out or writhe in our misery. And without that certainty, all is without value, is empty and void, is sheer and insubstantial vanity, without foundation anywhere, and our lives born to no purpose living or dead.

In Proverbs, chapter thirty, verses eleven to fourteen, we read:

There is a generation that curseth their father, and doth not bless their mother.

There is a generation that are pure in their own eyes, and yet is not washed from their filthiness.

There is a generation, O how lofty are their eyes! and their eyelids are lifted up.

There is a generation, whose teeth are as swords, and their jaw teeth as knives, to devour the poor from off the earth, and the needy from among men.

I ask the congregation to pray together for our deliverance.

The magistrate sat in the front pew, to the far right of other dignitaries, first and unequal to the others. His thoughts were not constrained within the church, headed out to the green land; he knew that summer was passing now, soon autumn would be over too, who could tell if sea ice would not fill all the fjords and block the harbours, creating an endless netherworld of white castles and towers and plains of sheer ice, the whole country engulfed in snow and the earth everywhere unyielding, everything white and cold; and the night endless and black.

Monday

And then the holy day was over. The day of rest, whom did it bring rest? Respite from what?

New times of work flow on with the sand in the hour-glass.

The hearing was still going on in the same room as before. And still attended by the same men. Those, that is, who were still the same as before.

We must conclude this, said the judge. I shall ask you, Saemundur, to conceal nothing so that the matter may be concluded.

Now everything proceeded swiftly and the pen was kept busy. It was stated when the accused first had carnal relations with his sister, whereupon this took place at intervals until the spring when she bore the child. He firmly maintained that he had in fact gone to bed with her three times at night after that, but that nothing of that sort had taken place.

Why not?

It was sort of beyond my control.

Let us record it as some kind of involuntary act.

The accused nodded several times.

And furthermore he repeated his earlier testimony that the subject had arisen between him and his sister after she had told him that she was pregnant, of them concealing the birth even at the price of the child's life.

Was it discussed whether the child should be killed if such action were necessary to conceal the birth?

It was not discussed, no. But I knew for certain one of us had to kill the child.

Have you considered since, or realized, that such a crime would rather be for her to commit?

No.

Really?

Well, I can't deny thinking it would have been more natural. It struck me that she ought to do what we had decided on. As soon as we had decided to do everything we could to conceal the birth, she said to me: Either I kill the baby or I kill myself. I tried to talk her out of what she was saying, killing herself. I couldn't bear the thought. I thought it would be much worse to lose her than to lose the baby.

Did you discuss the matter further, later? Afterwards, said the judge carefully.

I don't think we did.

There was no tension between them any more, rather a kind of accord such as when distant relatives meet after an accident in the family and feel they ought to know each other.

The accused continued, unprompted: I also remember her talking about trying to get some medicine from the doctor to abort it; she was going to tell him that her blood wouldn't clot. I know she consulted the doctor. Later I fetched some medicine from him but she used only a little of it. It didn't work. When she was talking about it I remember what a good idea I thought it was, compared with the alternative.

And your resolution remained unswerving, all the time as . . .

Yes.

Did you never think of any other way of preventing word of the birth spreading than killing the baby? That is, if it was a live birth?

No.

Never? No other plan? And your resolution never wavered?

No.

Never? Not once?

Never.

What about finding someone else to admit paternity? Wouldn't that have been worth trying? You perhaps tried that?

No, no.

Then let us turn to the birth. Now you will try to tell me clearly about . . .

Well, it was some day in the spring, I was coming back after

200

tending the sheep, it was at lambing time I remember, she told me she had had the baby. But it was not really until later that we went into the shed together. There was a trunk there where she said she had put the baby. Then I was really quite sure that she had killed it, I hadn't heard it make any sound and . . .

But you did not open the trunk? You didn't look?

Not then.

And then what?

Well, it was probably about a fortnight after she had told me, then I buried it.

A fortnight? said the magistrate, with more surprise than accusation in his voice.

Then it was recorded that he had been in a very deep depression after he began having carnal relations with his sister, right up until the present day. Although he had not shown it very much. He said it was caused by the feeling of terror at his crime and repentance for it happening. Although he was unable to abandon his resolution.

Did you know or were you aware, from anything else than what you have told us, that your sister would take her own life?

No, he said, hiding his face in his hands.

No hint?

No, he said, lowering his hands, and his eyes were dry.

Then the question arises how she could have obtained the poison to do what she did.

Well, in my trunk, there was a phial there, she had access to the trunk. With fox poison in it.

He recognized the key that had been taken from his sister's pocket when she was remanded.

Yes, to my trunk.

Did you encourage her to do it?

No. Not in the least. No.

But why did you keep the poison there?

It just was there.

Perhaps to help her put the plan into effect?

Not at all, the thought never occurred to me. I just didn't check. I had to keep it somewhere. I just didn't think of it. I suppose I must have forgotten about it. Yes, I think I must have done.

Did you agree to take your lives together?

No. No. But I was always afraid. That she would. If anyone found out.

Why?

I just felt it, after what we had talked about.

But the fox poison?

I got that from the master of the house. Some time last year. To poison foxes. There was just some left in the phial. I had poisoned seven ptarmigan with it.

And is that sort of poison left lying around all over the place?

Yes, I know of some other places. But no one else gave me any. I didn't mention it to anyone else. I just remember going out hunting with the farmhand from Beyla. We both had that sort of poison.

Court adjourned.

Return

Rock in the rain.

Now it was raining steadily on them. They had not spoken to each other, for a long time.

The cliff faces rapidly darkened. Everywhere that grey rock that wrinkles out of the land, jerks itself out of the grown surface of the earth, in some places with sharp edges that cut the green cloth to arch up a ridge or clump of stone; rend the vegetation with its delicate alternate yellow and green; at the top of a grey stone sat a small bird; the sky grey over a low hill.

The rocky peaks rose from a ridge or a plain with their faces turned up in masks of stone, like captured divine archetypal beings with human airs. They lay there, unable to do otherwise than accept the gentle rain, into their moss-clad senses.

He saw how his companion's brown horse had turned almost black in the rain. There were still snowdrifts in the mountains; he thought he saw an eagle hovering around the ledges, perhaps guarding an eyrie, clouds rose and abolished peaks; in many places, screes spread down the gullies on the mountainside, swelling towards their feet, and green strips stretched up the slopes; and here and there, brooks and rivulets threaded their way, stumbled across edges and rims, dashed over ledges and pillars; and beneath them stood lakes and pools; marshes of sedge at the bottom with waterlogged, bright reindeer moss; and the rain combed the stretches of moss and low hills, and showers swam over the fells; dark clouds thrust across the grey sky, reflecting in standing pools.

They could still see, if they cared to, out towards the sea, almost completely smooth; with the hint of eddying currents around islets and skerries. Birds swam in flocks at the limits where the land was reflected beyond, where the green of the meadows spread out into the fjord, and the dark banks steep and high.

His companion examined the man of authority furtively, darted sideways glances at him, not feeling assured about addressing him. He did not recall ever having seen a man alter so much in such a short time.

The ground was damp and soft everywhere where there was no dark rock, and the hoofprints filled up rapidly and splashed with a spongy slurch; and the brooks murmured as if the Almighty had sunk all existence into some bleary nostalgia, the man of authority thought to himself, and felt it pointless to strive after a subject for a poem, after the way the journey had turned out.

Later in the day they reached the ferry point, and met the farmer who was pulling the boat on to land after a trip. They loaded their belongings on to the craft and drove their horses out into the river, where they swam ahead of the ferry. The ferryman tugged at the oars with his enormous hands, jerking them downstream at a slant, glaring at them with grey eyes from beneath his beetling brow, tough and quick, with black hair but white on his cheeks and the stubble of his beard, his mouth open with an unflinching grin playing across his broad swollen lips; and a red scar right over his upper lip from the top of the wing of his nostril, big-jawed with dark specks in his furrowed chin; his forehead short rather than broad. He spat brown saliva into the eddies that rocked the boat, adjusted his course when they ceased, and headed even straighter into the current so they bobbed about in their flimsy craft, and water seeped in, and splashed over the low side of the boat at its roughest. You can bail out the slops now, he blurted out; if you care to go any further.

The others said nothing. Thórdur picked up the bucket and began bailing. The horses had emerged when they made land, and were standing there shaking themselves.

The ferryman took his cap from the thwart, put it on his head and tugged it down over his forehead, letting the peak hide his grey eyes and malicious face. The magistrate paid the ferry toll, and he kept his hand stretched out after being paid.

What's wrong, said the magistrate; wasn't that enough?

The ferryman rocked his huge shoulders, with his round trunk and long arms, and rubbed his left hand across his long chin and ruffled his grin, in silence; until he said slowly: Well, magistrate, that's the way it is. Aren't you going to pay for her too?

The magistrate's knuckles whitened as he gripped the shaft of his horsewhip where it met the strap.

He did not reply.

Summer Over, Autumn

Yet he still remembered how autumn had arrived.

Evening, summer had suddenly ended, autumn had come.

In the stillness and the cool it brought, in the air's cold colours; where dark grey clouds and teasings stretched across the cream dome above us, red-combed wisps. The hills were dark with a gloomy blue, and the dark-misted mountains, but the walls of the chasm even darker, the moon full.

Perfect calm.

At precisely that moment, autumn had arrived. Yet the vegetation had not changed colour; the moss grey and green, grass admittedly beginning to wither; but still no red in the heather or leaves of the shrub.

The waterfall sang in its rocky seat, and the calm evening sent a mighty echo back.

Nowhere silent.

Could he not hear the song of swans on the heath?

The waterfall had moved closer, the murmuring of the river stretched out towards him on one side. He had reached the heath, and knew of the water in a low dip, although the dusk was so close that the valley could not be seen, only the mountains above him, their soft contours inscribed wavily into the sky, pressed warmly together; the sharply defined forms dark against the orange glow in the air; which blurred away into green and blue-green with a bright light beneath.

The swans' voices repeated three notes with their trumpets, answering each other with variations on these three notes, sometimes changing the final one, until the whole ensemble of swans joined in. And the air rippled with the rhythmical trumpeting from the long necks of the swans, which he could not see in the dusk delivering their farewell to summer, death awaiting them all. Autumn.

He proceeded until he reached a riverbank at the foot of a steep slope.

The river meandered, fanning out into a delta on the sands below; farther up, it flowed between grassy banks, and split by a bar or tongue of sand still higher up; here it flowed in a single stream.

The sandy hill stood out against the sky with strips of grass that stretched up to its rocky face, and he knew there were dark rifts down them which could no longer be seen in the falling darkness.

He made himself ready on the riverbank, to the murmuring of the water that assumed authority there, and filled the register resounding and echoing to leave nothing but a theme with endless combinations and variations, growing louder and spreading everywhere, charging every vein, resounding on low and high, and hidden voices grew clearer and began to make themselves heard; voices that were either muffled, or wrapped deep inside an infinity of sound, and swept forward ever more powerful in this all-embracing flux . . .

He slept a dreamless sleep; when he awoke from the cold the blades of grass were tinged with frost, and sparkled, furry with their hoary fetters; the soft soil had stiffened as if the whole earth had tensed itself against all-pervading disaster.

Then it was bright, the full moon beginning to lose its sway over the earth though it still remained contented, high in the sky, whitening and stripped of its magic, and would soon fade away.

Where there were clouds borne in the sky, they were white as snow in billows and folds; up from the glacier to the west stood a white column of steam straight up into the pure morning air, a pillar from its shoulder; otherwise no cloud in that direction. The sea sprightly with its clear blueness, which bound his evening farewell into rhyme when this same bright blueness lay in a narrow belt under the glacier and end of the ness at its foot, the turquoise sash of the sea as if a focal point had been found there to charge the whole image with colour, and the rest created through exotic reference to that curious blueness.

But the sea was a more closely related colour now, for it had spread everywhere; therefore quite different. Yet was perhaps almost the same colour, but previously had possessed magic in its isolation, hidden force in its limitation, modesty.

Farther afield the sky above the mountains was striped with narrow red streaks against a yellow background.

Everything so quiet; no one about.

And the hoary mantle of the land thawed, the ground was moist in the sun-charged day, and the soil turned soft again.

Day.

And autumn.

The Verdict

The blue chests of the mountains stood out across the green and blue and brown bay, snowdrifts inched their way from ledge to ledge, the bare heads of the mountains had turned white overnight. The earth was covered in frost, the grass withered and sparkled when morning came on the day of judgment. Now the ground was no longer soft underfoot. It was autumn, winter was approaching.

Ásmundur the magistrate had not been sleepy that night. He had stayed awake with a bouncing puppy that never tired of demanding play and more play, scarcely obeying even when spoken to sharply, and preferring above all to have the man's finger in its mouth. It followed the magistrate when the chance presented itself and stayed up with him that night, and it seem to be able to read his mind, for now it was well behaved. It was past ten o'clock when the magistrate went outside, walked down the bank to the bumpy meadow, threaded his way in the dark over the moss on to the edge of the sea with the dog; and they sat on the rim of the land high above the steep-sloping beach. Beneath them, a wave splashed over skerries and rock stacks, and rolled on between stones over the sand in the bay, growling and sucking, then foamed over the land up to the boulders, noisily bringing seaweed, kelp and driftwood.

And then the first hint appeared in the sky of the green glow from approaching wrathful fire, which grew slowly at first, suddenly becoming a riotously coloured flood of flame thrown all over the heavens in spurts.

The northern lights lit up the night, speeding their unruly course across the firmament.

The first frost of autumn.

The puppy stopped its tricks, calmed down. It stood behind the man who was sitting at the edge of the bank, snuggled up to him, rubbed its snout against his shoulder as if enquiring something of him, afraid, and sought trust and protection of him. And the judge thought such company was better than none.

Beneath them the tide billowed, and the bank was wet and glittered in the light cast by the sea spray.

When day dawned, he had to pronounce his first sentence. He feared the night coming to an end, yearned to be able to tarry time, hold it tight, stop it. The mountains stood out vaguely across the bay, moving closer the more they whitened. One man and his dog; the sea and the sky, land. And the northern lights reigning over everything in the world.

But now it was day, and everything in different hues from then. The night had changed everything. And not just the night.

The sheriff was speaking in the new courtroom, another room from the one where they had met before, beside the same infinite ocean; other mountains, other countryside.

The magistrate's residence. A timber house, tall and narrow like a stooping elder relinquishing office after a long life.

The magistrate felt drowsy while the sheriff, the appointed counsel for the defence, pleaded clemency with flowery words and quotations from the Bible and idyllic classical poetry. And when he was swept farthest away on the wings of imported verse a holy aurora crossed his face, and his eye twinkled as if blind. He was long-faced with thick shadows under his eyes, high cheekbones and a fairly long chin, thick protruding lips with a curling moustache, well trimmed, bald with the short hair on his cheeks turning grey, and pinkish fluff on the top of his scalp, and a large carbuncle at the top of his forehead like a horn about to sprout. He was largish in build, with plenty of wind for rhetoric; the speech flowed out of him like a wide gushing stream running slowly and powerfully over mud flats in countless still streams, just pouring ahead without obstacle. The magistrate grew increasingly drowsy as the obligatory speech for the defence continued. He tried to take deep breaths to keep himself awake, and perhaps it was his apprehension about pronouncing the verdict that weighed most heavily. He stole occasional glances at the young defendant, who remained completely unmoved; sat stooping in the same position, not moving, except that his head lifted up from time to time without his expression changing, as if prompted by a thought travelling like a breeze over a blade of grass. Then his head bowed back. He sat with his left elbow on the table, that shoulder pushed forward and his hand hanging down, sometimes clutching his other hand between his knees, on the verge of pressing himself together with his other shoulder thrust back.

But then the counsel for the defence began describing the accused's background, and the judge's drowsiness seemed to wear off and he listened. He was the illegitimate child of two workers on a certain farm which he claims he was too young to remember when he left for another farm called Eydi. He stayed there with his mother until the age of six, and his father was not with them. Then he moved again with his mother to another farm, Brekka at Nes, and spent a year there, and went from there to Thórarinskot, all in the same district where he was born. By his eleventh year he was living in another district and spent the next four years there, then followed his mother to Kollavíkursel, to the district where these tragic events took place, the sheriff said. After one year there he moved away from his mother, in his sixteenth year. He spent three years at his next place of residence, then returned to Thórarinskot at Nes and stayed there for a year, then another year at another farm in the same district, then yet another year at the farm next to the vicarage where these tragic events took place, said the sheriff. And then he was reunited with his mother after a long separation and they lived there together and left there together, and went to stay at the vicarage where he had been since but which his mother left after a year. He had never lived at the same place as his father except at the place of his birth, and was too young to remember that. He had begun to work for a living in his tenth year, at Thórarinskot. The sheriff mentioned on behalf of the accused that the local parish had never supported him and both his parents had provided for him when he was too young to do so himself. Regarding his education, the sheriff said he had begun reading the Scriptures at Thórarinskot, and had been confirmed the following year. Then the sheriff said, quoting the defendant, that he had often felt a

211

sore lack of general knowledge after his confirmation and had felt a longing to study, but his poverty, and in particular the fact that he had needed to earn his own living as soon as he was old enough to do so, had prevented him learning anything more than to read and write, apart from his childhood religious instruction.

After this rigmarole it was time for the sheriff to display his eloquence in the room at the magistrate's residence before the small group of gloomy men, while the cool winds of autumn stroked the wide, calm bay; the sun softened the frozen ground on the first day that so clearly boded the winter.

They are as you can see just like any other godforsaken wretches. In fact most people are turned feeble by the conditions which the common people face in this country, which still is the colony of another nation and ruled by a foreign king who never comes to look at us. And we still live in misery in spite of the hope of liberty and partial improvement brought about by the farmers' organization, our co-operative society which has elevated us somewhat although obscure forces would welcome its demise. But we will not be turned back. Now we sell our sheep on the hoof and are paid in gold. We who never saw money for centuries on end but for the odd coin and what we could earn from illicit trade with sailors who came here in secret behind the profiteering of the royal monopoly.

The judge made do with clearing his throat while the speaker rambled on and made broadsides at his absent father and the King. Then after a pause he said slowly, without sharpness: Would the counsel for the defence please confine himself to the case in hand.

There was a hint that the speaker stumbled in his blazing sermon. He cleared his throat as well, although not so openly, almost choking. But he recovered quickly and said: I feel that this does concern the case in hand. There is much to bear in mind when sentence is passed on a man. All the conditions, even the future prospects and expectation of liberty of which this unfortunate is deprived but others enjoy. All nations are rising up around the world; the common people are breaking off their fetters and demanding their rights, and will not be stopped. The ancient order is crumbling, the chains are broken one by one and tossed into a heap to make a mountain of broken chains like a monument to the dark age which has passed. And this criminal is deprived of that, since prison awaits him; bearing everything in mind, since we should rather show mercy towards his infringement and his part in these tragic events which we cannot avoid discussing here. May I, ignorant as I am, having been appointed to his defence, implore that he be shown mercy; that we treat his case in Christian charity and sympathy, to which we owe everything that lives and draws the breath of life. I have related the circumstances of his entire upbringing, I have stated how sorely he feels his ignorance and lack of learning. And how might they who have received no instruction be able to distinguish between right and wrong?

The sheriff paused in his defence and looked proudly over his audience, one magistrate and poet, two arch-enemies from the trade war in the district, the village merchant and co-operative shop manager, and three pillars of the farming community; most of whom had stared at the table or the floor or their hands as they rubbed them, and some stretched their fingers and pulled them, and one who was endowed with such a talent had made them crack; the merchants stared out of the window as if waiting for a ship to see whether they had goods on board it; although both inspected the snow that had fallen overnight on the mountains across the bay. The criminal sat with his expression unchanged and thought about the first time they met in Kollavíkursel, he so young and she already a mature woman. And the sheriff rewarded himself for his performance with a hearty pinch of snuff, spreading a wide line across the back of his hand and sucking it up without haste to allow the impact of his speech to reach its full power in the minds of those who had heard it.

This young man's tragedy, he said, nasally after his dose of snuff, his eyes moist from the gift of God that divine tobacco is; I consider his distress more than ample without increasing it with harsh judgment by us; who are also frail men. May I perhaps remind you of the attitude of Jesus Christ, the most perfect man we know ever to have lived, indeed confirmed as the Son of God among the faithful. That phrase about he that is without sin, let him first cast a stone, which I hardly dare repeat,

213

so often have scoundrels and evil-doers taken those words to absolve themselves from just sentence. Though I shall remind you of this in the hope that it has not been wrung dry by overuse and misuse; he that is without sin among you, let him first cast a stone. These words were spoken because of a whore whom the entire rabble in the city felt worthy of sentence and stoning; and in this country we have so often placed stones on the cairns of unfortunate men and women without trying to understand their misfortune.

The origins and development of this young man who has confessed himself guilty of a terrible crime, all that has been duly recorded. But what do we really know? What do we know of what has dwelt in the hearts of these hapless people who are so devoid of fortune as the present case has revealed? They have committed a crime against the laws of God and man. Against nature too, we say. But what was their motive? Perhaps love. And if love is whole and heartfelt, is it not sacred? Is it not sacred, in spite of everything? This young man who has never had anything except, if my suspicions are correct, love, how much has he also lost? Perhaps we shall never be able to answer what is none the less the crucial question: What is love and what is fornication? I ask the judge to be light in his punishment and show him mildness in the spirit of the age which is dawning.

At this point the judge called a short adjournment before delivering his verdict.

When the court reconvened the magistrate delivered a long speech, describing the case in considerable detail and summarizing what had been revealed in court, and mentioned that there was a strong probability that the child had been murdered although this had not been proven, and that the half-sister of the accused had not told him that it had died in any manner, nor told him anything to the contrary and the conclusion, supported by medical opinion, was that the child had died from unknown causes. And here the judge was beginning to seek out extenuating circumstances, such as the lack of proof that carnal relations had taken place after the birth, and earlier that the accused had committed his crime of incest when not in control of his faculties. He described the crime as having been committed with singular daring in the midst of the people on the farm, and even after the accused had learned that he was under suspicion, and also after it had produced the ultimate consequences; yet he pointed out that the trial had revealed that the first step towards this criminal activity had not been taken by the accused, but rather he had been induced to it by another party; and he reminded them that even though he was the illegitimate half-brother of the deceased, they had not been brought up together. He could not absolve him of responsibility in the conspiracy against the child's life, but mentioned that, according to his testimony, he had ample reason to suppose that his half-sister would commit suicide if the birth were discovered; and that threat had aroused such fear within him as to have a decisive effect on his resolution to kill the child if necessary.

The magistrate had spoken at length with frequent pauses, sometimes in mid-sentence even though everything was clearly and legibly written on his papers, but then only momentarily. It was mainly the co-operative shop manager and sheriff who stole glances towards him; the others showed no sign of whether they noticed his hesitation or not. The accused did not look up, except once; and that was at this point, and the pause was much longer than those before. Then he finally looked at the magistrate for a while, until his head sank down again, and his gaze towards the point which no one saw except him.

Then the magistrate read out: Finally it should be borne in mind when punishment for the accused's misdeeds in their entirety is determined, that he has been reluctant to admit to complicity, but on the other hand has received a favourable recommendation for good behaviour from those of his masters who were able to make report, and also a fine report from the vicar who confirmed him, and that his upbringing, driven in poverty from one farm to the next with his destitute mother, has been very inadequate.

Now the magistrate paused again, and appeared to take another look at his papers, and darted his eyes as if searching for something said earlier, perhaps he was not looking at the papers; perhaps beyond them furtively, perhaps at nothing in particular. He was silent for so long that his audience, who had been completely still and motionless, began for the first time to rock in their seats or rub their hands; and the one who could make his fingers crack did so once but was embarrassed at the noise and the damage that such cracking could have caused in this special silence. Those who had been looking out of the window did so no more, as if they had abandoned hope of their ship coming in, in favour of more urgent business in this haven.

Was time finally standing still? Had the moment been captured? At last?

Then the ticking of the clock began to be heard. It was always the same when it was heard. So it stood still too. And the pendulum always moved the same, never farther in one direction than the other.

No boat on the sea, no clouds in the sky.

The shadows did not move. A solitary horse could be seen down in the meadow, grazing without looking up.

The snow that had fallen overnight was pure and clear, the whitest of white.

The blue chests of the mountains, thought the magistrate, now they are white. Have I ever seen anything as white and pure as that snow, those drifts that are like a redemption? In the mountains opposite; the mountains across this calm bay. Were I sitting on the bank by the sea the waves would perhaps whisper something to me, far below on the rocks and skerries and boulders off the beach. Far below.

He took a deep breath. They thought they heard him sigh; but were not quite sure. Then he began speaking, in such a low voice that they leaned forward to hear, everyone except the subject of the case, who never changed his position except perhaps that his head sank slightly lower.

No objections to the defence.

It is hereby deemed just that the accused, Saemundur Fridgeir Björnsson from Kaldbakur, serve ten years' forced labour. Also that he pay all the legal costs incurred in the prosecution of this case, including a fee of 6 krónur to the appointed counsel for the defence, sheriff Halldór Halldórsson from Bard.

Bower Scene

The notes found their way through the haze towards this man who sat alone over a bottle of wine on a forested beach far from the great stage, and closer to him the palm trees glittering in their shiny copper tubs. He sat at the same table as before, but a new century had turned since then. He was back in that city; and had mingled with the masses that he did not care about, and were unreal to him, similar to the dense haze that was awakened every Hallowe'en from the mass graves of distant lands; yet he saw what was here with sharpened vision, saw it but could not relate to it in any fashion. It was as if he were under some veil which separated him from what was none the less so close, making it distant, remote. He could in no way relate to what he saw and perceived so over-intensely. A divided man. Split. He was more there, far away; at a vast distance. No, he was sitting on a bank by a gentle stream with straws and wizened grass awaiting yellow-white the spring beyond; a river flowed in forks, mixing together voices from many. And the dog nudged his shoulder, expecting something. As if feeling that the man had been silent for too long. Or sensed how he felt, his master. And wanted to remind the man that he was not alone, that he was accompanied, accompanied by something other than what the dog saw and knew the man feared. It left the swan in peace, no longer chased or frightened it. The dog was black with a white chest in the snow-covered land. Before it had played several games of chasing the swan off the ice that covered the pool, making it race away in commotion. Now it was quiet beside the man, ready to defend him. If it could serve its master.

And the man in the bower of the restaurant hid behind his cigar in a thick cloud of smoke; and felt he heard the complex rhythm of music stirring unexpectedly within him, and the musical offering of that place give way to it. What also kindled within him was linked to the other place which he could visualize, a land far away, where he was much more than here. A veil he had thought before, perhaps he saw what was here through glass, outside – or was he outside himself? Sitting beside that brook in a time long past; feeling from it what was so far from coming into being. No, not a brook – the river instead. The river that was his childhood.

Why were his thoughts carried there? From the empty table at an angle in front of him he felt he was being constantly watched. He sensed a woman sitting there watching him. And he stole frequent glances in that direction. There was no one there.

Who was that woman?

What was the reason he thought of his mother here at this crowded place in the boisterous carousing of the city? He could not visualize her. He could scarcely remember her at all. Had she perhaps never spoken to her son? He had a vague recollection of an elegant woman, and cold, he felt. Headstrong. Then he could remember no more. And on the other hand, his father always needing to tell him something with wingèd words and ancient poetic diction, to teach him all he knew, deranged by a long drinking bout; that was his childhood.

Then a childhood memory stirred of weaning the lambs from the ewes. The tragedy in the bleating of the ewes fenced off in the milking-pens, when their lambs were taken away from them, so that man should have milk; and the lambs driven off to the mountains to eat rich pasture instead, running constantly whimpering, orphaned; were they perhaps crying if man listened to them? Had he forgotten this? That he felt so painful, dreaded summer after summer of his childhood. And in the autumn the lambs returned grown; and had forgotten their sorrow; when they ran in flowing sheep streams down the slopes to the farms, their bleating as griefless as the news of the day, merging with the shouts of men on horseback and the barking of dogs. He imagined the farmers weighing the lambs in their arms to decide whether they should be slaughtered, or foddered for the winter. And the milking ewes also seemed to have recovered from their maternal grief. So everything heals. So it appears. Man alone can die of suffering; but only on rare occasions.

He drove these thoughts away; and called out for another bottle of wine.

The man sat with a terrifying silence within him and another grindingly slow time which treated him cruelly, and found no peace in the boisterousness that filled the wide hall, the thumping of tankards, clinking of glasses and murmured babbling, laughter. And shadows flickered across darkened windowpanes, separating and spreading on the matted glass.

As his bottle gradually emptied, the distinction between brightness and shadow became clearer to him; individual features encroached on his perception; a finger in the shine from a lamp, a wine glass and a hand in the candlelight, the sharp blue twinkle of an eye; a dark lock tumbling from beneath a purple scarf, transporting the eye's brightness from the light into the darkness within him.

And the painting hung on the gable changed; he saw into the soul of the artist; what he dreamed of saying, what he intended; the mission ablaze on the pyre of fettered pain. Now this prisoner of his time was rotting in the earth among worms.

You are sitting opposite a failed work of his, much later, composing the verse that is needed to unlock the long-forgotten repository of his spirit, decipher from it the secrets of a soul that blazed with yearning in its tabernacle, screaming for the grace of understanding in order to survive; but never receiving the full measure for a picture. And the babbling grows, and the thunderous laughter becomes louder, tumbling copiously around him, cascading in foam, smashing and frothing against skerries; and your silence grows tighter; low, dark notes awaken there, branching into a tapestry; threads are woven together, themes awaken anew, and other new ones. And the colours come alive, a glow in a glass; shedding its lambency on to the cloth-less table.

A man's back is bare unless he has a brother. You recline, your back against the wall, and no one can reach you there; not eyes looking at the nape of your neck. And the evil eye of sorcery is power-less. And with the dulled glint of sleep, the eyes of the lascivious women of this nocturnal abode close around their fleetingly sacro-sanct ground; some of them blue, touching you for an instant, or green, never black; roam like a wing soaring over the crest of a wave; turning blue, turning white in the instant of a blink; or like the beam of a lighthouse across a dark sea; even lighting up a bird in its solitary swooping.

And still he was being watched from the empty table. He walked out leaving the empty bottle.

The night was warm, the pitch-black heaven within short reach. No stars.

Say something beautiful to me, said the woman, opening a view into her soul in her blue eyes beneath black hair; since you are leaving. Why do you need to leave?

I leave everyone. Except one, he said, toying with her sex with his toes.

Stay.

He did not reply. She knew that he would leave.

Say something. Just for me.

Autumn, he said then; wind. And the leaves dart astonishedly in new colours from the trees, fly, but lack wing, and fall to earth, lose their course, and land in a heap; and an end to it.

Later a new spring will come, without them.

As he was saying this, he saw wondrous happenings in her eyes.

But there will be new leaves, she said.

True, he said; but that's another matter. A different story.

He was sitting on a bench, the platform empty.

Except that he sensed around him, rather than saw, that someone was moving about close by. The night was large, like a great hall, not like the nights back home which ended nowhere. Here the sky was like a roof. Not immeasurability. What about the space between planets?

Then he recalled having met a broad, ponderous man on the steps with his head down on his chest, as if he were trying to stick it under his wing.

It was dark there, the man's face could not be seen; his hair was matted and long. He was wearing a thick overcoat in the summer heat, with a large upturned collar; a rip on the shoulder which could have looked like a seam, held together with a safety pin.

His clogs clattered absurdly on the iron-rimmed steps, ridiculously in the midnight silence, at the end of the fateful tolling of the bell, twelve strokes.

With an eloquent clapper in broad bronze casing.

He sat on the bench and waited for the bustle of the crowd to fade from his senses, so that he could face the night. And whatever it might offer from the hoard of memories, or a promise, a hope, even dreams.

The visitations of what he wanted to forget had dwindled after he left the boisterous bower, its empty rollicking.

A hint of burning still remained in his soul. But the night was warm and fell with a fluffy blackness, dispatching him from the piercing cruelty of unavenged deeds which followed from afar, from a different stage of vastnesses and cold dignity.

This night coddled, without the depth of fears or the vast perspectives that tensed and braced his mind.

Here it was too soft and shallow for spectres. His ghost retreated beyond the narrow range of the limelights here.

In this momentary peace he was sitting there, a visitor incapable of finding a permanent abode.

Then suddenly an arm reached over his shoulder and tried to tighten around his throat, and in its clenched fist a stiletto blade pointing towards this chest. And a toothless mouth muttered into his ear: Money, money. And, more nasally, slobbering the same words: Money, money.

He felt a spasmodic twinge in this arm which tried to tighten around his neck and constrict his gullet without raising the razor-shape knife which was pointing at his lower ribs but aimed for his heart.

Later when he recalled the episode he could not imagine how he had managed to throw this envoy of the night over his shoulder without being hurt by the knife; apart from thinking that by losing

221

the purchase of the foot he had placed forward, his assailant lacked the means of exerting power to direct the knife where it was intended. The next thing he knew was that the man was lying on the platform in front of him with the knife still in his hand.

When they stood facing each other afterwards they were poles apart in endowment and advantage, had it not been for the knife.

Himself, he stood silent, bowed slightly with his arms stretched forwards and his fingers spread as if holding an invisible yarn being wound into a ball.

Although he had never wrestled in this way before, he seemed to be granted the knowledge of how to fight, keeping his elbows tight to his sides, tensed there but elsewhere as supple as a cat about to pounce, ready to face attack by the man who had risen to his feet with the knife and was rocking clumsily like a wounded ape with one leg shorter than the other, tossing the knife between his hands.

He stood ready to face attack by his knifed assailant, suddenly threw his arms in the air as if he had abandoned the yarn for a rock which he raised, poised to toss down; and he gave a scream. Which resounded through the emptiness, and echoed through the large hall above, where tardy birds of night huddled and a handful of railway station guards were beginning to lock up for the night when the trains had stopped running.

What did that scream contain? Much, perhaps, which he felt that, in spite of everything, he could never tell, not even conceal in a poem.

Whereupon his adversary was startled away, and fled like a nightmare chased off with mighty sorcery, back home to its darkness and emptiness.

The poet stood with his arms aloft, his fingers spread out towards heaven, and his scream exploded in the night.